THE TIN
TRIANGLE

THE TIN
TRIANGLE

inspired by true events

Linda Abbott

FLANKER PRESS LIMITED
ST. JOHN'S

Library and Archives Canada Cataloguing in Publication

Abbott, Linda, 1954,- author
The tin triangle / Linda Abbott.

Issued in print and electronic formats.
ISBN 978-1-77117-515-9 (paperback).--ISBN 978-1-77117-516-6 (html).--
ISBN 978-1-77117-517-3 (html).--ISBN 978-1-77117-518-0 (pdf)

1. Canada. Canadian Army. Newfoundland Regiment--Fiction.
I. Title.

PS8601.B26T55 2016   C813'.6   C2016-900198-9
                                             C2016-900199-7

© 2016 by Linda Abbott

PRINTED IN CANADA

MIX
Paper from responsible sources
FSC
www.fsc.org   FSC® C016245

This paper has been certified to meet the environmental and social standards of the Forest Stewardship Council® (FSC®) and comes from responsibly managed forests, and verified recycled sources.

Cover Design by Graham Blair

FLANKER PRESS LTD.
PO BOX 2522, STATION C
ST. JOHN'S, NL
CANADA

TELEPHONE: (709) 739-4477   FAX: (709) 739-4420   TOLL-FREE: 1-866-739-4420
WWW.FLANKERPRESS.COM

9 8 7 6 5 4 3 2 1

  Canada Council for the Arts   Conseil des Arts du Canada   Newfoundland Labrador

We acknowledge the [financial] support of the Government of Canada. *Nous reconnaissons l'appui [financier] du gouvernement du Canada.* We acknowledge the support of the Canada Council for the Arts, which last year invested $153 million to bring the arts to Canadians throughout the country. *Nous remercions le Conseil des arts du Canada de son soutien. L'an dernier, le Conseil a investi 153 millions de dollars pour mettre de l'art dans la vie des Canadiennes et des Canadiens de tout le pays.* We acknowledge the financial support of the Government of Newfoundland and Labrador, Department of Tourism, Culture and Recreation for our publishing activities.

For my brother, Bob. You fought a long, frightening battle for your life, somehow never losing hope or your sense of humour. An inspiration to us all.

SING YOUR DEATH SONG
AND DIE LIKE A HERO GOING HOME.

— Chief Tecumseh

JULY 1, 1916
NO MAN'S LAND

I never imagined I would die this way. Young, surrounded by thousands, yet alone and far away from home. I thought I would be afraid, but I'm not. Only ten minutes ago, I was crouched in our trenches, anxiously smoking Woodbines, waiting for the whistle to signal our launch into attack. The pain in my chest has dulled to a mild ache. The ground is firm beneath my back. Funny, the firmness is comforting, like the rugged ground of my country, Newfoundland. Maybe if I close my eyes I'll see my home, see Mom one last time. Her sea-green eyes filled with tears as she waved to me from the dock. She'll be upset if I don't say goodbye. Dad stood tall as I marched with the other volunteers to fight for the Empire. He'll understand the sacrifice I made for king and country. And little Joanie. She'll miss me the most, I think. Her big brother always made time for her. I open my eyes and my breath comes out as a shudder. Can I still be here among the dead and dying in this barren place? This no man's land?

The sun is ribbed like a pumpkin, warming my face, but

why is the rest of me so cold? The earth trembles as the big guns drum louder than the roar of a thunderstorm. Bursts of black smoke tarnish the velvet blue of the vast sky. Rocks and earth shoot up, balloon out, then rain down. Shrapnel flies overhead with a zing and cuts into flesh, gnaws at chins, cheeks, foreheads, with the ferocity of starving rats. A man nearby, scarlet blood oozing from gaping holes, grabs at what's left of his face. How do you eat without a mouth? Screams of anguish and pain tear at my soul. The black clouds are growing, dispersing into black fog. It's difficult to see through the haze.

Something warm and sticky is trickling down the side of my face. If only I could reach my hand up to touch it. My ears pulsate from the cries for help all around me, harder to bear than the steady roar of the big guns. Something hits my shoulder and I try to turn my head to look. There, it's taken a long time, but I've done it. My heart sings! It's Joey Baker. He's a buddy of mine from St. John's, lying on his stomach and staring at me. Oh God! The top of his head is gone.

I want to cry for him, yet the tears won't come. Beyond Joey is the gnarled tree. We Newfoundlanders call it the Danger Tree. Bodies are piled up around it, arms and legs angled out as if double-jointed. I had hoped to make it farther.

The screams are closer, more piercing. A blast pounds into the earth and the ground shakes. Dirt flies up and splatters my face. My mouth is filling with clay, but I spit before swallowing too much. I cough with a gurgling sound. The sweet smell of burnt flesh and urine soaks the air, suffocating me. Another explosion, and a leg with a boot attached flies past me. Did I really see that? My stomach lurches, bile rising to my throat. I struggle to keep from vomiting.

Men run past me, their battle cries strong, relentless. Some jump over Joey, their chins tucked into their chests like they're heading into a snow blizzard. One lad, surely no more than fifteen or sixteen, stares down at me. Does he recognize me? My unblinking eyes stare back. He blesses himself. A crow caws close by. A rat's tail flicks across my face.

Dream, my sweet boy, of chocolate bunnies in a land of candy. Okay, Mom. I close my eyes and listen to her soft voice singing me to sleep, the way she did when I was a small child. Her hand gently caresses my cheek. I sigh. The cries and screams are fading into the distance, like echoes in a long tunnel. The ground is still, the heat ebbing from my body. Peace envelopes me, softer, warmer than my grandmother's quilts. I'm drifting away. All is quiet. Soon I'll be home in Newfoundland, where sun rays crown thy pine-clad hills.

CHAPTER 1

I tried to sleep an extra few minutes, but the sun slipped through a hole at the top of my curtain, spreading across my face, waking me to dust particles dancing in the stream of light. Mom patched it twice, but I removed it each time. At night it's like peering at the stars through a telescope. Last month I completed grade eleven with honours at St. Bonaventure College. My cousins Frank and Henry Corcoran, fraternal twins, barely passed. Henry hasn't stopped bragging about us three as the newest educated "townies." The smell of bacon motivated me to get out of bed, and I dressed in a hurry while my stomach gurgled with hunger. I noticed Dad had already picked up the morning paper from the front step as I walked down the narrow hallway toward him.

"Ah, Ron," my father said, placing a thick, strong hand on my shoulder. "You're up nice and early for your first day of work." He leaned in close to my ear, his six foot three frame equal to mine. "Burke and Sons are the finest barristers in town."

His eyes twinkled, and I couldn't bring myself to say what

1

I really thought about becoming a lawyer, so I forced a smile. "That's what everyone says. Don't want to give a bad impression by being late."

Dad squeezed my shoulder. He was right, of course. Mr. Burke and his four sons had excellent reputations. I should have considered myself fortunate. Still, writing was my love, and becoming a journalist my dream.

"Breakfast is getting cold," my mother called from the kitchen. Her voice conveyed a smile.

The patter of running feet behind me signalled that my eleven-year-old sister Joanie was up. She grabbed my hand, dragging me into the kitchen. "Mom made toutons and bacon," she said, as if my sense of smell was damaged.

My mother placed a plate overflowing with toutons in the centre of the table. She pointed a finger at me and Joanie. "I want every one of those eaten."

Joanie's mouth was already too full to speak.

I plucked up two with a fork and poured molasses over them. The thick, dark brown sauce took its time leaving the carton.

Dad opened the *Daily News*, the paper crackling as he did so. "Good God!" he said. "I don't believe this."

Joanie and I stopped chewing and stared at him. Mom swung away from the stove, the kettle in her hand. "Tom, what is it?"

"Anne, love." He laid the paper on the table, his eyes on her.

The caption was written in big, bold type. "'Balkans ablaze,'" I read out loud.

Dad swallowed hard and glanced at me. His expression told me he knew I understood. "Austria has declared war on Serbia."

Mom swayed, dropping the kettle back to the stove with a loud thud.

Joanie's forehead creased from a frown. "What's wrong?"

Dad rushed to Mom while I explained to my sister, half my attention on my mother. She'd gone awfully pale. "Seeing as Jack's in Austria, Mom's worried about him."

"Austria will let him come home, right? Uncle Jack . . ." Joanie's voice faded as she gazed at our mother's complexion, which was whiter than sugar.

Dad led Mom to the table and, with an arm around her small waist, helped her into a chair. "Don't upset yourself, Anne. I'm sure Jack isn't in any danger."

Mom pulled a handkerchief from Dad's shirt pocket and dabbed at her eyes. "I didn't want my only brother going all the way to Europe to study medicine in the first place."

My heart fluttered and my palms had gone sweaty. My uncle Jack Furlong was twenty, a scant three years older than me.

Dad was as pale as my mother. "Jack isn't involved in the trouble over there. He'll be all right."

My mother's parents died from tuberculosis three months apart. Jack came to live with us when he was five. So close to my age, I didn't refer to him as uncle. I saw him more as a brother. Dad often praised his "oldest son's" accomplishments to his buddies.

Mom stood up, running her hands repeatedly up and down her blue and white checkered apron. "He's not Austrian, so maybe you're right, Tom." She returned to the stove and moved the kettle to the front damper. A sliver of steam rose from the spout.

Dad smiled, but it didn't reach his eyes. "Eat up," he said with a sidelong glance at me. "Or we'll both be late for work."

Joanie dug into her food. "I'm glad Uncle Jack's all right," she said, a piece of touton hanging from her fork.

Mom put four strips of crispy bacon on my plate, every trace of fat gone, the way I liked it. Her natural rosy colour was returning. "Jack's a sensible boy," she said to no one in particular. "He knows how to stay out of harm's way."

Joanie chomped down on a long piece of bacon, swinging her legs under the table. "Me and Betsy Tyler are going to Bowring Park today."

My father scooped out a big chunk of butter and spread it across a slice of well-done toast. The scrape, scrape of the knife over the bread, part of the morning ritual, was comforting. "It was very generous of Sir Edgar Bowring to bestow the parkland to the city." He tweaked Joanie's chin. "Wasn't the opening ceremony a grand affair?"

"Yeah, but it went on for too long."

My mother's face relaxed. "That was to be expected," she said, joining us at the table. "Especially since the Duke of Connaught came from Canada to open it. He was a lovely, gracious man."

Joanie's feet scuffed the canvassed floor with each swing of her legs. "Who is he again?"

"The Governor General of Canada," I said. "Remember, he planted a tree in the park?"

Joanie shrugged. "That's not so special."

I left the house before Dad to avoid further discussion about Jack's safety . . . or lack of it . . . and headed toward Duckworth Street to the offices of Burke and Sons. My father and Mr. Burke were old school chums, and Mr. Burke had taken me on as a favour to him. I'd remain silent for now about my desire to be a journalist. The unrest in Europe was troublesome for my parents, more so now that Jack was living in a country at war. I turned my thoughts to a pleasant subject—the St. John's Regatta, scheduled to take place one week from today at Quidi Vidi Lake. It was a national holiday held on the first Wednesday in August, and already I was looking forward to a day off work, and more precisely to the boat races. The Regatta Committee crossed their fingers for sunny skies with light or no wind. No one wanted the races cancelled until the next fine day. I wanted to row in the regatta, but Dad insisted the long hours of practice would take away from my studies, which surprised me, as my father was once a rower himself.

Mrs. Lawlor, the secretary, was in her early forties with five grown sons, all teaching in different outports. Her hair was completely grey, a stark contrast to her reddish complexion. She closed the *Daily News* when I arrived, her bottom lip quivering slightly. "Ron, did you read the paper this morning?"

"Yes," I said, my eyes on Mr. Burke's office door. It was closed, but muffled voices filtered out from inside.

The secretary followed my gaze. "He's terribly anxious about losing influential European clients."

"That's too bad," was all I could think to say.

Mrs. Lawlor handed me two folders. "Mr. Burke's instructions are to go over these documents in detail and jot down any questions or concerns you have about them."

I sighed inwardly at the many boring hours ahead and went to the desk assigned to me in the corner. The task kept my mind off Uncle Jack's predicament. By noon my stomach rumbled like a set of drums. Mr. Burke hadn't come out of his office, not even to say hello. I went home for dinner, meeting Dad at the front door. He worked as a stevedore unloading the cargo ships. His dream was to be a barrister, but due to his father's sudden death from a heart attack when Dad was fourteen, he quit school to earn a wage for his mother and five younger sisters.

Mom flew down the hall and hugged us both, an unusual greeting, then waved an envelope in front of our noses. "Jack's coming home." Her voice was as musical as a harp. "He leaves August 5. He's been uneasy for some time now about the unrest over there and wants to get out while he still can."

Joanie bounded in from school, and we enjoyed a dinner of pea soup with dumplings, debating over which rowing team would win the championship race at the regatta.

A rumble of footsteps in the hall and sniffing noises announced the arrival of my twin cousins, Henry and Frank Corcoran. Henry lifted the cover from the pot, steam rising to his face. "Smells good, Aunt Anne. We're just in time for dinner."

"Like every other Tuesday I make pea soup."

Frank took down two bowls from the cupboard while Henry pulled out a chair next to me. "Frank and I are going to win the races." Henry feigned a hurt look. "How can any of you doubt that?"

Joanie stuck her tongue out at me. "That's what I told them."

Frank dumped soup and dumplings into each bowl. He placed one in front of Henry before sitting down across from Joanie.

Henry winked at her. "You're our girl, always rooting for the right side."

Joanie giggled and slurped a piece of carrot into her mouth.

Mom tutted, inspecting the hands of both twins. "Look at all those calluses. Sandpaper is softer." She brought over a homemade coconut cream pie from the kitchen counter. "Common sense dictates one wears gloves when rowing."

My father laughed softly. "Anne, they're not five years old."

My cousins were as different in personality as in looks. Henry was dark-haired with the Marrie high colour, and outgoing with a wicked sense of humour. Frank had light hair and a pale complexion. People often mistook his reserved nature for shyness. He accepted Henry's dominant personality without envy or complaint.

At one o'clock I returned to the office, where Mr. Burke greeted me with a hardy handshake. "How's your day going so far?" he asked, his eyes almost hidden beneath grey, bushy eyebrows.

"I've read a lot of documents." I hoped he wouldn't perceive it as a complaint. To tell the truth, I was a little uncomfortable looking down at my boss. It wasn't my fault I was taller than the average Newfoundlander.

He tilted his head to the side and stared up at me from underneath those heavy brows. "Your father has high aspirations for you, my boy." He removed wire-rimmed glasses and cleaned them with a handkerchief. "As do I."

I registered the subtle warning that I'd better meet his expectations and not disappoint my father. With that in mind, I returned to my desk. Mr. Burke put his glasses back on. "Ron, bring the documents into my office. We'll go over each one together."

The rest of the week progressed in the same manner. I read a document, then Mr. Burke explained all the relevant points. He was enthusiastic about his work and wished I could reciprocate for my father's sake.

The day before the regatta, at home for the midday meal, Joanie ran into my room carrying a jar filled to the top with coins. "Look, Ronnie. I earned lots and lots of money doing chores around the house and for the neighbours. I'm going to spend it all at the regatta." Her long brown hair hung in ringlets down her back. I was cursed with the same curls, but thankfully my hair was short.

When we went downstairs, Dad was sitting at the table with Mom, her hands covering her face. The *Daily News* spread out before them.

Joanie trod softly across the kitchen floor. "You got another migraine, Mom?" she whispered.

Our mother lowered her hands. Her face was flushed, the fine lines around her mouth more pronounced. "Look at this headline." She grabbed the paper. "Germany invaded Belgium yesterday. England has given them until midnight today to get out. Austria is an ally of Germany." My mother was a teacher before she met my father, and she stayed up to date on current events. She slapped the paper back down on the table. "Newfoundland is part of the British Empire. Jack will be regarded as an enemy." Her voice rose. "Maybe taken prisoner or even killed."

Joanie leaned into me. "Ronnie, they can't do that," she sobbed. "Please don't let the bad men hurt Uncle Jack."

Dad lifted her onto his lap. "Jack will be home in three days." He lightly brushed away her tears with the back of his hand. "And he'll tell us wonderful stories about Europe."

Mom kissed Joanie's cheek. "Your father's right, sweetie. I'll bake a chocolate cake and invite Henry and Frank over to celebrate his homecoming."

At work, Mr. Burke's oldest son, Will, twenty-five and recently married, read over a report with me. "You know, Ron," he said, pausing in the middle of an explanation about a point in the document, "I think war is inevitable." He sighed and sat back in his chair. "Germany won't leave Belgium on Britain's say-so."

He had voiced the thoughts people had been afraid to contemplate. "I agree. Germany surely is aware Britain has a treaty with Belgium."

Will slowly got to his feet, walked to the wide-open window, and stared out at the street. At five foot seven, he was a little taller than his father. The day was warm, and voices of passersby drifted in. "Germany will move across Europe and eventually invade England. You realize what that means for Newfoundland?"

"If England declares war, we're at war as well." I was excited and scared at the same time.

The clock on the wall ticked away the seconds. "Enough gloom for one day," Will said. "It's almost five, Ron. Go home and look forward to the regatta tomorrow." He straightened his tie and the muscles in his arms bugled out. "My brothers are determined to win the championship race." His words didn't match the drawn look on his face.

I slept fitfully during the night, dreaming. Jack was swimming in the ocean, trying to get back home. The water was calm and the moon lighted his way. Then, out of nowhere, a small fishing boat appeared, with two uniformed men holding long rifles aimed at Jack. He dived below the surface, the fluttering shapes of the men visible through the surface. Unable to hold his breath any longer, he swam upwards. As his head broke the surface, rifle shots blasted. I startled awake, my heart pounding so hard my chest hurt. Through the hole in my curtain a circle of stars winked at me, reassuring me the nightmare wasn't real. I closed my eyes and prayed for Uncle Jack's safe return.

The first rays of sunlight warmed the room, and I yawned, groggy, more tired than when I had slipped beneath the covers. Dad whistled as he shaved in the bathroom next to my room. It was the same tune every morning, "Jack was Every Inch a Sailor," but today the rhythm was less lively.

"The regatta is going ahead! The regatta is going ahead!" Joanie chanted, skipping past my room. The dream about Uncle Jack flooded in. I shivered. Was Britain and her colonies at war? Was the Regatta Committee occupied with the same concern when they made their decision? We attended the regatta as a family, with neither of us mentioning the crisis in Europe. The grassy banks of Quidi Vidi were lined with booths and concessions, people milling about them, eager for the boat races to begin.

A variety of cooking smells filled the air: hot dogs, fried onions, hamburgers, french fries. Enticing, inviting. We pushed through the masses, the heat from the sun and the closeness of sweating bodies oppressive. I accidentally elbowed an elderly lady. "Sorry," I murmured. She hadn't even noticed.

My father and I walked behind my mother and Joanie. "There's a restlessness in the air," he said.

Smiling faces surrounded me, yet the atmosphere was smouldering with tension. "We might be at war, for all anyone knows," I said.

"Don't repeat that to your mother," Dad whispered. She was holding Joanie's hand tightly. Was she afraid that if she let go her daughter would vanish?

We made it to the water's edge as the gun fired to start the first race. Will and his brothers were in one racing shell, Frank and Henry next to them. Mr. Burke was a few feet away and waved to us. Of course I had to pretend to cheer loudly for his sons. The crowd held its collective breath as the crews took off, oars splashing into the calm water.

Joanie jumped up and down, clapping her hands, screaming until she went hoarse. My cousin's team rounded the buoy in third place and quickly pulled into second place. Inches from the finish line, Henry and Frank's shell glided into first. Frank stood up to shake hands with the skip. An impish smile crept across Henry's face, no surprise to me, as he shot his hand out and pushed Frank overboard.

Dad slipped away, with me following a few feet behind. He hurried through the spectators, hastily greeting acquaintances and co-workers alike with a brief nod without slowing his pace. More than a little surprised by this, I continued to trail him. He approached Mr. Tucker, a friend who worked at Government House, sitting alone on the grassy hill apart from the crowd. He was staring into the water.

Dad sat down next to him. "Good day, Owen. Enjoying yourself?"

Mr. Tucker turned to Dad, his face a blank. The moment passed, and he ran a hand through his thick, red hair. "Sorry, Tom, I didn't see you there."

"You've heard something." My father's flat announcement betrayed the reason he'd sought him out.

"Afraid so. At nine twenty-five last night we received a message from the Secretary of State for the Colonies."

My legs almost buckled beneath me, and a middle-aged man asked if I was all right. I nodded, unable to speak.

Dad pulled his knees to his chest and rested his elbows on them. "Britain has declared war on Germany," he stated quietly.

Mr. Tucker was a widower with five grown sons. "The last British garrison withdrew from Newfoundland over forty years ago. We're unprepared to fight in a war."

"There's the four groups of cadets."

"They are composed of teenagers led by local men, who for the most part have no military training."

"They instruct the boys in drill and how to use a rifle." My father's shoulders slumped forward. "But you're right, Owen. There's no use deluding ourselves. That's not enough."

Mr. Tucker made a fist with his right hand and held it up high. "Regardless of our inadequacies, we'll answer the call to fight for Britain."

"Indeed we will," Dad said. He took a packet of cigarettes from his pocket and offered one to his friend. The two men lit up and puffed thick clouds of smoke.

CHAPTER 2

The regatta had been a success, even though neither my cousins nor the Burke brothers claimed the championship race. For many hours, we freed our minds and hearts from the brewing concerns in Europe. True to her promise for Jack's homecoming, scheduled for the next day, Mom baked a chocolate cake. Joanie helped, or hindered, depending on your perspective, and we invited my cousins, Henry and Frank. The twins were related to me on my father's side, the sons of his eldest sister, Elsie, widowed when the boys were ten. The other four sisters married men from the around the bay and came to St. John's once or twice a year. The twins spent more time at my house than their own.

They arrived with Aunt Elsie, each with a tray of her delicious chocolate fudge, which every neighbour on the street had tasted many times. My mouth watered at the very mention of the treat.

Mom flitted around the kitchen like a butterfly with a broken wing, rechecking that the best tablecloth was laid out, that her grandmother's china dishes were properly set. The large Welcome Home sign Joanie had spent a day colouring with green and red crayons hung from the centre of the living room. She'd placed it there herself, my participation limited to securing the stepladder.

The celebratory chocolate cake was never eaten. Instead of Jack showing up at the door, we received a telegram. When he had landed in England, rumours about the impending war with Germany were widespread, and he'd enlisted with the Royal Army Medical Corps (RAMC) in the British army. "To fight for Mother Country," as he put it. Mom was tight-lipped about Jack's decision, but the next morning her eyes were red and puffy.

There had been plenty of activity since the announcement of the war, which was why I was sitting on the stairs by the front door waiting for the paperboy. On the twelfth of August, Prime Minister Morris called a public gathering at the Church Lads' Brigade Armoury to discuss Newfoundland's role in the war effort. Mr. Burke had given me a file to peruse overnight, and my mother insisted it was more important than attending the meeting.

Several hours later, Dad threw open the door to the house. He grinned like a child with a new toy.

"It's decided." He tossed his salt and pepper cap on the living room sofa. "We've approved a resolution giving Governor Davidson the authority to appoint a committee of fifty men who will enlist and equip five hundred troops for service overseas."

My mother dusted the mantel top, humming softly. "That's grand news. Does this committee have a title?"

"The Newfoundland Patriotic Committee. Governor Davidson is the chair, and he called a meeting for Monday." My father's grin widened. "I'm on the committee."

"We'd expect nothing less from you," Mom said, and when I didn't comment, she whacked me gently on the arm with the dust cloth. "Isn't that right, Ron?"

"Yes, Mom." A bicycle bell jingled outside, snapping my mind to the present, and I bolted from the stairs. I whipped open the front door and snatched up the *Daily News*. Dad had hinted since the meeting on Monday that there would be an extremely important proclamation in the paper on the twenty-first. No matter how much I begged and pleaded, he remained silent, which was probably the reason why he was chosen for the committee. There it was on the front page. I ran to the kitchen, where everyone was seated around the table.

"Don't stand there like a lovestruck boy who's lost all power of speech," my father said. "Read the proclamation out loud."

Every muscle and nerve in my body tensed.

"By His Excellency Sir Walter Edward Davidson, Knight Commander of the Most Distinguished Order of St. Michael and St. George, Governor and Commander-in-Chief in and over the island of Newfoundland and its dependencies.

"Your King and country need you!

"Will you answer your country's call?

"At this very moment the Empire is engaged in the greatest war in the history of the world.

"In this crisis your country calls on her young men to rally 'round her flag and enlist in the ranks of her army.

"If every patriotic young man answers her call, Great Britain and the Empire will emerge strong and more united than ever.

"Newfoundland responds to the homeland's call and promises to enlist, equip, and dispatch to England the First Newfoundland Regiment of five hundred strong. We want to send our best, and we believe that Britain's oldest colony will gain greater honour and glory for her name.

"If you are between nineteen and thirty-five years old . . ." I coughed to hide the disappointment coursing through me like an electrical charge. Why couldn't I be two years older? I cleared my throat and continued.

"If you are between nineteen and thirty-five years old," I repeated, "will you answer your country's call? If you will, go to the nearest magistrate and enrol your name for service in the fighting line. If you live in St. John's, go to the CLB Armoury and enter your name at the Central Recruiting Office, on any evening between eight p.m. and ten p.m.

"Tickets to St. John's will be provided by the magistrate free of cost.

"The terms of enlistment are: to serve abroad for the duration of the war, but not exceeding one year. It is intended the men shall leave within one month of their enrolment, and that in the meantime they shall receive a course of instruction and training in St. John's.

"A complete outfit will be provided.

"Each private will receive pay at the rate of one dollar per day and free rations, from the date of enrolment to the date of return, a portion of which will be paid to the dependants left behind, or it will be allowed to accumulate for their personal benefit until termination of service.

"Volunteers from the outports will be given free passage to St. John's.

"Any applicant for service, forwarded by the proper authorities and not accepted after arrival at Headquarters, will be provided with a free passage and maintenance back to his home.

"God save the King.

"Given under my hand and seal at Government House, St. John's, this twenty-first day of August, A.D. 1914, by His Excellency's Command, John R. Bennett, Colonial Secretary."

My father took the paper from me. "Enrolment begins this evening in the Regiment headquarters at the CLB Armoury. Davidson cabled London, informing them we'll have five hundred volunteers within a month."

My mother continued to place strips of bacon in the frying

pan. "Ron, thank the Lord the war will be over before you're old enough to join."

I fiddled with my rolled oats, which, though coated with brown sugar, had lost their appeal.

My father laid the paper aside. "I don't think our boy shares your sentiment, Anne."

Mom spun around to me, a ladle in her hand, fat dripping from it. "Whether you do or not isn't important. You're out of the war, and that's that." She flipped over eggs sizzling in the second frying pan. "Jack's more than enough from this family."

I went to work, my head hung low amid the air of excitement all around me as I walked, catching snippets of conversations. "Our boys will rally to the call." "We'll keep the motherland safe." But not me. My heart was heavier than ten feet of snow on a flat roof. Will Burke's brothers, Ted, Wayne, and Gus, all of proper age, buzzed as well about joining the fight to save the mother country from oppression. By suppertime my appetite had returned. I'd made a decision I wouldn't confide to my parents until the deed was accomplished.

At seven o'clock I left the house with the excuse I was going for a stroll, which wasn't a complete lie, as I often walked around the neighbourhood after supper. The CLB Armoury was ten minutes from my house, but I wanted to get there ahead of the crowd. I rounded the corner and came to a full stop. The sidewalk and the entrance to the armoury was crowded with young men just like me.

"Ron," Joey Baker, a good buddy of mine, called from just outside the entrance. A head shorter than me, he could easily beat me in an arm wrestle. Five other underaged fellas from school lined up behind me. "My parents don't know I'm here," Joey whispered. "Neither did Henry and Frank's mother."

"How do you know that?" I searched the crowd for them. "They're supposed to be here."

"They were waiting for you when their mother happened along. Talk about mad enough to spit nails. She dragged them aside and warned if they didn't leave with her she'd march inside and report they were underage." Joey leaned in closer to me. "She told them to show some sense, like you."

I didn't panic quite yet. My cousins would never betray me.

"My parents think I'm out for a walk," I said as the line started to move. "What will we do if they ask for our birth certificates?"

Joey grinned. "Easy," he said, keeping his voice low. "We'll tell them they were burned in the 1897 fire."

We signed up, Joey receiving number 60, myself 61, out of seventy-four men—a substantial crowd for the first night of registration. We swore to guard the secret until we were due to report for training.

The next morning, Joanie got hold of the paper to read the comic section. She screamed so loudly my parents stumbled over each other getting into the kitchen.

My father looked from me to Joanie. "What on earth is the racket about?"

She stared at him with her big green eyes. "Ronnie enlisted."

My mother snatched the paper from her. "What nonsense! He's too young."

My mouth went dry, my heart stuck in my throat. I never considered the possibility the *Daily News* would publish the names of the enlisted men.

"Joseph Baker, number sixty." My mother's voice penetrated into my thoughts. "Ronald Marrie, number sixty-one." Her tone was controlled, like she was citing the weather report. Dad's hand lightly touched her shoulder. She didn't even blink as she lowered the paper to the table, folded it neatly, and went into the hall. The front door opened and closed.

I shoved my chair back and tore after her. "Mom," I yelled,

chasing her down the street. I caught up with her at the corner. "Where are you going?" A stupid question. "Mom, please listen to me."

"You're too young to fight in a war." She stepped off the sidewalk, her head high, eyes ahead. "You can't talk me out of this."

I grabbed her arm. "Mom, give me a chance to explain why this is important to me."

She pulled away and hurried on. "Your safety is my first concern."

"Mom," I shouted. "If you report my age I'll never speak to you again."

She stopped dead in the middle of the road, turned, and walked back to me, each step slow, unsteady. A light wind blew strands of hair around her head. "Ron, you can't be serious."

"Please, Mom. Don't force me to shut you out of my life."

She stared into my eyes and saw I meant every word. A pigeon flew overhead and perched on a pole wire. "You take care of yourself over there." She slipped her arm through mine and we walked back to the house in silence.

I passed the physical examination, which was rigorous and thorough, easily surpassing the minimum requirements of five feet inches in height, 140 pounds in weight, and a thirty-four-inch chest. My attestation notice arrived on a printed card. Dad read it to the family, his voice oozing pride.

"First Newfoundland Regiment, number sixty-one, R. J. Marrie, Private. You have been passed by the medical authorities as fit for foreign service. You will parade at the CLB Armoury for attestation at seven thirty p.m. Monday, the thirty-first August, 1914. Colonel A. Montgomerie, Secretary, Recruiting Committee."

My mother cooked all my favourite meals over the week,

rarely referring to my impending departure. Joanie clung to me like a wet leaf. Mr. Burke praised me for doing my duty and assured me my job would be waiting when I returned. I thanked him, but something negative must have resonated, because he said in a most pleasing manner, "If that's what you desire, of course."

My father was busy with the recruiting committee and kept me apprised of the situation at Pleasantville, where I was to begin training. "It's getting into shape," he announced during supper several days before I was due to report. "The government and private businesses have donated the tents for the recruits."

Joanie stuffed half a potato in her mouth. "Nellie's father . . ." The rest of her words were a muffled garble. Bits of potato and saliva stuck to her bottom lip.

"Donated a tent," Dad finished for her.

My mother hadn't uttered a syllable all during the meal. "I heard they've stripped the sails from ships in the harbour and made them into tents."

"That's right, Anne," Dad said. "The whole town is participating. They want Pleasantville ready for occupation by the second of September."

And it was. On the sixth of September, having consumed such a large breakfast I was stuffed, I tiptoed out of the house. I didn't rouse Joanie to say goodbye. She'd have a hard enough time dealing with the reality of my situation when I shipped out. I met up with Joey Baker and arrived for duty at eight o'clock.

The night before, my mother had packed a few items for me despite my objections. "Mom, I'm sure the army will supply all my essentials."

"Listen to me," she said, packing a toothbrush wrapped in a face cloth, a razor and blades, and a bar of Sunlight soap. "It doesn't hurt to have a ready supply just in case." Before closing the small carrying case, she added a pencil and writing paper. "You'll be a journalist someday." She buckled the case. "Regardless of what your father wishes."

Pleasantville had beautiful, open grounds across the road from Quidi Vidi Lake. It was now lined with tents, cookhouses, marquees for quartermaster stores, an orderly room, and a canteen, leaving ample space for parades.

"There's a squad for men who've never had any experience with the military," Joey said.

"I guess we'll be spared that squad," I said. "The Catholic Cadet Corps taught us about taking orders and marching properly with right and left turns on the appropriate foot."

We were greeted by a soldier and given instructions. First we registered at the orderly room, and from there went to the quartermaster's marquee to be fitted for a uniform and be issued equipment. Each of us was given a khaki drill uniform, two khaki shirts, a cardigan, a pair of boots, two pairs of socks, drawers and singlet, two blankets, an enamelware plate and mug, knife, fork, and spoon. We were fitted with outer coats, one size fits all. Joey's hands were hidden under the sleeves, the tail going down to the tips of his boots. There wasn't any official army head gear available, so we wore what we brought with us.

A guide escorted us to a bell tent, where we'd live with eight other men for the next four weeks. We changed into our uniforms and proceeded to the orderly corporal, who then led us to the parade ground, where we were assigned to a squad.

The next morning, a bugle blasted and I bounded upright, my heart pounding, my vision blurred with sleep. The smell of the tent wafted up my nostrils as I stared around. Where was I? Who were all these people? Joey sat up, stretching and yawning. Another man grumbled and threw off his blankets. "Six o'clock," Harold Bartlett said. "Time to get up, boys."

His bed was across from me. I remembered him from the

night I enlisted. He was nineteen, with black hair, and sported what my mother called a blue beard, where shaving didn't erase the underlying dark hair. An inch or two shorter than me, he was thinner than a needle, with protruding ribs. I'd never seen a malnourished person before, and it occurred me there were probably many in St. John's less fortunate than me. We ate breakfast at seven, consisting of oatmeal porridge with brown sugar or molasses, marmalade which the cook said was locally manufactured, bread, and tea. Harold gobbled down the food as if he thought someone would steal it away.

The day was divided into one-hour and sometimes half-hour instruction in squad and platoon drills on how to use a rifle, and skirmishing. The lectures on discipline and the care of weapons fascinated me, as did those on health and hygiene. Living with nine men in a relatively confined space widened my knowledge concerning various insects I'd never before encountered, and their tastes for human blood.

By noon I was starved. My appetite waned, though, when presented with a concoction of what appeared to be gristle, grease, bone, and undercooked potato. Joey gagged a few times but got it all down. More instruction and lectures ensued, followed by supper at five thirty, which turned out to be quite scrumptious: salt cod or corned beef hash, bread, jam, and tea. Harold nearly fainted when the cook stacked his plate with extra food.

Each day, evening passes from six o'clock to ten o'clock, were granted to a third of the men, taken in rotation. Joey and I weren't part of the first night's one-third. Lights out at ten was difficult for me, as that was the hour I read every night. The next day, and every following second day, we marched for five miles. The second time out, we'd walked for an hour and my feet ached. Joey limped alongside me, wincing with each step. "I got bloody big blisters on every toe."

"Fall out! Ten minutes!" The order bellowed through the air like an explosion.

"Thank Jesus," Joey said, falling down on the side of the road. He pulled out a packet of Gems from his pocket and tapped at the bottom end until the tip of a cigarette appeared. "These are produced locally by Imperial Newfoundland Limited, where Dad works." He poked the packet in front of my face. "Want one?"

"Don't smoke," I said. "Didn't know you took it up."

Joey glanced around at the men spread out along the side of the road. "I didn't until I joined up," he said when he was sure no one was close enough to overhear him. "Smoking relaxes me." Hundreds of cigarette butts littered the ground as we set off again. Another hour of walking, then another rest break. Each time, a haze of smoke floated in the air like thin clouds.

The third day I was granted a nighttime pass. Joanie shot into my arms the instant I opened the front door. "I missed you something awful," she murmured into my chest.

"I missed you, too." The absolute truth, even though I'd only been gone a few days.

"Are they feeding you enough?" my mother asked, and didn't linger for the answer. "I'll put the kettle on."

"Tell us everything," Dad said. "How's life at the camp?"

"Well . . ." I paused a moment, thinking about where best to begin. "There's going to be a concert once a week, and the talent will be provided by musicians, singers, and performers from St. John's. And get this, Dad, every Sunday there's a compulsory church parade, where we'll be positioned according to religion."

"Did you really think you'd escape religion in the army, son? Tell me about the training."

"I've done a musketry course at the regulation range on the South Side Hills and qualified on the miniature range at the CLB Armoury. We used the long Lee Enfield rifle."

My father frowned. "That means the rifles the government ordered from Canada haven't arrived yet."

Joanie snuggled next to me on the sofa. "You're a crack shot."

My father winked. "He sure is. Just ask any of the moose he's shot."

Joanie laughed, her plump cheeks red and her eyes nearly squeezed shut from the effort. Dad tickled her ribs and she rolled onto the floor, letting out great hee-haws that cut off her breath.

Mom came with a pot of tea, buttered raisin buns, and molasses bread. She eyed Dad, sending him a silent message. He quickly pulled his exhausted daughter to her feet.

"Daddy's really funny," Joanie said, scrubbing away the laughter-induced tears.

Mom laid the tray of food on the coffee table. "Eat up." She gazed at me. "You're looking too thin."

I didn't have the heart to tell her I was full, so I drank a cup of tea and ate one of the buns to please her.

Harold was given leave the next night and sneaked food out with him. "Is his family really that poor?" Joey asked as we lay in our bunks.

"Look how thin he is, and you've seen the way he wolfs down every meal."

Joey sucked air in through his teeth. "His father died when he was three, and as soon as he was able, he worked to feed the family. I don't know if I could've done that."

"He never went to school, either." I folded my hands behind my head. "He's not ashamed about his upbringing and doesn't pretend to be anyone other than who he is."

Joey didn't comment and I turned my head to look at him. Just like that, he was sound asleep, letting out a soft, whistling snore. Harold was poor and uneducated, yet one of the smartest people I'd ever met. The first night we'd settled into our bunks he asked my opinion about the government's claim that the war would last mere months.

"The government knows those things," I had said, believing Harold wasn't bright enough for an in-depth answer.

"What makes you say that?" he had thrown back in his easygoing manner.

"Well, the men in power oversee the running of the country. They have to allocate monies, regulate the fishery—"

Harold cut me off in a quiet voice. "But what does that have to do with stating the length of the war with arrogant accuracy?"

I raised my eyebrows at the high level of thought he had put into his question.

"I taught myself to read and write," he said. "It helps you forget about being hungry."

"The army money will help out your family."

Harold's eyes glistened in the flickering candlelight by the side of his bed. "Mom won't struggle anymore to feed the family."

Joey's snoring attained a roof-raising pitch, and the boy at the end threw a bible at him. Joey snorted and stirred but didn't wake up.

As the weeks progressed, my physical endurance improved to the extent that a five-mile march required little effort. Fortunately for Joey, his blisters healed, leaving him with tougher skin. We were becoming real soldiers, ready to serve our country in the battle for freedom. Harold had gained twenty pounds and his chest measurements increased by five inches. On the morning of October 3, I awoke before reveille like a typical townie. I'd never been in a boat of any type, and here I was preparing for an overseas voyage on a huge ship.

The last camp parade was held, where each of us was given a New Testament. Whether Catholic or non-Catholic, we appreciated the symbolic gesture of good faith and the hope for our safe return. My mother would be more than pleased I would be carrying the word of the gospel into the war. At 4:00 p.m., with bands from three different religions before us, we left the Pleasantville encampment and marched past Government House, en route to the wharf.

The streets overflowed with well-wishers, family, and friends, as more than 300 of the volunteers originated from St. John's. My parents stood with them, Dad holding Joanie's hand to prevent her from rushing at me. People surged in among us, disrupting our orderly march as they sought out their son, brother, husband, neighbour, or friend. I looked for Frank and Henry among the growing masses jostling me about.

A tall, thin woman with dark hair darted in front of me. A young girl about Joanie's age followed close behind, both female versions of Harold. The young girl held the hand of a five- or six-year-old who limped, one leg obviously shorter than the other. An eight- or nine-year-old held the other hand. We were almost at the wharf, when weeping women threw their arms around their sons, preventing further movement. Joey blushed and pulled away from his mother. Joanie wound her arms around my waist, and as I tried to board the *Florizel*, she tightened her grip. "Please don't go, Ronnie. I'm afraid you won't come home." Her heart was pounding.

Dad gently extricated her as more people pushed and shoved to reach their loved ones. Our marching lines were gone. Some of us were lumped together, while others had spread out. Mom whispered in Joanie's ear. My sister simply nodded and looked up at me. "I love you, Ronnie," she said in her little girl voice. "Promise me you'll come home."

Innocence is a powerful shield. I stared at her, shock rifling through me: I might never come home. I might never live to see another summer.

Dad clasped my hand. "You take care, son, and make Newfoundland proud."

Mom hugged me. I didn't speak. A soldier on his way to war shouldn't have tears in his eyes, or in his voice. I parted from the ones I cared for most in the world, and fought through the throngs of well-wishers to reach the *Florizel*. Seconds poured into minutes as I wove in and around fellow soldiers attempting to extricate themselves from weeping mothers, sisters, and wives.

Henry and Frank appeared out of nowhere. "I'll see you over there in a few months," Henry said. "Save some Germans for me to kill."

Frank stood to the side. "Don't worry about Joanie. We'll look after her."

Then, finally, we were aboard, standing on the ship's deck and looking down at the crowd on the dock. Harold stood next to me. "There's no turning back now."

Joey clapped a hand on each of our shoulders. "Either of you boys get seasick?"

Before I could answer, a cheer rang up to meet us, and like a rolling wave, every soldier waved his cap in the air.

CHAPTER 3

Ten o'clock Sunday night marked a marvellous autumn night. The wind was calm and the moon shone down, tracing a silver path along the water as the *Florizel*'s engine churned in preparation to leave St. John's harbour. My stomach was fine for the moment. Perhaps it would stay that way.

I'd never given much thought to the numerous hills that comprised St. John's. From this vantage point, the city was nestled on a rolling slope with luscious trees intertwining among the buildings. The major fire of less than twenty years earlier had left no visible scars. The great Cathedral, designed by a famous German architect, stood out like a welcoming beacon. A sudden pang of longing stole over me. When would I see home again?

Families and well-wishers had gone home hours earlier, leaving the wharf empty . . . lonely. The next day, the ship moved beneath our feet as we glided smoothly toward the Narrows. I glanced back at the city when the ship slipped out into the open water. As if propelled by an unspoken command, waves swelled and washed against the side. The *Florizel* rose and fell like a rocking cradle. I grabbed hold of the railing, swallowing to keep my stomach in place.

"Where are we going to sleep and spend our time during the voyage?" Joey asked. "The *Florizel* usually carries cargo and normally accommodates less than a hundred passengers. There are only a few staterooms on the main deck. Which undoubtedly will be given to the officers."

"The ship's officers have put us to the hold." I wrinkled my nose against the smell of seal fat rising up. "It'll be our home for a while, so we might as well get comfortable down there."

Lately my life was a series of new experiences, and the vastness of the ocean was a little overwhelming. I wasn't sure if I was scared or thrilled to be there. "We might as well turn in for the night," I said, and climbed down into the hold of the ship.

"Comfortable isn't the right term," Joey said, jostling close to me. Not because he wanted to, but because there was so little room. The men smoked, covering our clothes in the foul, stale odour. They talked about the great adventure ahead, but my nervousness kept me awake far longer than if I had been in my own bed.

Huge waves tossed the ship from side to side, and I woke up dizzy and nauseous, unable to get to my feet. Cramped together with more than 500 men, they were lucky I didn't lose any of my stomach's contents. I prided myself on being strong and healthy, yet in the morning, when greasy food was lowered by rope, I scrambled up on deck just in time to retch over the side.

Harold's head also hung out over the water, his face as grey as I assumed mine must have been. He swayed from side to side, holding tight to the rail. "I might not survive long enough to fight. I'm so dizzy I can hardly stand upright."

I suffered just as badly, but was too busy throwing up once more to say so. At the end of the day, I ate a little bread. Harold declined even to look at food. It wasn't until the next morning he drank a quarter cup of tea and kept down the one bite of dry bread.

Joey walked down the deck toward us like he'd been raised on a ship. He stood at the rail and breathed in the salty air. We were fifty miles off Cape Race and in calm seas. "Take a look at that!" he said, staring out over the waves. "Have you ever seen so many ships?"

I wiped my mouth with a handkerchief. "Chaplain Murray said we're supposed to meet up with a Canadian convoy of thirty-two ships with over 32,000 soldiers on board, as well as more than 6,800 horses." I whistled. "It certainly is a magnificent sight." Seven warships escorted the fleet.

I settled into the routine life aboard the *Florizel* with sentry and lookout duty on alternate days. Water was rationed out, and I often found myself so thirsty my tongue stuck to the roof of my mouth. Joey complained about the toilet facilities, a protest which every soldier wholeheartedly chimed in on. It wasn't unusual to find ourselves standing in lineups for over an hour. "We got to find a better solution," Ches Abbott, a medium-height, stout, thirty-year-old fisherman from Bonavista, said. He was married with three children. "Me bladder can't take much more of this." He slapped his backside. "Me rear end, either."

"Got any ideas?" asked Gord, Ches's younger brother by five years.

"I'll have a word with the Battalion's pioneers. They're a smart group of lads." The next day a lean-to was constructed, extending six feet out over the stern of the ship, able to seat six men at a time. "Well I'll be," Ches said. "Good thing we're at the back of the convoy." Every man bent over with laughter.

With my ongoing battle with seasickness, one day dragged

into the next. Some days weren't so bad, though my pants had loosened around the waist. Harold went from grey to green and sought out medical help to keep down water. On October 14 we reached Devonport, England, situated on the south coast, seventy-five miles southeast of London. I raised my eyes to the sky. "Thank the Lord," I murmured under my breath.

Harold urged, a hand over his mouth. "That goes double for me."

"Weren't we supposed to dock at Southampton?" I asked as we steamed into port.

"Submarines were spotted in the English Channel," the chaplain, a tall, lean man with a cultivated moustache, said, "so we've been ordered here." He sighed. "Which poses a huge problem. Devonport's not equipped with railway facilities or anything else we need to disembark and get under way."

To my dismay, we were confined to the ship for an additional six days. Around midnight, we marched seven miles in pouring rain to Salisbury Plains, located in the southern central part of England. The chalky land was empty of trees and the ground was a sea of mud. Three hours later, with twelve men to a tent, we fell asleep in wet clothes. In the morning, Joey ran into the tent after breakfast. "Our Ross Rifles are finally here, and we're getting new khaki uniforms along with caps and puttees." He brushed dried mud from his blue puttees. "It's too bad we won't be referred to as the Blue Puttees anymore."

I shook my head. "The name is part of who we are now."

The rain pelted down for five days, and the tent didn't provide much protection from the cold and damp. We trained in the higher ground, trudging through mud, sinking down to our ankles, then each evening spent hours cleaning our puttees and boots for morning inspection.

Canadian soldiers were stationed two or three miles from us. I became acquainted with Simon Townsend, a lad my age from Ontario. "I've been here two months and haven't seen the sun one time," he said, offering me a cigarette. The tips of his fingers were shrivelled, like they'd been soaking in water. "The rain hasn't let up long enough to build huts so we can get out of the godforsaken tents." He inhaled, drawing smoke deep into his lungs. "Look at my boots."

"Good Lord. They're rotting off your feet."

"That's no surprise, since the heels are made from compressed paper. These are what Sham Shoes supplied for the troops."

"Sham Shoes?"

"That's what we call the government minister who issued the boots." He tapped the heels of my boots. "At least yours are sturdy." Simon flicked his half-smoked cigarette away. "We tried to set up a large tent so we'd have a place for some needed re-creation. The goddamned wind blew it down every time."

That night I sat on the icy, muddy floor of my tent to write a letter home. My hand shook so badly I didn't get past "Dear." The next morning the walls of the tents shimmered with ice and my breath was a thick mist. I lit a candle, dreading the thought of stepping out into frozen mud, when lively whistling carried into the tent.

"Who the hell is happy at this ungodly hour?" Ches Abbott barked, his blankets tucked in around his ears.

I dressed in a hurry. Two tents away, Humphrey Little, a thick-chested man from Twillingate, stood shaving, stripped down to the waist. "Morning," he called. "I love a nice crisp start to the day."

I saluted him and went back inside. Gord shivered under the covers. "All that hair keeps him warm," he said when I told them about Humphrey. "The fishing grounds aren't this cold in mid-winter."

"Never knew fishermen were such sooks," I said, moving out of Gord's reach.

He threw off his covers and chased me outside. "Lord dyin' Jesus," he yelped, raising a fist to me when his bare feet sank deep into the ice-crusted mud.

The rain persisted for days and the ground became a muddied swimming hole. "Blast this rain and cold," Chaplain Murray yelled one night following a tumble into a puddle of water, up to his neck. This from a man who embodied patience and understanding.

"Amen to that," Ches Abbott said, stretching out his hand to help the dripping-wet chaplain to his feet.

I almost danced when on December 8, we were ordered to Fort George in Scotland, which stood on an isolated piece of land jutting out into the water eleven miles northeast of Inverness. We marched over a wide walkway, which had a drawbridge over a ditch to get to the entrance. And I did dance when shown into barracks containing cots and mattresses. The fort had the capacity to house more than 1,600 men, supported by a bakehouse, a chapel, a provisions store, and a powder magazine store.

Harold marched next to me. "I read that the fort has underground bunkers in case of an attack."

Joey Baker actually kissed the dry, hard ground. "Please never let me see mud again."

Ches woke up grumpier than usual a few weeks after our arrival. "This is a proper waste of time," he said, climbing out of bed.

I braved a question. "What is?"

He hauled on his trousers. "I came over here to fight. It wasn't easy leaving me wife and youngsters. It's been over three months and all we do is train." His large hands were scarred from the hooks on fishing trawls. "I should be on the fishing grounds, earning a living for me family."

"Ah, go on, Ches," Joey said. "Your war pay is earning a living for your family. Your wife doesn't need you."

Ches threw a pillow at him.

On February 9 we were ordered to Edinburgh and stationed in the famous castle. "I can't wait to tour the historic sites," I said, loading up my haversack.

"Sightseeing!" Ches said, as if he thought I'd lost my mind. "It's been almost six months and we ain't any nearer to fighting the Germans than the day we left St. John's. What's the holdup?"

"The leaders have a plan. They'll explain when it's the right time."

Harold tapped a finger against his chin. "It stands to reason that the Germans are efficient at warfare and Britain wants us extra-prepared to fight them."

Gord smiled and looked at his brother. "Don't worry, Ches. This time next year the war'll be over and we'll be back in good old Bonavista."

"Right," Ches hissed and went back to packing.

As we neared Edinburgh, every eye was drawn toward the huge castle towering on a rocky hillside high above the city. "If I didn't know better," Joey said, "I'd swear it was carved out of the rock."

"The place has loads of hills like St. John's," Harold said. "Gives you a warm feeling."

We reached the city and marched on a road that ran through the centre of Edinburgh. The brick buildings reminded me of Duckworth Street and brought on a surge of homesickness. The centre of the city wasn't very big, and I headed back there once we were shown to our quarters and assigned our duties. None of the locals stared at me. Obviously they were used to foreign soldiers on their streets. I stopped at a store to buy shortbread cookies, a treat my mother baked to perfection. When I was about to head back to base, a slap on the back nearly knocked me off my feet.

"Ronnie, it's good to see ya."

I whirled around to see the smiling face of my cousin, Henry Corcoran. I hugged him so tightly I took his breath away. "What are you doing here?"

"I shipped out with the second contingent from home. We arrived two days ago."

I looked past him for his twin, as it was odd to see one without the other. "Where's Frank?"

"He's still in Newfoundland. Mom had a fit when I signed up and threatened again to report my real age. Uncle Tom convinced her to keep quiet." Henry rolled his eyes. "She agreed on the condition Frank stay home. Which won't be long," he added with a cunning smile. "The age for enlistment is being lowered to eighteen next month. Henry will be eighteen by then, so Mom won't have a say."

A pretty girl in her late teens, with blonde hair down to her waist walked by. Henry tipped his hat to her. "A lovely morning," he said in a teasing tone. He was a handsome lad, and not many females resisted his charm. The young woman giggled and hurried on her way. Henry watched her until she rounded the corner.

"What are your duties, Henry?" I asked, drawing his attention back to me.

"We've been assigned to guard Edinburgh Castle, the first overseas regiment to be given the honour. What about you, Ron?"

"I'm detailed to the garrison military police, to patrol the streets at night to ensure soldiers are behaving themselves."

"Better you than me."

"I'd rather count the bricks in the castle, Henry, but the brass takes this assignment very seriously, even instructing us on how to subdue offenders. Worse, I have to guard prisoners of war in the hospitals and at the railway station." I shrugged. "At least I have the mornings off."

Harold Bartlett was my patrol buddy. It was a pleasant evening, not too cold for the time of year, and the streets were quiet.

"Ten more minutes and we're off duty," Harold said as we approached a pub frequented by the Newfoundlanders.

We heard a loud voice coming from inside. "Who are you calling a stunned bayman?"

"That's Ches Abbott," Harold said. "What's he up to now?"

"I am," another voice yelled back. "What are you going to do about it?" The door to the bar swung open, and a soldier as big as a bear flew out and landed at our feet. His nose and left cheek were bloodied.

Ches stood in the door, his fists held up before him. "That's what I'll do about it." He hopped from one foot to the other like a professional boxer.

The man jumped to his feet and started for Ches. Harold, ever agile, grabbed him by the arms from behind. "Take it easy, buddy."

"Let me go," the soldier shouted, twisting and contorting his body in an effort to free himself.

Ches moved forward. I put a hand on his chest. "Back away, Ches," I ordered, even though he could've decked me with one punch. I turned to the unknown soldier. "Your name?"

"What's it to you?" he growled. "This is between me and the bayman."

Ches dived at him. I stuck my foot out.

"Jesus," Ches yelled, as he tripped and fell onto his knees and hands. "Why'd you do that?"

The big bear laughed. "Serves you right."

Relieved there weren't any spectators. I walked over to the soldier. "I'll ask your name one last time." A scowl on my face, I stepped closer, meeting him eye to eye. "Don't make me mad."

He smiled. "Corporal Fred Thompson. 'B' Company."

Harold shoved Thompson toward Ches. "Forget about the argument and shake hands, or get written up and arrested."

Both men glared at each other.

"Listen good," Harold said. "Over here, whether you're bay-man or townie, we're all Newfoundlanders, so save your anger for the Germans."

Ches stuck his hand out to Fred. "Seeing as you put it that way."

Fred stared at the offered hand, his jaw tight. I stiffened and my pulse quickened as I got ready to arrest him. "All right, all right," he said, and shook Ches's hand. We accompanied the drunken men back to base in silence, as ordered by Harold.

When not assigned specific duties, we performed daily parades in front of the castle and continued our training at Baird Hills, a couple of miles away. We didn't escape the daily march-es, which were continued to maintain our physical condition. Henry was almost as tall as me, but a good thirty pounds heavi-er, with a larger build, and an avid hockey player.

Early one evening, Fred Thompson showed up at the barracks, clapping his hands and dancing a jig to the tune of "I's the B'y."

Ches threw his musical spoons at him. "Why in the name of the Holy Mother are you so cheery?"

Fred performed a poor imitation of a tap dance. "I'm get-ting hitched tomorrow, boys. You're all invited."

Gord's eyes bulged. "What? You never mentioned you were seeing a woman."

Fred retrieved the musical spoons from the floor and tossed them back to Ches. "Eileen's a real looker with the cutest pug nose."

"Hmm," Ches said. "Is she blind?"

"If she's not," Gord said with a nudge at his brother, "love sure is.

"What's this beauty's name?" I asked.

"Eileen MacMilligan." Fred tapped a finger to his lips. "Eileen Thompson has a fine ring to it, don't you think?"

"I do," Ches said, seriously. "Congratulations, Fred, and best wishes. I look forward to meeting your young lady."

The wedding was slated for seven the next morning at the house of the mayor, a childhood friend of Mr. MacMilligan. Richard Carter, Fred's best friend from home, was also on hand. The living room was small, with red velvet wallpaper, and overstuffed with three armchairs, two side tables, a coffee table, and a bookcase occupying the back wall. The mayor's wife—who wore a permanent smile, was a foot taller than her husband, and weighed close to 300 pounds—glided around like she floated on air.

Eileen, a petite young woman of nineteen, had flowing auburn hair. Long, dark eyelashes cast shadows on her flushed cheeks. She smiled and shook hands with each of us. Mister MacMilligan's eyes glistened with unshed tears when he kissed her forehead. He was a widower, and Eileen was his only child. She wore a cream-coloured dress and a yellow rose tucked behind her right ear.

The mayor put on wire-rimmed glasses attached to a chain around his neck. They magnified his small, squinting eyes three times. "Before we begin, I'd like to welcome the soldiers of the New-found-land Regiment into my home."

I cringed inwardly at his mispronunciation of my country's name. He didn't pronounce "found" as we did, running the words together, as in "Newfunland." It astonished me why foreigners had a problem with that.

The mayor continued. "My wife and I are delighted to marry Eileen to such a fine gentleman."

"I thought she was marrying Fred," Ches said.

"Thank you, Mayor. Ignore my jealous friend here. You do me a great honour."

Eileen, arm in arm with her future husband, smiled at us. "I'm pleased Fred's friends are here to share in the happiest day of our lives."

Fred winked at her. "Let's get this ceremony under way."

The vows were brief, and once the rings were exchanged, the mayor announced them as man and wife. He hosted a delicious breakfast consisting of eggs, ham, homemade bread, and strong tea. His wife had baked a vanilla cake covered with a white frosting, which I reluctantly admitted rivalled my mother's.

Fred was granted two days leave and booked into a hotel immediately after breakfast. Every free moment in the following months he visited his bride at her father's home, where she continued to live.

On the fourth of May another contingent, "C" Company, arrived from Newfoundland, bringing our numbers to 1,250 men. We spotted Frank Corcoran in the second row of troops as they marched past the castle. "It's about time you showed up, brud," Henry said, his voice quivering ever so slightly. I put that down to the coldness of the wind.

"It's grand to have you both here," I said, my own voice unsteady, due once again to the blustery wind.

Eleven days later we moved to Stobs Camp, near Horwick in North Hampshire. The camp sat in the middle of a barren land, closed in on all sides by bleak hills, where once again we lived in tents. I consoled myself that I'd travelled across an ocean to fight a war, not to view beautiful scenery or live in luxury. The three months of training were rigorous, leaving no time for missing people and feeling homesick. Some of the lads had brought along their tin whistles and mouth organs, and during leisure time we sang and danced the jig. Ches's tenor voice was good enough to perform on stage. His rendition of "It's a Long Way to Tipperary" had us all tapping our feet and clapping our hands.

One night after lights out, Ches pulled out a bottle of whiskey from under his pillow. He had smuggled it in right under our noses.

"Take it easy," Gord said. "You know how you are when you're drunk." He glanced at me. "He can be a bit of a rabble-rouser."

"Go on with ya," Ches slurred as he downed another swig. He bounded to his feet and started to dance, singing "I's the B'y" at the top of his voice.

"Keep it down," Gord said. Ches dodged his brother's outstretched hand and ran outside, singing at a deafening volume.

"Jesus," Gord said. "No telling what he'll do now."

"We're trying to sleep," Captain Wakefield called out.

"Well now, that's too bad," Ches roared.

Gord flew out the door with me behind him. The captain stood in front of Ches, half dressed, hands on his hips. "Give me the bottle, go back to your tent, and sleep it off."

Ches leaned into the officer's face, nose to nose. "Make me."

The captain snatched the bottle from Ches and beckoned Gord forward. "Get him out of my sight."

"Sorry, Captain, he's not himself when he's drunk."

The next morning Ches was presented with a five-day "CC"—confined to camp. He scratched his head and shrugged it off. "It's better than being thrown in the brig."

The second of August we transferred to Aldershot in England for another bout of training. Frank and Henry's companies remained in Scotland. "I wish we were going with you," Frank said. He sat on the edge of my bunk, toying with his hat between his fingers. "The army says we need more basic training."

Henry produced his usual grin. "We'll see each other on the battlefield in no time at all."

Fred remained silent as we marched away from the city. "Take heart," Ches said. "You'll see Eileen again."

The first night in Aldershot, Joey ate very little. "We've been over here almost a year," he said, "and we haven't been involved in any aspect of the war."

"Jesus Christ," Ches swore. "I'll die of old age before I lay eyes on a German."

Harold Bartlett ran into the barracks. "I have great news. Lord Kitchener will be here tomorrow to inspect our division!"

Ches's eyes went wide. "He's the field marshal. I'd wager he's going to tell us we're off to France or Belgium to fight the Germans!"

"He'd better," Gord said. "It's high time to get this war over with."

The next day we performed a series of fake attacks and military manoeuvres for Lord Kitchener and the civilian population, then stationed ourselves at the end of a long line of British soldiers. When Kitchener trotted on his horse to a position in front of our battalion, the others were ordered to leave. "I knew it," Ches said. "He's got big plans for us Newfoundlanders."

Kitchener sat tall on his horse, his huge black moustache very striking. "Your performance was exemplary," he called out, his voice booming across the field. "You men have been well-trained. I'm sending you to the Dardanelles very soon."

The men cheered as Kitchener galloped off. Harold stared after him. "That destination can't be much of a secret."

"Why?" I asked. "He's only told us."

Harold indicated the townspeople a short distance away. "Do you suppose they're all deaf?"

Ches grimaced like he'd bitten into a rotten crabapple. "Where the devil are the Dardanelles?"

Frank and Henry were as befuddled as I. We all stared at Harold when he spoke up.

"It's a narrow waterway joining the Mediterranean Sea to the Black Sea. It's essentially the border between Europe and Asia."

Harold's knowledge of the world fascinated me, a so-called educated person, but my knowledge of the world paled compared to his.

Ches undid the top button of his shirt. "What's that got to do with the war?"

Harold continued. "If we attack Turkey and take the Dardanelles from them, the Russians will be stronger and better able to fight the Germans on the east."

"That makes sense," I said. "The Germans may have to send reinforcements, which will weaken the German army in France and Belgium, giving the Allies the upper hand."

Ches scoffed. "Whoever came up with that stunned idea is an arsehole, in my opinion. A war to protect Europe should be fought in Europe, not in some place no one's ever heard of."

Gord pursed his lips. "Wouldn't it be better and safer if the navy battled for the straits?"

"They tried and failed," Harold said.

Ches gritted his teeth. "That's just grand. We have to do what big hulking ships couldn't."

Within the next week we were subjected to all sorts of inoculations and vaccinations against diseases we'd never heard of, ailments which were apparently easily acquired in tropical regions such as the Mediterranean. Fred spat on the ground. "If I'd known about all this nonsense I'd never have signed up. That malarky is for sissies and old farts. I was nine when I made my first run to Barbados for rum. No silly talk about inoculations and vaccinations in those days." He smacked his lips together. "Nothing better than good rum to warm the belly."

Had I heard correctly? "Nine years old! Your father allowed you to go off on a ship to a foreign country?"

Fred spat again, a dark look on his face. "Don't talk to me about fathers. My mother died when I was eight. My old man skipped out on me and moved to Halifax. The man next door didn't want me ending up on the streets a criminal, so he took me with him and his son on his runs. The best training for real life anyone could get."

Three days before departure, Fred slipped into our barracks just after breakfast, interrupting Ches, who was playing the spoons and singing "My Wild Irish Rose." "How would you boys like to nip out tonight for a few swallies before we ship out?"

Ches laid his spoons aside. "I'm in."

"Count me out," Gord and Joey piped in as one voice.

Harold buckled his belt. "Me and Ron have patrolling duties."

Fred wiggled his eyebrows. "Leave that little problem with me."

I'd never broken a rule, and the prospect of doing so made my blood pump a little faster. "How are we going to get past the guards at the gate?"

"Rick Carter's on duty with Johnny Rendell. He's a good buddy as well. See you boys at seven by the gate."

At ten to seven we left the barracks, hurrying toward the gate. Rick and Johnny greeted us with warm hellos and turned their backs while we casually walked out of the castle. We made our way across town and ended up in a bar I hadn't come across on my nightly patrols. The patrons greeted Fred with handshakes and huge smiles.

The bartender, a big-bellied man with a bushy beard, spoke up. "Freddie, me young laddie. Ye haven't been 'round for a while." I hardly understood a word of his thick Scottish brogue. He eyed me and the boys. "I see you've brought along some friends."

Fred hauled me and Harold toward him. "McTavish, this is Ron Marrie and Harold Bartlett from St. John's, townies like me. He's from around the bay, but don't hold that against him."

The smell of beer and stale cigarette smoke hung in the air, along with the acrid smell of pipe smoke. A man, taller than a giraffe, played the piano in the far corner. The slow tune, unknown to me, was at odds with the vibrant conversation and laughter.

McTavish whipped a cloth from around his neck, polished four glasses, and brought out a bottle of dark rum from under the counter. "Only the best for Newfoundlanders," he said, filling each glass to the brim.

Fred thrust a drink into my hand and Harold's, then passed one to Ches. "There's plenty more where that came from."

"Enjoy," McTavish said. "The first bottle is on the house."

Fred and Ches threw back their heads and emptied the glasses in one take. I stared at mine several seconds, then with a sidelong glance at Harold, did the same. I gagged and coughed as the rum travelled into my nose from the inside.

Ches pounded me on the back. "I'll be dammed. That's your first taste of liquor."

I was too busy catching my breath to reply. Harold hadn't touched his drink.

I sipped the next round while Fred and Ches finished off theirs. Harold gulped down his first and glowed red in the face. "It has some kick to it," he said, rubbing his chest. "Burns all the way down."

Time sped by as the locals asked questions about our small island nation, stating that Harold and I had an Irish accent while Ches had more of a cockney dialect.

By midnight I was dead tired and more than a little drunk. "We'd better get back," I said through a yawn.

"Aye, laddie," Ches said, imitating to perfection a Scottish brogue. He stood up and stumbled into me. "I got you," Harold said, steadying Ches with one arm.

Fred had polished off two-thirds of a second bottle of rum, and with a steady hand he brought another drink to his lips. "I'll see you boys back at the castle."

Between the two of us we kept Ches upright as we walked. "Poor Fred misses Eileen already." He hiccupped. "I'd give any- thing to see my wife, Isabelle."

Early next morning Captain Wakefield visited our barracks. Gord, Harold, and Joey were playing cards. Ches was playing "My Wild Irish Rose" again with spoons. "Fred Thompson is missing. Either of you have an idea where he is?"

"Fred?" Ches said. "He's supposed to be on guard duty."

"He didn't show up. I take it he went to replenish his supply of rum?"

Two days later Fred strolled into the castle and came straight to my barracks to be confronted by Captain Wakefield. "I thought you might show up here to have a chat with your partners in . . ." He paused. ". . . partners in absconding without official furlough."

"No, sir. I stayed behind on my own. The boys had no idea what I'd done."

"Private Thompson, do I look stupid to you?"

"No, sir."

"Good. Five days confined to barracks and the loss of a week's wages are in order." The captain turned toward me and Ches. "You lot have the luck of the Irish. We're about to ship out, therefore confinement to barracks is out of the question. The same for Harold Bartlett. He's shipping out with you."

He spun on his heel to face Fred. "I'll forgo the loss of pay as well."

"Thank you, sir. You're a fine gentleman."

"I won't be a fine gentleman if this breach of policy happens again."

He placed his cap firmly on his head. "By the way, men, I forgot to mention one minor detail about Gallipoli." His gaze stole over each of us with such intensity my heart beat a little faster. A slight grin curved one corner of his mouth. "You'll all be sporting shorts instead of long pants."

Before any of us could react, Ches dropped like a brick onto a chair. "Jesus Christ, Cap'n, tell me this is a joke."

CHAPTER 4

EGYPT AND THE GALLIPOLI CAMPAIGN IN TURKEY

A long sea voyage wasn't appealing, but the idea of an exotic city was compelling and overshadowed my dread of seasickness. Postcards of the *Megantic* were plentiful, and men bought them as precious items to send home. I purchased one knowing Joanie would be thrilled to see a picture of the steamer. As there was limited space on the back, I chose my words carefully.

> Leaving England tonight on this ship most likely bound for Egypt, then on to Khartoum. Two thousand soldiers aboard. Thirty-four officers. Going to Dardanelles to fight the Turks. Will write when I reach destination.
>
> Love, Ron

Harold Bartlett came in as I sat at the table with a steaming cup of brewed tea. He tapped his postcard against the corner of the table. The back was blank. "I'm not sure it's a good idea to write home with details of our mission, especially on the card showing the ship we're sailing on."

"Anyone can buy this postcard." I read out loud what I'd

written. "Do you really think someone would leak the information to the Germans?"

"I wouldn't want to risk it. Then again, Kitchener blurted it out for everyone to hear." He pulled out a chair and plunked his elbows onto the table. "You'd think troop movement would be confidential."

Harold tore his postcard in two and I ripped up my postcard despite the fact all vital information had already been posted to Newfoundland by most of the troops. At least I hadn't contributed to the spread of military information.

At nine o'clock the next morning, August 20, we boarded the SS *Megantic*. "Turkey," Ches Abbott said, and gobbled like one. "Who ever heard of a country with a bird's name?"

Charlie Paterson, just a youngster, from Goobies, tilted his head to the side in deep thought. "Maybe it's the other way 'round."

"Now, laddie," Ches said in a fatherly tone. "Stop blabbering such nonsense."

Harold moaned, stricken with queasiness even though we hadn't left port. "If seasickness does me in before we get to the Dardanelles, don't toss me overboard as fish food. Bury me on land. Promise!"

Ches placed his hands on his hips. "If we were going to France you'd suffer for a few hours. Instead, we'll be on the open seas for days." Harold groaned louder. "Sorry, lad. Didn't mean to rub it in."

I was more concerned with safety issues. I glanced toward the lifeboats. "What if we're hit by a bomb in the middle of the ocean? Are there enough of those for everyone?"

"Yes," Joey Baker said, coming up behind me. "The chaplain reassured me there's plenty to hold every man on board."

Fred patted the bulge under his breast pocket. "Never mind lifeboats. A good rum is more reassuring."

While we waited to ship out, I decided to write a letter home. I found a secluded spot near the lifeboats and had taken paper and pencil out when the chaplain stood over me.

"Mr. Marrie," he said, "I ran into your uncle Jack in London recently. He was quite shocked to hear you'd enlisted." The chaplain glanced down as if searching the floor, an odd habit of his. "He sends his regards and orders you to keep your head down."

"Thank you, sir. Now I have more good news to tell my parents."

I went back to start my letter. I had just written "Dear Mom and Dad," when Joey showed up.

"I'm worried about Harold," he said. "We haven't left port and he's already throwing up." He held up a paper bag. "This is mint candy. I gave Harold some. Mom swears they help with seasickness. I suggest you take a few."

Guarded by two destroyers, we steamed out into the English Channel at seven in the evening. Every inch of the rail was taken up by soldiers, squeezed together like clothes in an overpacked suitcase, all waving back at the hundreds of civilians who'd come out to see us off, as if we were royalty. The weather was relatively calm during the voyage, much to Harold's relief, who endured the occasional bout of sickness. Perhaps Joey's mint candy had worked a miracle.

The second night, Harold went missing from our quarters. I found him stretched out on the deck gazing up at the stars. "Still seasick?" I was quite well myself, having somehow hardened my stomach to the toss and roll of the ship.

"Not too bad. It's hot enough below deck to boil molasses." He sat up and took out a folded sheet of paper from his pocket. "You know I never went to school like you and Joey Baker. Neither did any of my sisters." There wasn't a hint of resentment in his voice as he continued. "Ma's done her best to bring us up by herself." Harold indicated the paper he held. "She always found someone to read my letters."

"That's good," I said.

"Teaching myself to read and write wasn't easy, but I was determined." Harold passed the paper to me. "Would you look this over and correct my spelling?"

I read down the page, underlining very few mistakes, trying not to concentrate on what was written. Personal thoughts were just that, personal, but the name caught my attention. Harold rewrote the words as I spelled each one out.

"Elizabeth is . . . was my girl," he confided. "Her father is a teacher and wants more for his only daughter than someone like me."

"How does she feel?"

"She doesn't care what her father thinks. I won't have her worrying about where the next meal is coming from like my mother does." Harold erased the last spelling mistake, corrected it, folded the letter, and returned it to his pocket. He lay back down and gazed at the stars once more.

Without fail, we had lifeboat drills every day. As much as possible, Harold, Joey, and I spent most of the time on deck, even sleeping there as the hold grew hot and stuffy—a situation sure to ripen another bout of seasickness.

British soldiers were aboard, the game of poker their preferred recreational activity, which they played with astonishing skill. It chased away Ches's grumpy mood, despite losing just about everything he owned on the third night out.

"Now what are you going to do for money?" I asked, expecting he'd want to borrow from us.

"Old Ches is never down and out." He took a penny out of his pocket and tossed it in the air. "This is me lucky charm." He smiled, showing off even, white teeth. "Maybe it's time to put it into action." Whether it was the coin's magical powers or not, Ches won the next night, tripling the amount he'd lost.

Guard duty wasn't enough to keep us busy, but even Joey, who had an aversion to any form of gambling, finally indulged. "That's me boy," Ches said, the fourth time in a row Joey cleaned the men out of their money. "Beginner's luck isn't an old wives' tale after all."

One night when Ches was on guard duty, Charlie Paterson decided to try his hand. "I never played before," he said to the English soldiers gathered around a small table. "It looks easy enough, though."

In the first hand a veteran player bluffed and beat Charlie's three of a kind with a pair of sixes. By the fourth hand, I suspected from the sidelong glances the British players cast at each other, that they were conspiring to fleece Charlie. He'd gambled away half of his money before I convinced him to quit.

I informed Ches what had happened. "What?" he roared. "Those no-good sons of fish bait took advantage of a boy." He stormed past me and went down below. We heard a scuffle, then Ches came topside and handed Charlie back his money. "Listen, boy. Warn me the next time you get the itch to play."

"Thanks, sir. Ma doesn't abide with cheaters."

"Charlie, call me Ches. You're a soldier like the rest of us."

As we neared the coast of Morocco, Joey wiped streams of sweat from his forehead. His hair was plastered to his head like he'd just come aboard from a swim in the ocean. "This heat drains my energy quicker than a twenty-five-mile march. We'll melt away before we fight in the war."

We closed in on the many warships, and Ches and Fred came up from below as we came upon one of the hospital ships returning from the Dardanelles, carrying sick and wounded soldiers. Two soldiers stood by the rail, one a head shorter than the other. The taller stood with his arms behind his back.

The shorter man lit a cigarette and put it in his companion's mouth. He puffed several times before the other soldier took it from his mouth as the man blew out smoke. The same process repeated.

"Jesus Christ!" Ches said in a breathless voice as we pulled alongside. "The poor bugger's arms are gone." He slumped against me and my legs almost gave way. The sleeves of the man's shirt were pinned up to keep them from flapping in the wind.

Joey opened his mouth, but made no sound. Harold blessed himself. "He's no older than me," he said, his eyes never leaving the soldier. Fred pulled a bottle of whiskey from his pocket and took a long swallow, his hand shaking. As the ship moved on we stared at each other in silence.

On August 26 we reached Valletta Harbour, the capital of Malta. The sun sparkled on buildings that looked like they'd been fashioned from white sand. The domes on the mosques reminded me of swollen buns of bread dough. We stayed aboard the ship overnight, the officers the only ones granted permission to go ashore.

"It doesn't bother me to stay aboard," Joey said. "The chaplain said the hospitals are overburdened with sick and wounded soldiers. I don't fancy bumping into more armless men."

Local people sailed around the ship in small skiffs, selling fresh fruit, a treat even in back home in Newfoundland. Ches peeled an orange, his callused fingers digging into the orange skin. "I'd rather be dead than lose me arms." Juice squirted onto his shirt, staining the pocket with pin-sized spots. He tossed the peel into the water with a heavy sigh. "How's that poor bugger going to earn a living?"

We departed the next morning and arrived at Mudros on the Greek Island of Lemnos. Forty miles from the firing lines, it was the base for the Dardanelles operation. The harbour was congested with hundreds of troopships, battleships, submarines, cruisers, hospital ships, and cargo vessels. We avoided looking at the hospital ships.

Harold turned his face toward the sun. "I'm looking forward to getting off the ship. My stomach deserves green earth beneath my feet."

"Sorry, lads," Chaplain Wakefield said. "No one's permitted ashore. Orders have been changed, and we move on to Alexandria tomorrow."

Ches growled deep in his throat. "We left home almost a year ago. What's the problem? The generals can't make up their minds how to run the war?"

The captain rolled the ends of his moustache between his fingers. "An accurate conclusion, in my opinion," he said, and wandered off.

Fred Thompson rammed his fist into the rail. "Who gives a shit what orders are? I'm getting off this boat and getting me some rum." He massaged his knuckles. "Hey, Harold. You should come with me. You need a break from this floating barge."

"If I get off I might never get back on."

Fred took off his boots, tied them together, and hung them around his neck. After one glance up and down the ship, he climbed up on the rail. "See you later, boys," he said, and dived into the water.

We'd finished eating supper when Fred sneaked back on board, dripping wet, with three bottles of dark rum.

"They must've cost an awful lot of money," I said.

"Not a penny, boy. Not a penny."

"How—" I snapped my mouth shut. Better to be in the dark.

Once in Alexandria, we finally set foot on solid ground and headed for Abbassia Barracks on the outskirts of Cairo. To my surprise, the barracks were made of stone and didn't have a single piece of furniture. We slept on the stone floor, which I never got used to, our haversacks the only pillow. Training consisted of a march from six in the morning to seven thirty in heat like an oven. We stumbled back, exhausted and dripping wet.

"We're on the move again," Ches said, and we were transferred to Polygon Camp in the desert outside Heliopolis. "Farther and farther away from the fighting." We shared huge tents with a capacity to house over sixty men.

Fred leaned against the wall and slid down to the floor. "Never thought I'd be happy wearing shorts." He flicked a pebble at Ches, and didn't crack a smile. "Ches, your missus must be jealous of your smooth, hairless legs. Do all the Abbott men shave their legs?"

Gord opened his mouth to speak but Ches cut him off. "Another word about shorts or my legs will land you . . ." He stared down every man in the room. ". . . a whack up the side of the head."

Truth be told, Ches's legs really were almost hairless and he had been enduring endless teasing. Even fifteen-year-old Charlie Paterson had more "manly" legs, as Fred duly noted the first time we donned shorts.

After sunrise one morning, Joey's gaze roamed over the sand that extended into infinity. "I don't like the desert," he said with a slight shudder. "The air glows and shimmers like flames of fire. No place on earth should be this hot."

Sand infiltrated our food no matter what was done to stop it. Even the drinking water left sand residue on our lips. During one of our marches, sweating profusely, we stopped to rest at an oasis. Palm trees surrounded a pool of water, their leaves as unmoving as trees in a painting. There was always a short supply of water in the camp, and our throats were parched. The men swarmed to the edge of the pool, anxious to indulge.

Ches's head rotated like a chicken as he sniffed the water.

"Hold on, boys. Do you smell that?"

Harold ran his hand through the water. "All I smell is over-heated bodies that need a good wash."

"No," Charlie said. "Ches is right. This water reeks like an animal's been dead in there for a week."

We all stared at the water, licking our parched, sandpapered lips.

"I'm warning you," Ches continued. "That water's not fit for drinking."

We listened to Ches and thanked the Lord we did. The next day Harold Bartlett came off duty, his face grey as steel. "Some of the men in the other unit drank from that oasis yesterday. They's all sick with stomach cramps and diarrhea."

"I told you that water was off," Ches said.

Harold sat down and took off his boots. "The pool was drained to check it out. You'll never believe what they found on the bottom. They pulled up the carcasses of three horses and a human skeleton." He ran his hand over his mouth to squelch the urge to vomit.

Charlie sprang to his feet and ran outside, great heaves racking his body. Ches poured water into a tin cup. "Poor lad. He'll need this."

On September 14 we boarded the SS *Ausonia* for Mudros. Joey squashed a fly on his arm with the palm of his hand, producing a loud smack. "Why are we going back there?" Another fly pitched on his cheek. He slapped it away, leaving a speck of blood. "It's like we're chess pieces being moved around by men who haven't a clue how to play the game."

"Think about it like this," I said. "Despite the heat and shortage of water, the marches have kept us in excellent shape for when we do get to the front."

We landed at Mudros three days later and were given 200 rounds of ammunition, blankets, and greatcoats, all adding up to eighty pounds. Ches was as excited as a newlywed. "Maybe now we'll see fighting and help end the war."

The armless man flashed before my eyes.

Joey lifted the haversack onto his back and stumbled forward. "This weighs almost as much as me."

"You're bent over like a feeble old man," Charlie said, laughing so hard he almost fell down. Although I was only three years older than Charlie, I thought how childish he looked despite the unknown dangers awaiting us.

We came ashore at Kangaroo Beach in Suvla Bay on the Gallipoli Peninsula late the following night. The roar of shells exploded around us as we ran for safety. Gary Newman from Stephenville was blown upwards, then tumbled down on his back. Blood soaked through his upper right arm. I dropped down next to him, pulling bandages from my kit. He looked dazed.

"You'll be all right," I said, keeping my voice steady.

Ches hurried over. "Let's get him to his feet." He draped Gary's good arm around his neck and pulled him up. Sand flew into the air as we sidestepped the impacts from shells and the holes left behind. Ahead of us, two men fell to the ground, not hurt, but obviously stunned, and were helped to their feet by passing soldiers.

A short time later, a lifetime to me, we took refuge in a shell hole crater that was nothing more than a slight hollow in the sand. We gathered the wounded, fifteen altogether, and treated them as best we could. No amount of training had prepared me for hurt and bleeding bodies. I slept fitfully, awakening to more shelling, the sound like claps of thunder. Later that day, after the wounded were taken away, we made for Essex Gully, a more protected shelter farther inland.

We dug deep trenches in the support lines during the long, cold nights and slept during the unbearable heat of day, to avoid snipers and shelling from the hills a little farther ahead. "The rear lines are no safer," Joey said after we'd completed our first ten days. "If I spit it'll reach their front line."

He wasn't exaggerating. To make matters worse, sickness and insects claimed more lives than the constant shelling, sniping, and scarcity of water. I woke each morning fearful about the next victim to fall prey to dysentery or jaundice. The day before, Ben Saunders from South Side Road fell down, grabbing his stomach. Sweat beaded on his forehead. "Oh God," he cried, curling into a fetal position. "I'm sorry, boys."

"What for? You can't help—" I wrinkled my nose as the fecal odour wafted toward me.

"Don't be embarrassed, lad," Ches said. "Others haven't made it to the toilet in time. Let's get you cleaned up."

I counted out loud the slugs crawling up the side of the trench.

Harold Bartlett scratched the side of his neck until it bled and squashed horned beetles camped out on his boot. "I should let the insects crawl all over me," he said. "At least they'll eat the lice." He scratched his chest. "As poor as we were, Ma always kept our house clean."

Itching from head to foot, I scratched until my skin hurt. "A swim in the ocean might slow down the lice."

"Why not?" Harold said. "And if we get shot, maybe we'll float back to Newfoundland."

Somewhat refreshed and itching considerably less, we returned to the trench, our clothing air-dried by the time we arrived. Ches and Gord, and Private Sid Tremblett, a fellow fisherman from Bonavista, were digging in a trench shoulder-to-shoulder across from me when a shot rang out. I dropped my shovel and dived to the ground along with the three men next to me. A howl of pain pierced the air, akin to a dog's cry at the death of its master. Two more shots, then silence.

"Everyone all right?" I yelled, a knot in my stomach.

"Sid Tremblett's been hit in the head," Charlie Paterson called out.

I scurried to the side of the trench and peered over the top. Ches moved along the ground, crouching low with his rifle slung across his back. The moon illuminated him like a spotlight. I grabbed my rifle and followed, slithering along the ground.

"The shots came from up there," Ches whispered, pointing up the hill. His hand was covered in blood.

"The sniper must be gone by now, or he would've picked us off like ducks on a pond."

"He can't have gone far." Ches raced up the incline, his rifle now held out before him. I charged after him. A cloud passed over the moon and Ches disappeared from sight. Another shot rang out and I sank to the ground, my skin tingling.

A Turk emerged out of the shadows, his hands behind his head. I'd never seen the enemy close up. He stopped, his lip bleeding and swollen, his eyes dark, mirroring the expression on his face.

Ches shoved him forward with the butt of his rifle. "Keep moving."

I fell into step beside Ches. "What happened?"

"He was eating some weird-looking fruit when I sneaked up on him. He managed to get off a shot but missed." Ches glanced briefly at me. "Never kill when you don't have to."

I blinked. I'd misjudged this gruff, outspoken fisherman in more ways than one.

We returned from delivering the Turkish prisoner to find Sid Tremblett sitting up in the trench, his head bandaged. "I got the fright of me life," he said, gently fingering the wound. He was whiter than the gathering clouds above us. "They're sending me to a hospital ship." He stood up, took one step forward, and slumped down into a heap.

"Charlie," I said, "there's blood on your face. Are you hurt?"

"No, that's Sid's blood," he said, wiping it away.

Joey and I carried Sid to the dressing station. "My head's busting," he said, and we set him down on his feet. He passed out again.

Joey knelt beside Sid. "Doctor, he was conscious until a minute ago." The doctor removed the bandage to reveal three-quarters of a bullet protruding from Sid's forehead above the right eyebrow.

"I did my best to clean the wound," Joey said.

The doctor replaced the bloodied bandage with a fresh one. "Was he coherent?"

"Yes," Joey said.

"A good sign," the doctor muttered to himself.

"He did complain of a headache," I said.

"The bullet doesn't seem to have penetrated too deeply into the bone. It's likely his brain hasn't been compromised."

Sid moaned and opened his eyes. "You fellas still here?"

"We couldn't leave without seeing you off," I joked, stepping aside to allow two men to place him on a stretcher. Sid waved as he was carried toward a tug bound for one of the hospital ships.

We continued with the never-ending task of digging deeper trenches, unearthing more slugs, and fending off insects I couldn't name. Rain fell as dawn approached, with flies buzzing around Joey's head. He made a futile attempt to flick them away. "My feet will never be dry again, and these damned insects are driving me crazy."

An animal the size of a puppy moved in the shadows next to me. I whacked it with my shovel, and with a loud squeal a large rat scurried away. "Bloody rodents!"

"They'll eat us when the food's all gone," Joey said. "That's if we don't die of thirst first."

A shell whistled close by, followed by a loud blast. The earth shook, knocking me off my feet. An avalanche of dirt poured over me, its weight pressing me to the ground, squeezing tighter and tighter. My face was buried deep in the debris and I couldn't move. Everything was dark and quiet. My lungs didn't have enough room to expand. My brain screamed for help.

Ches's muffled voice penetrated through the debris. "Ron, Joey, hang on."

"We'll get you out." Harold's voice was thick, as if he were speaking from under water.

Other men's assurances reached me, their ragged breaths betraying the soothing words.

A pair of hands caught me under the armpits and lifted me to my feet as I coughed and spat out dirt. Harold pulled Joey by the legs from under a mound of rocks. Two men threw their shovels aside when Charlie Paterson's boots appeared, and dragged him out. His eyes were open, but there wasn't any expression in them. Ches sat him against the side of the trench wall and cleared dirt from his face. "Come on, Charlie, talk to me."

He didn't move, didn't make a sound. Ches slapped him. "This isn't the time to fool around, boy."

Transfixed, we stared at Charlie, a boy of fifteen, his head resting against Ches, his wide eyes greener than grass, his arms hanging loosely to the ground. We'd never witnessed a human being die before. I saw a tear on Chaplain Murray's cheek when he whispered a prayer before Charlie was taken away for burial in this foreign land. His mother would never have the opportunity to visit her son's grave.

Ches drew a knee close to his face, draping one hand over the side. "He was too young to be here." He spoke to no one in particular. "The child didn't even shave."

"Our baby brother better not join up." Gord stood up and staggered against the side of the trench. "Must've got up too fast."

Ches leaned back his head. "A good stiff drink wouldn't go astray."

The next day while working on the trenches, Gord toppled over onto his back.

I ran my hands over him, checking for a bullet wound. "What happened? Are you hit?"

He opened his eyes and sat up. "I felt weak and then everything went black." He held onto his stomach. "I've been having awful cramps. I got to get to the toilets, but I can't make it on my own."

The lineup was impossibly long, with men grunting and groaning, trying to hold their bowels, clutching their stomachs.

"I got diarrhea bad," Gord said. "I don't know if I can hang on much longer."

"Hurry up." It was an Australian voice.

"What's keeping you?" An English soldier this time. "You've been in there ten minutes."

A hush came over the men when the man in the toilet didn't answer. The Australian and Englishman exchanged looks, then kicked open the door. A soldier sat slumped over, his pants down around his ankles.

"The poor lad's dead," the Brit said, and with the help of the Australian he pulled up the man's pants and took him away.

The next morning Gord threw up non-stop, and by noon he was vomiting blood. Ches held the water bottle to his brother's lips. "Try to drink a little."

Gord swallowed a mouthful but couldn't keep it down. His face burned red. "Sorry, Ches. Looks like I won't be here to watch out for you like I promised Isabelle."

Ches flinched like he'd been slapped in the face. "We'll get you to the doctor. They'll set you right."

Gord lay on a stretcher waiting for transportation to Valetta Hospital. Ches, forcing a smile, smoothed sweat-soaked hair out of his brother's eyes. "We'll see you at the front in France." Gord was too weak to smile back. Another victim of dysentery, the illness now sweeping through the ranks causing life-threatening fevers.

Endless days merged into an eternity of digging, sickness, dying, and not enough food to eat. Storytelling became a favourite pastime. Fred related a tale about the first time he'd tasted liquor and got dead drunk at the age of twelve. "We traded for rum in the Bahamas. One night I had the worst thirst of me life and slipped down to the hold and pried open a barrel of rum." His eyes lit up. "A finer taste you'll never find. I started to feel dizzy and made my way back on deck. The sea was calm, but the ship swayed back and forth under me feet. The next thing I know I'm in the ocean yelling my head off for help. Old Ed, that was the man who took me under his wing, hauled me out of the water by the scruff of the neck and threw me in my bunk."

"Was he mad at you?" I asked.

"He didn't say a word, although he was quite pleased with my hangover in the morning. I vomited for two days straight. Old Ed stayed with me the whole time. He passed on with a heart attack when I was eighteen. I miss the old fart."

Ches recounted how he'd met his wife, Isabelle. "She's a townie, you know. Came to Bonavista at Christmas with her sister to visit their cousin. They were walking along the rocky beach when some young fellas pelted them with snowballs."

"And you came to the rescue," Harold said, holding back a grin.

"Normally I wouldn't spoil the youngsters' fun." Ches whistled, a long musical sound. "Isabelle was cuter than a baby seal, so I stepped in to help her."

"And the hero won the lady's heart," I said.

"Not exactly. A snowball smacked her sister right in the eye. Isabelle blamed me and told me off in style. Later that day I, uh . . . let's just say I persuaded the real culprit to confess to her. She came back during the summer and lost her heart to me." Ches placed his hands over his own heart and sighed. "She couldn't help herself."

Sid Tremblett, who'd returned a week earlier, fitter than ever, threw his hat at Ches. "That's a fairy tale if I ever heard one."

Ches slapped the hat back on Sid's head. "One more wise-crack from you and you'll end up with a matching scar over your other eyebrow."

The rising of the sun meant warmth, enabling us to stretch our cold limbs. It also meant snipers had resumed their favourite pastime . . . using us for target practice. One morning, Fred Thompson scanned the open ground. "There's a group of Turks not far off." He grabbed his rifle and shot three times. "That's three less to worry about." He spat out tobacco juice, the brown mess blowing back into the trench.

Late one afternoon, Captain Wakefield, using a periscope, focused in on a knoll several yards up the hill. The enemy occupied the spot as a sniper post. "I'm sick to death of being picked off from up there. It's time we arrange a surprise for the Turks. They do a lot of their dirty work in the night. Tonight we'll have a surprise for them."

Harold, Fred, Humphrey Little, Rick Carter, Johnny Rendell, and I accompanied the captain to the knoll. As night fell, the Turks' soft whispers and quiet chuckling drew near.

Fred's eyes smouldered. "The cocky bastards think we're easy marks again tonight."

Two Turks appeared, walking as if on a relaxing stroll, rifles in the crux of their arms.

"Hello," Captain Wakefield said, his pistol trained on them. "Lovely night for a walk."

One Turk froze, the other ready to raise his rifle.

Fred blurted out, "No you don't," and aimed just above the man's head. The bullet went through the top of his headdress. The Turk dropped his rifle and raised his hands on his head.

The next day Captain Wakefield sent reinforcements to safeguard the knoll and came across a Turkish patrol. Fred opened fire. "Let's show them who owns this hill once and for all."

"Look at them run," Humphrey Little said. "They got the message this hill isn't theirs anymore."

Harold slung his rifle over his back. "I say we name this Caribou Hill, since we Newfoundlanders ousted it from the Turks."

The weather grew cold enough to take out our greatcoats and blankets. Trench foot became a real concern in the constant damp, unsanitary conditions, and from wearing the same wet socks for weeks on end. Captain Wakefield had seen a case of severe trench foot where gangrene had set in. He'd insisted that soldiers be paired off to check each other's feet daily, and he even distributed whale oil to help prevent infection. More than once Fred Thompson was heard yelling at Rick to take off his boots or he'd get a kick in the head.

We Newfoundlanders survived better than the Australians, who, for the most past, had never seen snow or experienced below-freezing temperatures. At the end of November I awoke, kicking and splashing to stay afloat in my heavy clothing. "What's going on?" I gasped, coughing and spitting out water. Rain picked at my face like the tips of a hundred knives. The wind howled, and blew strong enough to rip away a caribou's antlers.

Joey Baker stood up but slipped as his feet came out from under him. Harold yanked him up with one hand. "The water's gushing down the hills like a busted dam," he shouted over the wind.

Joey clung to Harold. "We're trapped with nowhere to go."

We climbed the side of the trench, slipping backwards like we were on a playground slide. Ches intertwined the fingers of both hands and as we stepped onto this human rung, he catapulted us over the top. Harold, the last one out, gripped Ches's hand and pulled him into the newly formed lake. We went down the line toward the shouts and cries of men scrambling from the other trenches, trying to haul comrades with them. Some had died in their sleep, while others drowned trying to save their buddies. We were hip deep in water as we rescued the living.

"Jesus Christ," Ches screamed. "We didn't come over here to drown like sewer rats!" He closed the eyes of an Australian who was no more than eighteen. "This lad's parents will learn their son drowned, and wasn't killed in fighting." Ches kicked at the ground, splashing water into my face. "Where's the honour in that?"

Chaplain Murray made the sign of the Cross over the boy. "I'll see to it personally that his parents are told he died in defence of freedom."

"Sorry, Chaplain," Ches said. "I didn't mean to overreact."

"No apologies required."

Two nights later the temperature bottomed out and the water in the trenches froze.

Harold rested against the side of the trench, shivering in his wet clothing. "I'm used to the cold." His breath formed whiffs of clouds with every word. "But never like this. Even the hairs on my arms are cold."

Ches growled. "So why the hell did they issue those sissy shorts?"

"Isn't it obvious?" I asked. "It's because of the extreme heat here."

Joey Baker's lips were a pale shade of blue. "Thank the Lord," he said through chattering teeth, "my feet aren't cold anymore."

Harold bolted upright. "I'll be right back." The slush in the bottom of the trench didn't slow him down.

Joey tried to smile, but his mouth didn't quite achieve it. "Hope he makes it to the latrine in time."

Harold returned with a medical officer, who inspected Joey's feet. "Sorry, son," the middle-aged man said. "You have a serious case of frostbite."

Within the hour, Joey lay on a stretcher waiting to be evacuated to a hospital ship. Garth Duncan, an Australian suffering from trench feet, was evacuated along with him. His feet were swollen, with blisters and open sores along the ridges of the toes. The heels were red, the ankles dark blue. They smelled like decaying fish on a hot, humid day. He chatted with Joey like he didn't have a care in the world.

"Your feet aren't bothering you?" I asked Garth.

Garth sat up and pinched the puffy skin. He didn't even flinch. "My feet are numb. I know they'll be good as new once the swelling goes down."

I spun around to agonized screams. A man writhed on a stretcher, his feet twice the normal size, with reddening of the toes.

"That's my mate," Garth said. "The pain is excruciating, but a good sign the swelling is going down. I hope I'll be as lucky as him."

"Lucky," I said. "He's in agony!"

Garth stared down at his deformity. "I may have waited too long. My feet might have to be amputated."

Two stretcher-bearers arrived. "Good luck, Garth," I said.

He half-smiled. "Thanks, mate."

Joey gave me a long, searching look. "Don't count me out, Ron. I'll be back with the regiment before you know it."

"Tom, wake up!" The cry rang out from the trenches as stretcher-bearers carried Joey and Garth away.

Another of Garth's mates had frozen to death.

Food had been scarce since our arrival. The Australians had been here much longer, and they much closer to starvation. I stopped counting at one hundred the number of men who'd perished in the harsh weather. As they presided over the burial of each drowned or frozen Australian, the chaplains looked more haggard than the men who'd dug the graves. These men of God all served the war effort by offering counsel and prayer, aiding their fellow man through tragedy and grief. Who would counsel them?

Dozens more Newfoundlanders and Australians suffered frostbite. Ches became jittery and slept fitfully. One night after a man with a severe case of frostbite had been loaded onto a hospital ship, Ches tossed and turned in his sleep. "Don't stop!" he cried out. "You'll freeze to death."

Ches jerked awake into a sitting position, white, panting and gasping for air, his hair soaked with sweat despite the cold weather.

Harold scurried to his side. "It's just a dream, Ches. You're all right."

"Are you worried about getting frostbite?" I asked.

"No. I was dreaming about the seal hunt of nineteen fourteen."

From coast to coast, every Newfoundlander remembered the horrific disaster that occurred on the ice floes that year. Inquiries had been ongoing when I left home.

Ches's breathing slowly returned to normal. "The seal hunt is a godforsaken hardship at the best of times. Icefields collide into each other, crushing the sealers, blizzards push boats away, and men perish in storms. The shipowners are too miserly to furnish proper clothing or equipment. You're forced to eat nothing but tea and sea biscuits for weeks and months at a time. It's not too long before the drinking water stinks from seal fat and blood." He ran his sleeve across his forehead. "You townies don't know how fortunate you are."

Ches pulled his blanket more tightly around himself. "We slept in the holds of the ships, and later on top of the seal pelts once they were gathered in. If a man got injured he recovered or died without any medical aid. One hundred and thirty-two of us were left stranded for two days and nights on the icefield. Of course, we weren't properly dressed for the Arctic weather and had little food. Snow blinded us, and the wind cut through us as easily as a hand through water. The only way to hold on to a measure of heat was to keep moving."

The rumours and accusations about who was responsible for the tragedy abounded. I'd never spoken to an actual survivor before.

The blood drained from Ches's face. "Men cried out in pain, a few going crazy from it. Some stepped into the water to relieve the agony. Seventy-seven froze to death by the time help arrived. One died later in hospital. Seventy-eight men. Many others had their feet amputated due to severe frostbite."

"There were ships close by that had no idea what was happening," Harold Bartlett said.

"That was Captain Kean's fault, as far as I'm concerned. He was a mean bastard who cared more for money than his own men. Captain Randell of the *Bonaventure* found us. I'll never forget the look of horror on his face when the frozen dead were brought on board."

Harold folded his blanket around Ches's shoulders. "I was among the thousands on Harvey's waterfront when the *Bellaventure* sailed in. It was eerie how so many people never made a sound."

Ches rocked his feet from side to side. "I walked aboard the ship with a little help, thankful there was no permanent damage. My uncle died an hour before we were rescued."

"Joey's feet," Harold said. "Will he—"

"He'll be all right. My feet were in a worse state than his."

I pictured the scene Ches had described. Dark human forms struggling to walk on floating white ice, lumps of freezing flesh surrounded by frosty water and more ice. I'd been stranded in a blizzard for five hours as a boy. My eyelashes became coated with ice and burned my eyes. Although I was warmly dressed for winter weather, the howling wind stung my skin like needles. Thawing in front of a blazing fireplace, I whimpered like a newborn from the intense pain of warm blood pumping freely through numb extremities. Ches and the sealers had survived a living nightmare. I drifted to sleep with a deeper respect for fishermen and the burden of their everyday lives.

The routine of guard duty, digging trenches, being shelled by gunners, and shot by snipers dragged on. One morning, orders were given for all troops to withdraw. "Here we go again," Ches said. "Another guess on the chessboard. I could teach them generals a thing or two about the game."

The Newfoundland Battalion was the last to leave, but not all at once. Men sneaked away at dusk, and more just before dawn, while fifty of us remained in the trenches, quickly changing position to make it seem like there were hundreds of us, in order to fool the Turks. Ches and the other men fired their rifles intermittently while Harold and the rest of us set booby traps, which we timed to go off at precise intervals.

Once that was accomplished, the other half of us slipped away. Ches, Harold, and I were among the remaining few charged with setting more delayed-action devices. Ches rigged the last bomb. "All right, boys, let's get the hell off this godforsaken land." Satisfied smiles on our faces, we boarded the very last lighter to leave the pier in the early hours of the morning. We had tricked the Turks into believing we continued to be available easy target practice.

We landed at Lemnos, and as far as I was concerned, we had arrived in paradise. There was enough hot food to satisfy the hunger of ten polar bears waking up from a long winter's hibernation. We were sheltered from the weather, with no more duty in front line trenches.

More Newfoundland recruits arrived from England, bringing our forces to 400 men. I wasn't sure if I was happy or disappointed Henry and Frank weren't among them. A little over a day later we shipped out without being told the destination.

"Lord jumpin' dyin' Jesus," Ches roared to the sky when we went ashore at Cape Helles on the Gallipoli Peninsula. "We're back in the hellhole we just left."

Captain Wakefield addressed his men, walking back and forth in front of us, his voice clear and strong. "We're expecting the Turks to launch a massive attack against us very soon. You along with other units, will prepare the defences."

"Ron," Harold said when the captain left, "all we've done is dig ditches and move from one place to another, presenting ourselves as target for the Turks. I've a gut feeling the generals don't even have maps of Gallipoli, but merely an impression about the lay of the land."

After two weeks of working harder than soldier ants to dig trenches, the attack came. We endured forty-four hours of artillery bombardment. "My bones can't stop rattling," Harold mouthed, covering his ears with his hands. "Not to mention my teeth."

Finally, the British infantry, together with support from warships, returned fire.

We braced ourselves for the onslaught of Turkish soldiers. It never came. "They backed off like the cowards they are," Ches said.

Fred Bartlett shook hands all around. "We did good work, boys."

Ches gripped Fred's hand a extra few seconds. "You did all right for a townie."

"A fine compliment, sir. Thank you."

We withdrew from the Gallipoli Peninsula for the last time and made for Suez, a seaport city in northeastern Egypt. The goal was to recuperate, as we were tired beyond reason, with many of us suffering the effects of illness. Our commanding officer, Colonel Hadow, was a strict disciplinarian who was determined that the Newfoundland Regiment's military standard equal or even surpass that of any other British regiment in the Division. As per his strict orders, we performed incessant drills, exercises, and route marches into the searing heat of the desert.

The letters I wrote home talked about the sights and beauty of the different places I'd been and about the friends I'd made. One night in early March, following a rather rigorous exercise program, more asleep than awake, I picked up a pencil and wrote to my parents, with no idea about what I would say.

Dear Mom and Dad,

The British forces have pulled out of Gallipoli with death and disease the only outcome of our presence there. Twenty-two Newfoundlanders are buried on the peninsula, killed by snipers, disease, or by the never-ending shelling. Ches always questions why we were sent where thousands were massacred for what he swears was a worthless endeavour. Is he right? I really don't know. Harold Bartlett has come to believe Britain saw the Dardanelles as an easy route to their ally, the Russians. The Turks were supposed to be neutral but joined with the Germans.

We're in Suez (Egypt) to recuperate, and believe me, it's well-deserved. I've witnessed men talking and laughing one second, then dead the next. Their lives, their futures snatched away by an enemy they never saw, never even met. Others drowned in their trenches or were smothered by sand and dirt. The cries of the wounded eats into my very soul. Seeing men killed who you've spent every moment of the day and night with is . . . I can't find the right words to describe my feeling.

We fought back but never achieved any significant advance. I don't regret signing up to fight for England, but I admit I never took time to really think about what was involved. How could I when the reality of war is beyond normal comprehension? I realize now that I was young in more ways than my age when I signed up, full of enthusiasm to do my duty for king and country. Gallipoli has taught me that a soldier's existence is fragile, exhausting, and meant to suffer unbearable conditions, especially for the Australians. More importantly, sheer luck is sometimes the only reason one survives. I promise you that, despite everything, I stay alert and try not to dwell on the danger that lies ahead.

I love you all.

Ron

P.S. Tell Joanie happy birthday from me. I'll write her tomorrow night.

I sealed the letter and crawled into my bunk. Early next morning, as we were getting ready for another bout of training, a British soldier entered our barracks and asked for Harold Bartlett. "Colonel Hadow would like to see you right away."

"Well, well," Ches said. "I'm usually the one in trouble. What have you hidden from us, lad?"

Harold turned to the soldier. "What does the colonel want with me?"

"I wasn't informed. He ordered me to escort you to him without delay."

Harold, pale, his arms rigid at his side, looked at me and Ches. "I'll see you on the training ground."

The soldier stepped aside. "After you." He followed Harold outside.

Sid moved closer to us. "What do you suppose that was about?"

Ches massaged the bridge of his nose. "Harold is an exemplary soldier, obeying every regulation without question." He drove his hands deep into his pants pockets. "This can't be anything good."

We marched into the desert under the sweltering sun, the taste of salty sweat on my lips. My legs ached with every stride, my arms hurt with every swing. I was stiff from the rigorous training that was the essence of our life lately. My muscles soon became immune to pain as I threw my heart into the training.

Ches, who hadn't said a word since we left camp, spoke up. "What's keeping Harold? We've been here over an hour. Something is wrong." None of us was willing to speculate on the reason for the colonel's summons.

The training concluded, we returned to base to find Chaplain Murray sitting outside our barracks. "Harold has been given compassionate leave," he said quietly. "I don't know the precise detail, but his mother and youngest sister were involved in a terrible accident. His sister is deceased, his mother in serious condition."

"Jesus Christ!" Ches blurted. "The poor bastard."

"He'll need our prayers and kind thoughts to get through this tragedy." The chaplain's comforting voice and gentle manner had eased many a soldier's last moments on earth.

Ches sat down on his bunk and stared out the window. "Your family getting hurt is the last thing on your mind. That's scarier than the Turks."

Fred produced a bottle of rum and placed it on the table. "Help yourselves, boys."

I wrote a brief letter to my parents, my insides shaking.

Dear Mom and Dad,

I've written so much about several of the men in my battalion you must feel like you know them. Harold Bartlett received the most awful news today. His sister died in an accident and his mother is badly hurt. He's been given compassionate leave and is on his way home.

I told you his father died years ago and Harold's remaining sisters are too young to be on their own. How frightened and heartbroken they must be. It would mean so much to me if you would check on them. They have only Harold now, and he'll need support as well. His family lives at 37 Flower Hill.

I don't know how I'd cope being so far away if anything happened to either of you or Joanie.

Love, Ron

I reread what I'd written, content that my parents wouldn't let me down.

CHAPTER 5

ST. JOHN'S, NEWFOUNDLAND

Mrs. Elizabeth Burke slowed long enough to check her watch, then rushed down the street. She gazed up at the steel-grey clouds that threatened a downpour at any second. The wind bit into her skin and dragged at the hem of her coat, pushing her forward. She held a hand to her hat, the broad rim flapping against her stinging cheeks. "Oh my goodness," she murmured, tightening the grip on the hat as a stronger gust almost lifted it from her head. Several large drops of rain spattered the sidewalk and the rain soon grew into a torrent, almost horizontal in the high winds. The sun had been glowing when she'd set off, and she hadn't anticipated this deluge.

Five minutes past nine she scurried up the steps of Government House for the morning meeting of the Women's Patriotic Association. She patted her cheeks with gloved hands to ease away the cold numbness. She pulled a tissue from her pocket and wiped the water dripping down her neck, opened the door to the building, and headed down the corridor to the drawing room. With fingers stiff from the cold, she unbuttoned her coat and pulled off her scarf.

Another woman walked with quick steps a few feet ahead, her boots echoing on the floor. "Mrs. Marrie," Elizabeth called in a slightly shrill voice. "Good morning to you. Glad to see I'm not the only one late."

She turned around to see Mrs. Burke tucking her scarf into her coat pocket. "Mrs. Burke, you look colder than an icicle."

"I'm frozen to the bone," she said. "On a foolish whim I decided to walk."

"You picked a rather blustery day."

"I'm a firm believer that brisk, fresh air clears the clogs from the brain. It kept my imagination at bay, for a few minutes, anyway."

"Is everything all right? You're rather pale." Women envied Mrs. Burke's naturally rosy cheeks.

She removed her hat and smoothed down her tousled white hair. "A trifle upset, to be honest. Mr. Burke and I haven't heard a word from Will or either of our other sons in over two months. This war is . . ." Her voice faded and she shivered. "Don't take me wrong. I'm proud they went to defend England."

"Mrs. Burke, I understand exactly what you mean."

"Forgive me, my dear. Of course you do, with a brother and son overseas."

Anne had gotten to know many women since becoming a member of the association. Most had sons, brothers, uncles, or husbands fighting in the war, and all wanted to help with the effort in any way possible. Some had daughters or nieces serving in hospitals. What she admired most about the association were the very members themselves. As a Roman Catholic and former teacher, she associated with and taught members of the same religion. Not a choice on her part, but an accepted feature of the denominational education system. Knowledge of other religions engendered understanding and tolerance. The ladies in this association were from diverse religions. Another amazing observation was the congeniality between the rich and the poor, the educated and uneducated, with no thought or concern to class distinction or background. Those working from day to day to feed their children and those who lived in luxury all shared the same goal: to aid the fighting men and their families.

The hum of conversation greeted them as they entered the drawing room. Tables took up every available space, some packed with shirts sewn by the women, while others held dressings, pillows, and underwear to be shipped off to soldiers and military hospitals. They were hoping to raise enough money to open a hospital in France for the wounded Newfoundland soldiers.

Mrs. Burke and Anne donned their official aprons, which displayed a large red cross symbol engraved across the front. Anne moved to the head table with Mrs. Burke and sat down. As the founder of this chapter of the association, Mrs. Burke remained standing and addressed the women.

"I've counted the money from the collection boxes we installed around the city two weeks ago. The passersby have been quite generous with their donations." She smiled. "Three hundred dollars and eighty cents." She took bills and coins from her purse, and laid the donations on the table, the coins clinking against each other.

Murmurs of approval echoed round the room.

Anne held up a copy of the Distaff magazine, published by the association. Rectangular-shaped, with a thick red line next to a blue one spread across the top and bottom and along each side. Each corner contained a cross. "The DISTAFF" was printed at the top, with a medical symbol directly below it. "In Aid of RED CROSS BRANCH Newfoundland" was printed under the symbol, and "W.P.A." at the very bottom. "The people will be pleased to read how much they contributed to our cause. And," Anne continued, anxious to announce the next piece of news, "my husband has arranged a hockey game for next week. The stevedores are looking forward to challenging the police."

Mrs. Young, a woman with fifteen grandchildren, chuckled. "My husband Carl would pay a pretty penny to see the police beaten."

Mrs. Burke returned the donations to her purse. "I'll bank this during dinnertime and give Mrs. Young the receipt," she said, referring to the association's secretary. Elizabeth Burke ran her eyes over the volunteers. "I think we should stop by Mrs. Sullivan's home this evening. She's by herself since her husband enlisted, and with the baby on the way she's awfully nervous about the birth."

Two women volunteered for the visit. "We'll bring her some groceries. The war pay won't go very far with another mouth to feed on the way."

Anne indicated the table to the side containing a single layer of knitted socks. "We're low on those. Maybe we should concentrate on knitting more this week."

"A good idea," Mrs. Casey, a dark-haired woman in her late thirties, said from the back of the room. "My son Tony can't stand cold feet. I get letters from him asking me to send more. He's been offered packs of cigarettes from Canadians for the ones I've sent him so far."

"That settles it," Mrs. Young said. "We knit socks."

They each collected a ball of wool from the supplies and whipped out their own needles. The morning progressed as they talked about letters they'd gotten from overseas.

Mrs. Young passed around a photograph of a pretty young girl with wiry hair, in her late teens. "My oldest grandson sent this. Donny met her in Scotland while in training. He plans to marry her when the war's over."

Mrs. Casey knitted, her fingers moving faster than the eye could see, transforming the ball of wool into a sock. "Tony says the Scottish people welcomed our boys like they were family. He's been invited to supper quite often by the townsfolk."

Anne learned about young men she never knew and would probably never meet. The stories warmed her heart nonetheless.

She excused herself at eleven, taking along her unfinished pair of socks, and ran most of the way home in the intermittent showers to fix sandwiches for Tom and Joanie. With tea steeped and everything laid out on the table, she left for the hospital. Anne had volunteered three afternoons a week, reading to patients, assisting others with eating their meals, and performing whatever other tasks were required. When four o'clock rolled around, she'd just begun to read to Mrs. Caul. Her husband had died a year after their marriage, and she had remained a widow, with no children. The youngest of five siblings, she was the only one left, and all her friends had long since passed. At ninety-eight years old, Mrs. Caul was as sharp-witted as Anne. She often shared Ron's letters with Mrs. Caul, and the elderly lady would compliment her on having such a lovely boy. She patted Anne's arm. "You run along, dear. Don't keep Tom waiting for supper."

Anne stopped off at Williams Grocery Store at the bottom of her street. A long, wide, one-storey building, it was stocked with every item from nails to tea. She had run out of salt and dared not forget it again today. Tom couldn't eat a single morsel of food without smothering it in the white crystals.

"This is outrageous, Mr. Williams."

Elsie Corcoran, Anne's sister-in-law, Tom's oldest sister, stood in front of the owner. Normally a soft-spoken, mild-mannered person, her tone surprised Anne. She hurried up the aisle to the counter. "Elsie, what's the matter?"

Her eyes blazed. "Mr. Williams has upped the price of a box of salt by fifty per cent."

Anne looked to the short, balding man. "Mr. Williams, that must be a mistake."

He wrung his hands. His clean-shaven face had gone white. "I've no other choice, Mrs. Marrie. The supply is down considerably, and I have to pay more than usual myself. I don't know how long before any of my other supplies will arrive. I've explained that a dozen times today." He looked like a puppy being chided for tearing up a favourite cushion. "I truly am sorry, ladies."

"I apologize, Mr. Williams," Elsie said. "I didn't meant to bark at you. Money is scarce as it is without adding extra costs of food to the burden."

"Mr. Williams," Anne asked, "do you know why the supplies are low? Tom hasn't mentioned anything."

"No, but I certainly would like to."

Anne purchased the salt and hurried home to find that Joanie had potatoes, turnip, and carrots peeled and boiling on the stove. "What else are we having for supper?" she asked, standing at the sink, scrubbing the carrot stains from her fingers.

Anne scooped bacon fat into a frying pan. "Fried cod."

Joanie slouched against the counter. "How come? We only eat fish on Fridays."

"That's a perfect question to ask your father." True to her inquisitive nature, Joanie demanded a response the minute her father came through the front door.

"Mmm, dinner smells delicious." Tom hung up his overcoat on the hall stand. "I'm starving."

Joanie followed him down the hall to the kitchen. "Dad, I'm still waiting for an answer."

Tom sat at the table and tweaked her chin. "The fishermen catch plenty of fish and we should support them by buying more." He pulled on his daughter's nose with his thumb and forefinger. "Even better, it's good for you."

Not to mention a whole lot cheaper than red meat, Anne thought to herself. It went without saying that Tom wouldn't have included that in his explanation to their daughter.

"That's all right, 'cause I love fish." Joanie picked up her fork and cut off a crusty portion. "My teacher brought in a map of France today to show us how close it is to Germany." She pushed a potato around her plate. "I'm scared for Ronnie."

Tom shook a large amount of salt onto his potatoes. "Your brother can take good care of himself."

Joanie ate a second helping of fish, and the instant she swallowed the last bite, she hopped up from the table. "I'm going to write Ronnie a letter about all the fish we're eating." She skipped down the hall, humming to herself.

"We're low on coal," Anne said to the sounds of Joanie's footsteps running up the stairs.

Tom pulled out the *Evening Telegram* from his back pocket. "One of the men at work told me the price has gone up again."

Anne stacked the dishes in the sink. "The price of salt is fifty per cent higher. What is going on?" She ran water and poured in detergent. Tom hadn't said a word. She dried her hands in her apron and sat back down. "Tom, what's bothering you?"

"There's been scarce few ships arriving with supplies lately. A rumour's going around the docks that the Water Street merchants are selling many of their largest steel-hulled steamers to Russia. One of the men heard the Russians need them to patrol their northern waters."

"Why would the merchants sell off their ships?"

"Who knows how merchants think? Maybe the war has cost them extra money and that's how they recoup the loss." Tom put his finger on the picture of a steamer at the bottom of the page. "I picked up the paper to show you this. It's not a rumour anymore. The steamship *Bellaventure*'s been sold to the Russians."

"I don't see the sense in that. Now they don't have enough

ships to import the products we need. It's obvious now why prices are suddenly increasing to a ridiculous amount."

Tom stared past her out the window, one hand drumming the tabletop. "Less ships to unload means less work for me and the boys. Some of them have big families to feed."

"Ron's war pay can help tide us over."

"Anne, we're not touching that money. It's his for when he comes home."

"If we get stuck, he'd want to help get us through."

Tom scraped a match along the bottom of his shoe and lit a cigarette. "We haven't fallen on hard times yet."

Anne smiled to herself. Hard times or not, her husband would never spend his son's money, especially money he'd earned risking his life. She washed the dishes singing "My Wild Irish Rose," Tom's favourite song.

"The war's done some good for Newfoundland," he said.

Anne glanced over her shoulder as Tom blew out circles of smoke. Joanie always caught them between her hands. "How do you figure that?"

"The fisheries, for one. Many of the nations at war don't have the time or men to fish like they did, therefore our fishermen have more markets available to them, including selling right here at home, since the price of imported meats is so high."

Anne pulled her hands out of the soapy water and threw a dishcloth at her husband. He put out his cigarette in the ashtray. "Are you trying to tell me something?"

"Very smart of you to reach that conclusion."

Tom whistled softly and picked up a plate from the dish rack. "You missed a spot," he said, and dropped it back into the sink.

She jumped back to avoid the splash of soapy water.

He grinned. "Sorry, Anne."

She pretended annoyance and dug out the plate. "I would

imagine the forestry and iron ore mines are taking advantage of the war as well. You can never have enough wood for buildings . . ." A thought raced through her head. "For hospitals, especially."

"Hank Dooley from Bell Island told me last week the mines aren't faring so well. Their best customer was Germany."

Anne moved hair from her eyes with the back of her hand. "I saw him at the hospital today. He's doing much better. The doctors are relieved the congestion on his chest finally broke up."

Tom picked up a cup to dry. "Thank the Lord it wasn't tuberculosis. He'd never get back to the mines, for sure."

"The Burkes haven't received a letter from either of the boys in two months. Mrs. Burke's worried." Anne pulled the plug from the sink and watched the water swirl and gurgle down the drain. "I didn't mention we hadn't heard from Ron for as long, either."

Tom pulled her into his arms. "Anne, I know it's difficult, but we can't start fearing the worst. It'll drive us to distraction."

CHAPTER 6

When orders came in March to begin the journey to France, Ches Abbott broke out in song.

On the twenty-fifth, we travelled by ship from the Suez to Marseille in France. Harold Bartlett had returned a week before our new posting. His voice was quiet as he explained how a taxi had knocked down his mother and his sister. Lucy had chased a ball into the street just as the cab came around the corner. With one leg shorter than the other, she couldn't run fast enough to avoid impact. "Ma was watching from the doorway and dashed into the street. She was thrown back onto the sidewalk. " His voice broke. "Lucy was only five years old." He paused, grief carved into his face. "She had so many terrible injuries, it was a blessing she died instantly. Mom sustained head trauma and was in a coma. Two weeks after Lucy's funeral, Mom came out of the coma, calling for Lucy." Harold stared down at his feet. "I had to tell her she was gone."

Ches blew his nose in one of the many handkerchiefs his wife had packed for him. "If she's anything like you, she'll be strong for the other children." A tear glistened in the corner of his eye.

"She's always had to be strong."

Harold gave me a letter from my parents. "They told me you wrote them about the accident. They took in my two little sisters and looked after them until Mom was discharged from the hospital."

"Did you see your girlfriend Elizabeth?"

Harold paled even more. "She came to the hospital with her father. He bragged about her engagement to a lawyer."

I silently cursed myself for mentioning her name.

"She's getting married next month. I wished her well."

Ches looked ready to punch something.

Harold pulled out a bag of Bullseyes from his jacket pocket. "Your sister Joanie sent these for you." He brightened a little. "She's a sweet girl and promised to keep in touch with my family." He never spoke of Elizabeth, his sister, or the accident again in the week leading up to our departure.

Late one night, when Harold was out of earshot, Ches questioned me about Elizabeth. "The least his girl could've done was write him about her engagement. Not shove the news in his face at his mother's hospital bedside."

"Her father didn't approve of Harold, and she agreed that he wasn't good enough for her."

"Hmph," Ches snorted. "By the sounds of it, Harold's better off without her."

The next morning we boarded the ship bound for France. I had somehow gotten used to the sea and was only mildly affected by the toss and roll of the ocean. Harold grew worse the longer we were aboard. Any suggestion offered by the doctor to relieve symptoms had absolutely no effect, and Joey's supply of mint candy had run out. Eight days at sea, Harold was almost as skeleton thin as when I'd first met him. "What's your secret?" he asked, standing on deck, head bent over the rail, his hand on his stomach. "I'll give you a month's wages if you tell me."

I chewed on a slice of bread dripping with molasses. "Believe me, Harold, if I knew I'd tell you for free." Harold didn't respond. He was too busy throwing up again.

In Marseille we boarded a train for Pont Remy, a village on the northern bank of the Somme River. The conductor's gaze went from Harold's gaunt cheeks to the dark circles under his eyes. "Ah, le mal de mer," he said with a knowing nod.

Harold swayed slightly. "I don't understand French," he said, holding the wall to steady himself.

The conductor thought a moment, then made gestures of rolling waves with his hands.

"You mean seasick," I said.

"Oui, oui," the conductor said, bobbing his head up and down.

Harold settled into a seat and slept soundly for the first time in a week. For three days the train moved across France, with Harold waking occasionally to take a little food. Though war-torn, France maintained some of the most magnificent, green, forests I'd ever seen. We passed through towns and villages that had retained their medieval appearance, with castle-like structures and cobbled streets.

I hated to disturb Harold when we reached Pont Remy station at two in the morning. "We have to cross the Somme River," I said, and hastily added, "We're walking across the bridge."

Five miles inland we gathered around Captain Wakefield, having marched across the bridge to stand on the opposite bank of the Somme. It was so dark we could hardly see his face. Ches puffed on a cigarette. "Where to now, sir?" Rain poured down with a sound like pennies bouncing on a tin roof. We shuffled from foot to foot to keep warm.

"You'll be billeted in barns at Buigny-l'Abbe, three miles from here." The captain sounded as tired as myself.

Ches put out his rain-soaked cigarette with the heel of his boot. "Let's get marching before I fall asleep standing up."

Fred Thompson hoisted his rifle to a more comfortable position on his shoulder. "You can say that again."

For the next week and a half we marched from one town to another, until we reached our final destination of Louvencourt on the fourth of April. The town wasn't far from the front line or support trenches facing the Germans at Beaumont Hamel.

I'd heard the French were an expressive lot and discovered it to be true first-hand when Madame Lemont, an elderly, big-busted, plump woman grabbed me by the shoulders and kissed both my cheeks. Ches turned the darkest shade of red when she planted her lips on him. "Faites comme chez-vous," she said to him. His face was a mask of bewilderment.

A tiny, grey-haired man next to the woman spoke up, his eyes as bright as the moon. "My wife, she want you to be at home here." The man took a step toward Ches.

"Good of you," Ches said, his head jerking back as far as it would go.

The man chuckled. "I no cheek kiss. Men hands shake."

Over the coming weeks, British and Canadian soldiers marched through Louvencourt on their way to billets in surrounding towns. Pump sets arrived from England, and men were assigned to lay pipes to take water to the front.

Ches pitched a shovelful of dirt over the top of the six-foot-deep trench. "Something's up. All this activity isn't for nothing."

Across from Ches, Harold dug at the earth with a pick. "I think you're right. Yesterday an English bloke told me railway tracks are being built to bring in equipment and supplies, some of which are designed to supply and support ambulances. Tons of ammunition has already been unloaded."

Fred Thompson shivered. "Casualty-clearing stations and cemeteries are being set up as well. There's a cemetery set up at

Acheux, five miles from the front lines at Beaumont Hamel. I heard over ninety thousand Frenchmen were killed when the Germans attacked Verdun." He gave a long, low whistle.

I rested my hands on the handle of my shovel, taking a break for my aching back. "There were probably thousands more injured. So many lives lost because leaders crave what doesn't belong to them."

Harold frowned, something he did often since his return from Newfoundland. "Power-hungry men always lead the innocent into death." He swung his pick into the ground. "Do you think we're getting ready to take back Verdun?"

Ches threw up his hands. "Who knows? We're simply the dumb followers."

Practice attacks began, intended to teach us how to correctly jump over trenches, which confirmed our suspicions that a major battle was in the works. One morning Captain Wakefield led us to a field of ripening corn. "We have to place flags and plough furrows to duplicate German trenches," he said, indicating the field.

Fred ran a hand through his hair. "Are you serious?"

"Afraid so," Captain Wakefield said.

Richard Benoit, a dark-haired man from Stephenville, pulled a leaf from an ear of corn. "That does not sit well with me," he said with a trace of the French accent.

Fred nodded. "You can say that again. I don't fancy the idea of trampling across the poor villagers' crops. We'll destroy them."

Harold stared at the faces of the Newfoundlanders grouped around us. "The people of Louvencourt treat us like family. It's not right."

A chorus of agreement rang out. I remained quiet, for my sentiments had been aptly expressed by the others.

"Ne vous inquietez pas." Monsieur Balai, the man with whom Ches billeted, smiled at us. "No worry," he said. "Tout le village comprend."

"Hey, Richard," Ches said. "What's he saying?"

Richard Benoit returned the Frenchman's smile. "Bonjour, Monsieur Balai. Nous ne voulons pas detruire le mais."

"Non, non, non, non," Monsieur Balai said with a shake of his head. "Vous etes ici pour liberer la France. Je vous en prie, faites ce qu'il faut faire." He placed a hand over his heart. "Je vous tous remercie de tout mon coeur."

"Well, Richard," Ches said as Monsieur Balai walked away. "What did he say?"

"He thanked us for trying to free France, and wants us to do whatever is required to achieve that."

We were less resistant to trudge through the field and start tearing up much of the crop, yet each of us was still somewhat bothered at the destruction we'd cause for people who had welcomed us like their own.

Once the mock trenches were prepared, I was about to take my first jump when Captain Wakefield called me aside. "Ron, German snipers are taking out men working on the front lines. I read your file and noted you did exceptionally well in target practice."

My voice rang with excitement. "You want me to be a sniper?"

"Yes. Come with me."

I was driven to the front lines, a mere fifty yards from the enemy, where a sniper nest was thought to be. The captain and I lay on our stomachs on a slight incline behind low bushes, and scanned the area. "Look, sir." To the right, a cloud of cigarette smoke floated upwards. I readied my rifle, anxious for the opportunity to prove my marksmanship.

"They hide better than moles," Captain Wakefield said. "Take out every one you can. Show them we're here to stay."

"Whoever's smoking can't be too smart, giving away their position like that." We waited and watched, neither of us making a sound, until my arms grew numb. "Sir, we've been here over two hours. I don't think they're going to show themselves."

The captain kept his gaze trained on the German trench. "Patience, my boy. They'll get to their dirty work sooner or later."

The cigarette smoke continued to drift up. "Sir, maybe they know we're here and plan to outwait us." Gusts of wind stirred the tall grass. It tickled my nose. A photograph flew into the air and floated to the ground a foot or two beyond the swirl of smoke, followed by an angry guttural sound. I tensed, my finger on the trigger. The top of a German helmet appeared and rose upwards until a pair of eyes came into view, searching the ground. The soldier checked the land in every direction, then quickly reached out for the photograph. I pulled the trigger, and as I did our eyes met. Terror, regret, and sadness flickered across his young face in the instant he knew he was going to die.

The bullet hit him square in the forehead and he fell back. My heart hammered. A wave of nausea came upon me as the cry of German voices split the air.

"Good work, Ron," Captain Wakefield said. "We'd better get out of here before we're spotted."

The photograph the German had risked his life to retrieve blew toward me. I snatched it up with a trembling hand and stared at the image of the man I'd just killed. He was smiling, with his arm around a young woman holding a newborn baby. Ches Abbott's words to me that night on Suvla Bay when he captured the Turks sprang into my head. Never kill when you don't have to. I tucked the photograph in my pocket and swallowed to loosen the lump in my throat. "Captain, I don't want to be a sniper anymore."

Men were selected from among British and Canadian troops to learn how to properly use bayonets. I was included and found myself in a field overflowing with rows of straw sacks lined along the ground. Above each sack, another one hung from a wooden structure. I stood with a tall, heavy-set Canadian soldier from New Brunswick. He shook my hand and introduced himself. "I am called Jean Lasalle," he said slowly, as if translating in his head. "I am with Company 183." He said each number separately.

"Ron Marrie," I said, explaining I had a French last name because my grandfather had emigrated from France with his parents as a small boy.

"We both have French blood. We are special, n'est-ce pas?"

The rims of his eyes were red, like he'd been crying. He dabbed at the edges with his fingers. "My eyes were burned by chlorine gas."

I remembered hearing that the Canadians had been among the first to suffer the effects of the inhumane treatment.

"I was one of the fortunate few who survived because I was at the rear of the unit." He sighed. "We had no idea what was happening. One minute the air is clean, the next, a horrible smell like dirty eggs and a fog-like mist." He paused briefly, without a doubt reliving that awful day. "The men ahead of me cried out that their eyes were burning and they could not see. They became confused, trying to turn back, knocking into each other to get away from the gas, which followed them like it was alive. My comrades stumbled toward the rear, gasping for breath, their tongues swollen, choking them. Many cried out that their chest and stomach hurt." He looked away. "A few men's faces turned purple. The sky was dark from the gas. My eyes began to burn and watered so badly I was not able to keep them open. Since then, wherever I go, I sniff like I have a bad cold, since the gas also affected my sinuses."

I hadn't experienced the poison gas every man feared more than the bullets, bombs, or shrapnel. Gas that would literally evaporate the lungs. I shuddered at the thought.

"So many of my battalion are permanently blind or have

damaged lungs that will eventually kill them in a few years. Now I tunnel in no man's land, like a mole, laying charges. Once, we reached the very edge of a German dugout and could hear them talking." Jean lowered his voice for effect. "A simple sneeze would have betrayed us."

"Must be hard work," I said.

"Because the ground is made of hard chalk, we have to use push-picks not to make noise. Near the enemy position we bore holes with a carpenter's auger and poured in vinegar to soften the earth. Then we scrape out the clay and catch it with our hands. Everything has to be done in complete silence, so we work barefoot."

"How do you get rid of the earth?"

"We pack it in sandbags and pass it along to a line of men who have to sit because the tunnels are only four feet high and two feet wide." Jean opened and closed his stiff fingers. "Advancing eighteen inches per day is normal."

I'd never suffered from claustrophobia, but listening to him made my heart beat a little faster.

Jean rubbed his forearms as if a cold wind had blown over him. "Gas is terrible, but fire has to be worse. I met a French soldier a few months ago who fought at Verdun. His brother was caught by a flame-thrower. The fire shot out like the tongue of a lizard for over ten feet. He has nightmares about his brother's screams of agony as the skin melted from his face. Soldiers disintegrated into charred skeletons. Those who survived are so disfigured they wish they hadn't." His eyes travelled to the straw sacks, the pretend-enemy. "War brings about terrible inventions."

"Pay attention," the instructor shouted. A red scar ran from his right eyebrow down his cheek and across his chin. "This may save your life." He proceeded to show us how to hold the rifle and charge at a hay sack. He thrust the bayonet into the sack on the ground, then into the one hanging from above with such vigour and determination he must've visualized real, living German flesh. Perhaps the soldier who'd sliced open his face. "The object is to disembowel the enemy. The more of them you kill, the sooner the war will end in our favour."

Lasalle's eyebrows drew together and he stared at me.

"Kill the enemy," I said loudly, thrusting my rifle forward in an attempt to make him understand. Perhaps the instructor had spoken too fast for Jean.

"Yes, I understood what he said." He looked toward the shredded hay sack. "I do not believe I will enjoy killing. We are all human beings, n'est-ce pas?"

"Even the cowards who used the poison gas on you?" the instructor spat out, before darting over to a lad having trouble inserting his bayonet.

"Jean," I said. "I see your point. But we have no other choice but to defend ourselves if we come face to face with a German."

Later that night, Sid Tremblett whistled "My Wild Irish Rose" while shaving. The bullet in his forehead had caused minimal damage to his skull but had left a thick reddish scar. He rubbed the deadened area. "The French ladies are drawn to this like cod to caplin."

Leave it to Sid to see the positive in an injury.

"Got a date?" I said, joking around.

"Sort of. Why don't you come along?"

"Why would you want me on a date with—" My mouth snapped closed. The date was at Madame Prudhomme's brothel. I would've crawled into a hole if one had been handy.

Sid made a clucking noise with his mouth. "You don't know what you're missing."

Ches hooked his thumbs in his belt. "The lad's busy tonight. He promised to help me write a letter to my missus. Then we're off to visit the Balai family. Mister has the fanciest accordion." Before anyone could comment, he tapped me on the shoulder. "Get out your pencil and paper, lad. I've plenty to say."

"I'm off, then," Sid said with a wink at me.

"How old are you?" Ches asked when we were alone.

"Eighteen."

"Listen here, lad. There's no telling if any of us will survive this war. Look at poor Charlie Paterson, dead at fifteen." He coughed and cleared his throat. "I don't normally abide paying to be with a woman."

My face burned hot enough to catch wood on fire.

"Don't be embarrassed, lad. You've been over here since you weren't much more than a boy, with no time for normal living." There wasn't even a glimmer of mockery on his face. "Go to Madame Prudhomme's." He took out his pipe, the one his daughter Lilly had saved up to buy him for Christmas. "Time to go outside for a proper smoke."

"What about your letter?"

"Another time, lad."

I sat awhile contemplating Ches's advise. It wouldn't hurt to visit Madame Prudhomme's, to . . . What would my mother think if . . . *Who's going to tell her?* a voice from somewhere deep in my brain countered. To clear my head, I went for a walk in town, and eventually I found myself outside Madame Prudhomme's house. My breath quickened as I knocked on the front door.

"Ah, cheri," a woman said, her bright red lips tilted upwards in a big smile. "Entrez." In her mid- to late sixties, she'd retained some of her youthful beauty.

I tripped over the step and stumbled onto the front porch. "Madame Prudhomme, I—"

"Mon beau garcon," she said softly, cutting me off. "I 'ave special girl for first time."

Was "It's my first time" written across my forehead in bright letters?

"Chiselle," she called up the stairs. "Viens ici."

A girl about my age with golden, blonde hair and sky-blue eyes appeared on the top landing. She glowed like an angel, wings the only things missing to make the picture perfect.

"Ah! Qu'il est beau!" she said, gliding toward me.

"Chiselle say you handsome," Madame Prudhomme said, then whispered a number in English in my ear.

I gulped, reached into my pocket, my palms sweaty, and passed over the money, my Catholic guilt nagging like an itch I couldn't scratch. Would that make this the first and last time I'd ever frequent a brothel in this foreign land?

Chiselle kissed me on both cheeks and her lilac-scented perfume made me giddy. She took my hand and led me up the stairs.

"Amusez-vous bien," Madame Prudhomme said. I glanced back at her. "Enjoy," she translated, sticking the money inside the top of her dress.

The next day we marched from our billets for our first five-day tour in the front line trenches. "Who the hell dug these?" Ches said after we'd surveyed the area. "The parapets are run down and won't give much protection from snipers."

"That's not the worst," Harold said. "Many of the trenches don't connect with each other."

Ches growled like an angry dog. "What were the bloody French thinking about when they dug these?"

"To be fair," Fred piped in, "most of the fighting has been around Verdun. I guess they didn't have enough men to keep this place in order."

We were assigned to connect a section of the front line trenches across from the German-held town of Beaumont

Hamel. The parapets protecting us from snipers were badly in need of rebuilding. Sid and several other men were assigned that task.

I chopped at the earth with a pick. "Ches, do you miss fishing?"

"I've been fishing since I was thirteen. You don't have the luxury to ponder whether you like it or not. It's expected if you want to make a living." He had more scars on both hands than wrinkles on the face of a hundred-year-old man. "It's damn hard work putting hooks on a mile-long trawl, hauling it in, and unhooking the fish."

"Is the pay good?"

Ches laughed, a harsh, unhappy sound. "That's the biggest joke of all. You receive barely enough to live on. The fish merchants pocket most of the money. They get back the pittance they pay us when we buy food and clothing from the stores they own."

"Sorry," I mumbled, ashamed that I knew very little about the life and hardships of a fisherman.

"It's not your fault." He glanced at Harold and Fred working on the other side of the trench we were connecting. "You lot are down-to-earth folk."

A single shot whistled through the air. I looked toward the parapet and saw Sid Tremblett drop to the ground like a felled tree, blood flowing from a gaping hole in the back of his head. Harold tried to pull him into the trench. Another shot whizzed past Harold as he dived to the bottom of the trench. All quiet, he got to his feet and peered over the parapet. A bullet hit the ground inches from his face, while another struck Sid's lifeless form, jerking the body.

"Bartlett," Fred called out. "Stay down, you'll get yourself killed!"

"I can't leave him like that."

It wasn't fair that Sid Tremblett should lie without the

chance to defend himself. Instinct took charge, and I made to climb out of the trench.

Ches blocked my way. "Don't be an idiot. You'll end up like Sid."

I grabbed my rifle and searched the open ground to catch sight of the sniper. From the corner of my eye I saw Harold raise his head slightly over the top of the trench. He extended an arm and pulled Sid in.

"The poor bugger didn't even see it coming," Ches said. "Just like the poor sods at Gallipoli. Another good soldier to be buried in a foreign country." He continued to gouge out earth with his pick as Fred and Harold bore Sid's body to the chaplain. "It's the one thing that bothers me most about dying over here."

Preparations for whatever major event was in the near future progressed under intermittent shelling and sniping. Beyond exhausted, we'd collapse into our dugouts for much-needed sleep. To keep it away from the rats, Harold tied his food to the ceiling with a string. "I won't starve so rats can have a feast."

Fred stretched out with his hands behind his head. A rat, the size of a tabby cat, the fur matted and damp, scurried over his feet. Fred pulled out a pistol and shot it, picked up the dead rodent by the tail, and flung it over the side of the trench, toward the German line. Another rat took its place.

The rats made my skin crawl, but I wouldn't admit it to the others. Falling asleep in the trenches was difficult for me because of those creatures. One night I awoke to find one nestled in the palm of my hand. I screamed like a child and was rewarded by being bitten. The men howled with laughter, and I joined in to cover my humiliation.

Sid occupied my thoughts, another reason I couldn't sleep. He'd been buried in one of the new cemeteries with a white wooden Cross to mark his grave. I missed his easygoing manner.

The stars glistened in the clear sky, and for a moment I imagined I was in my bedroom peeking through my curtain with my binoculars.

"Jesus Christ, help me!"

Every man in the dugout woke up, his weapon at hand. Panting and fumbling in the dark, we saw Ches on his back, a huge rat on his face. His hands were around the animal, trying to dislodge it, while blood poured down the sides of his face.

Fred Thompson knelt beside Ches. "Let go of the rat," he said, aiming his pistol, and with one shot the rat stopped moving. Fred eased the teeth out of Ches's nose. There was so much blood I couldn't tell if his nose had been bitten off. Harold and Fred accompanied him to the dressing station. Ches was a handsome man. How would his wife react to his disfigurement? Sometimes it amazed me the foolish things that went through your mind in such times.

I sat up, my rifle across my knees, listening to the squeals and sounds of rats scurrying about. The first light of dawn settled over the land when Harold returned.

"How's Ches?" I asked.

"He'll tell you himself."

Ches eased himself down into the trench, holding his head erect, with Fred behind him. Splotches of red seeped through the thick white bandage across his nose. "The bloody rat took the tip of my nose off."

Harold sat down on a sandbag. "The doctor said there wasn't any major damage, though he will have a scar."

Ches rested his head against the trench wall. "My face hurts all over." Traces of blue were visible under both eyes. "For a while back there I thought me missus would get a letter telling her I was killed by a rat." He blew out his breath. "How'd she be able to live that one down?"

"Speaking of letters," Harold said, "Ches received one from his brother Gord while we were at the dressing station."

"Don't keep us in suspense any longer," Fred said. "Read it!"

Ches pulled an envelope from his pocket and passed it to me.

I tore open the end of the envelope and took out two pages of writing. "This is a woman's handwriting."

Ches smiled. "I'd say good old Gord talked a nurse into writing that. He was always a bit of a flirt with the ladies. Go on, let's hear what he's up to."

Dear Ches,

I asked a pretty nurse to write this for me. She was very obliging and said she'd be delighted to help me. Says she loves my colonial accent.

Ches, my temperature was one hundred and five and I was so weak I thought I was a goner for sure. It took the longest time before I could even sit up in bed without help. I've lost some weight, although now that I can eat without vomiting I'll gain it back. My sea legs are improving, and yesterday I took a bus to Buckingham Palace. Ches, it's a grand place. You got to see it before you go home. I was awful tired when I returned and slept for three hours.

The doctors are draining my blood like them vampires in the picture book Lilly loves. They say they are checking to see if I'm cured of dysentery. I can tell them I am because I feel so much better now. I'm going to do some more sightseeing before I get back to the trenches.

Ches, I'm asking only one thing of you. Don't go getting yourself sick, wounded, or anything else stupid before I'm there with you and the boys.

All the best.

P.S. I almost forgot. Ron's uncle Jack came to see me. Heard I was in the First Newfoundland Regiment. He was on leave for a few days before heading to the front once more and was beside himself with relief to learn Ron survived Gallipoli. He heard the losses were massive, the Australians decimated (his word), and that the Newfoundland Regiment was the last to get out of there.

Well, that's all for now. No. One more thing. Just in case you haven't done so yet, I sent a letter to Isabelle and told her you're number one and not to worry about her man.

Gord

Ches's face softened. "She'll be delighted to hear from Gord."

Fred nudged Ches in the side. "When was the last time you sent a letter home? Come to think of it, I don't remember seeing you post one."

"I haven't. It's no one's business I can't read or write."

"Isabelle could've taught you."

"Fishing takes up too much time."

"I'm not a pretty nurse," I said to lighten the mood. "But I can write just as well."

"I'll send a letter when we get back to Louvencourt."

Relieved when the five-day tour ended, we returned to our billets, where we were able to wash our personal belongings and take baths. Ches was often asked what happened to his nose and replied with the truth, which I admit surprised me. "The bloody thing wouldn't let go. Fred here had to shoot the bugger."

"The darn things are worse than the enemy," a Canadian soldier said. "They keep at you like a child pestering for candy."

"Quite right," a British soldier added. "At least they don't try to use you for food."

"That's debatable." Ches wrinkled his nose. "It's so itchy I almost wish the bastard had taken it off."

We all laughed and Ches laughed the hardest.

One day, Chaplain Murray strolled over to us as we sat relaxing in the sun. He rolled his shirt sleeves up to the elbows and glanced at Ches. "I've got a few of those," he said, extending his right arm. Partially healed bites dotted the skin from the elbow down. "I've sent a few of the vermin back to their Maker."

I looked up at him, squinting from the sun. "Most of the soldiers call it the 'Somme Rat' due to its huge size."

"The scourge of the earth is more appropriate," the chaplain said, and sauntered off.

Ches rubbed his nose through the bandage. "Time for this to come off. Be back in a while." He darted away like he'd left a pot boiling on the stove.

I went for a walk across the field and sat under a juniper tree. I soon found myself drowsy and closed my eyes.

"Wake up." The voice was loud, commanding.

"What's wrong?" I cried out even before my eyes opened.

"Nothing at the moment. I told you I'd be back. My feet are as good as new." Joey Baker stood over me, a few pounds heavier, a big smile on his face. "I was luckier than most of the Australians with frostbite. One poor buddy had both feet amputated. Dozens more developed gangrene. Several lost a leg. Ron, you know I wanted to be a doctor like your Uncle Jack, ever since I was a youngster." He stretched out beside me. "I do now more than ever. They're faced with tough challenges."

I spotted Ches coming toward us and quickly filled Joey in about the rat bite. He steeled himself.

"It's not bad at all," Ches said. The tip of his nose was more flat than rounded and covered with a dry, scaling scab. "My missus won't mind, but it might take Lilly a bit of getting used to."

The next week, while marching to the front line trenches

for another tour, I noticed something unusual sticking out of Ches's backpack. "It's netting," he said, when I asked what it was. "The rats won't get another taste of me."

. Activity revved into high gear during the month of June. Tons more ammunition rolled in on trains, then were transported by horse and cart to the gunners. The three sets of trench lines were finally connected, with officers inspecting them two and three times a day.

Around seven o'clock one bright sunny morning, a British soldier was on duty at the small table in the radio communications dugout. From my vantage point I saw him come outside to greet his officer. I looked up when we heard the whistling sound of a shell flying through the air. A direct hit into the communication dugout sent equipment and earth into the air.

"Don't that beat all," Fred said. "The captain's unexpected visit saved the radio operator's life."

Late June, we'd returned to our billets for no more than twenty-four hours when word arrived that all troops in the area were to immediately head to the front line. Close to 60,000 soldiers marched on the dry roads, kicking dust into the air like smoke from a brush fire. The men coughed and gagged. I spat out dirt. "It's clogging my nose and drying out my throat."

Captain Wakefield conversed with the captain of another unit a few feet from us. Their exchange carried on the wind. "I'm worried about all the dust we're kicking up," Wakefield said. "It'll signal the Germans there's a large-scale attack pending."

"There's nothing we can do about that," the other officer said. "We have our orders."

We continued to march in the sun and heat. In the early afternoon the rumble of thunder sounded in the distance. Gathering black clouds rushed over each other, robbing the daylight, and the claps of thunder drew nearer. In seconds, rain poured down, churning the ground into a stream of mud, splashing onto the backs of our legs. We approached the communication trenches, which were filling with waist-high mud thicker than tar.

Fred tried to make light of it. "I can't swim. How about you boys?"

We waded in and crept through the sludge, lifting each foot with a sucking noise. Sometimes, if a leg was bogged down too deep in the mud, I was forced to use my hands to pull it free.

"Sorry, lads," Captain Wakefield said. "We'll have to stay put until dusk. Can't risk the Germans seeing us."

"What happens then?" Fred asked.

"We'll have to proceed over land."

Every inch of me felt like hungry insects were biting at my skin. I was chilled despite the warm weather. At dusk we dragged ourselves from the muddied trench and began the trek over land, our boots sloshing water with every step.

CHAPTER 7

NEAR MIDNIGHT, NO MAN'S LAND

The next day the artillery barrage from our side began a brutal, unrelenting assault on the German trenches. That night, pressed together with the others in dugouts no larger than a closet, unable to sleep, I thought about what my life would be like if I hadn't enlisted. Would I have gotten up the courage to tell my father about my dream to be a journalist? The war had changed me, and I knew I had the courage for anything. Two nights later, close to eleven o'clock, the bombardment stopped. "What's that about?" I asked, the sudden silence washing over me like a dip in cold water after a day's march in the dry, hot desert.

Fred lowered the letter he'd been reading by the light of the lantern hung above his head. The candle inside flickered out. He lit another and replaced the burned-out one. "Maybe we've run out of ammunition." He raised the letter to his nose and sniffed. "Eileen's sweet perfume smells like cherry blossoms."

In the brighter light I saw his face more clearly. "By that look I'd say you're still in love."

"Forever, Ron. Forever."

A wiry man with a tooth missing poked his head in. "Captain Wakefield wants to meet all of you in five minutes."

Handfuls of men who'd fought at Gallipoli emerged from their dugouts as we made our way through the trench. Rain pelted down, smacking the planks on the floor, which failed in their efforts to protect our feet from the mud. "I have a mission for you," Captain Wakefield said when the last man arrived. "Aerial reconnaissance is impossible in this weather. Headquarters wants to know the condition of the German trenches. We're to capture a few prisoners to find out about their strength and morale."

"The way I see it," Ches said, "you'd be a fool to have high spirits in this war."

Fifty-seven of us, trained in bayonets and hand bombs, prepared to cross no man's land. We carried a Bangalore Torpedo to cut through the German barbed wire. I'd been schooled in using the twenty-foot-long steel pipe, filled with explosives containing special igniters, which fired when you gave the torpedo a slight twist.

Armed with rifles and hand bombs, we climbed up the trench ladders and went over the top with Wakefield in the lead. I crawled through mud thicker than bread dough, holding the front of the torpedo, with Ches carrying the rear. Rain beat into my eyes, soaked through my clothing, and weighed me down. The terrain was rugged, pitted with holes from the shelling. My arms ached, muscles fatigued from the weight of the torpedo. Fred Thompson and Joey Baker flanked us while the rest of the men came behind, panting. The night was blacker than crude oil and the world a giant black hole. We moved in rows along the ground on elbows and knees like spiders chasing a prey, holding our rifles beneath us in our left hands.

Time stood still, and it could have been minutes or hours before we covered the vast distance, which I calculated to be at least a mile. Mud caked our legs, arms, stomachs, and faces, slowing our progress. Captain Wakefield stopped, and as I peered ahead I made out the thin outline of barbed wire. Every man became motionless. "It's a lot heavier than we thought," Wakefield said.

I twisted the torpedo. The explosive burst into the wire, cutting through only halfway. "Good Lord," the captain said. "The wire is extra thick. No time to waste. We'll have to do this by hand." He pulled out his hand cutter.

"The bloody Germans," Ches said, glancing ahead every now and again as he clipped away at the tough wire.

"Say, that—" Fred's cutter fell from his hands as he slumped face down in the mud.

"Christ, they've seen us," Ches said. Machine gun bullets sprayed inches above our prone bodies.

"Withdraw," the captain shouted. "We don't stand a chance here!"

Ches turned over Fred Thompson. One side of his face was smeared with blood. His eyelids flickered. "Hang on, buddy," Ches said. "I'll get you home."

A popping sound was followed by red stains spreading along Ted Williams's shoulder. Ted was a later reinforcement to the unit. His arm hung limply at his side. "Give me your rifle," I said, staying alongside as he pulled himself forward with his good arm.

"I can make it," he said.

"What about the torpedo, Captain?"

"We'll have to leave it."

Ted held his injured arm. "The sneaky sods wanted us to get close enough to pick us off one by one."

We scuttled toward our trenches like sea crabs. Ches trailed along after me, doing his best to aid Fred, whose face was covered in blood. The captain came in last, carrying Mike Vickers, who'd been shot in the foot. The wounded were sent to the casualty clearing station while the rest of us hunkered down in the dugouts.

I'd finally started to doze when Fred showed up, his left ear bandaged. "The buggers nipped me earlobe and grazed my neck."

The following day, the British resumed bombarding the Germans with unrelenting artillery fire. Ches scratched the flat tip of his nose. "I almost pity the poor bastards," he yelled over the blasts. "They must be out of their minds with the noise."

"It's bad enough here," I said. "Must be ten times worse over there."

Captain Wakefield stomped toward us, his face hard, a cigarette hanging from the corner of his mouth and the ashes dropping onto his jacket. I'd never known him to smoke. "Gather 'round, men." He threw the partially smoked cigarette to the ground and stepped on it.

Fred was sitting on a stack of sandbags. "Sir . . . Mike and Ted all right?"

"They're fine. The Brigade Commander has ordered another raid tonight. He's confident we won't let him down this time."

"Let him down!" Ches said. "The bloody damned idiot. What the . . . sorry, Captain. Sometimes my mouth kicks in before me brain."

"You're not the only one." An easy guess to whom the captain referred.

"Sir," Harold said, "we saw how fortified the German trenches are. Obviously the artillery fire hasn't done any serious damage. It's only made them more alert."

Joey stamped out the remaining butt of his cigarette. He'd become a chain smoker in the army. "Captain, don't you think the Germans will be more than ready for another sneak attack?"

Wakefield tapped his hat against his thigh. "I don't disagree, but orders are orders."

"No disrespect intended, Cap'n," Ches said, "but has the commander ever been face to face with the enemy?"

Wakefield remained close-mouthed, yet the tic in his jaw revealed his innermost thoughts.

With darkness upon us once more, fifty of us set out with two Bangalore torpedoes. The first Bangalore crew cut a six-foot-wide hole right through the outer wire. A little farther on we came to another belt of wire.

Captain Wakefield moved over to me. "Ron, get a move on before we're spotted."

I twisted the second torpedo. It didn't fire. "Just dandy," Ches said. With not a word spoken, the men took out their wire cutters. We worked hard in the rain, slicing and cutting at the wet, tough wire. Then we squeezed through, careful not to make any noise or let one of the hand bombs fall.

"Right, men," Captain Wakefield whispered. "You know what's required of you."

We slithered forward like snakes over rugged ground, littered with rocks and shrapnel that was as sharp as scissors. All was quiet. Too quiet. The hairs on the back of my neck prickled. As we were about to advance, Joey paused, a hand on my arm. "Ron, did you hear that?"

"No—" My voice caught in my throat as I heard popping sounds.

Joey turned to me with a look of acceptance. "We're dead."

A German flare shot up in the sky, illuminating the area as bright as a sunny day. I looked toward the German trenches and saw shadowy forms lining the parapet.

Shouts and cries echoed over the land as bullets sprayed all around us, shredding the ground, spewing up dirt and rocks. Up on our feet, we raced, zigzagging to avoid bullets. I saw the enemy's face, which was no different from mine. We fired back at men protected by the parapets of their trench. Ahead of me the Wheeler brothers from Gander ran together, bayonets extended, and jumped into the trench. Phil Morgan and Clarence Saunders had inched closer to the German trenches, and each tossed a bomb. When the smoke lifted, Phil flew backwards into the mud, his face gone. Clarence went down moaning, a bullet in his groin. The rest of us pressed on amid a hail of bullets flying around us, like snow in a blizzard. Hank Collins, a policeman from St. John's, fell forward grabbing at his stomach. Before he hit the ground his bowels spilled out. Bile rose in my throat.

"Bobby, get down," Fred yelled, and I looked in his direction. Bobby Whalen, a schoolteacher from Corner Brook, held both hands to his throat as blood spurted out in an arc.

I fired until my ammunition ran out. Adam Power, a burly thirty-seven-year-old from Placentia, ran over to me. "Son," he said, his eyes on the trench, "get in front of me."

No time to move, he threw me to the ground. A soft patter of bullets tore into his flesh and continued after he was dead.

"Ron, you all right?" Joey's breathing was ragged as he pulled Adam off me.

I stared at Adam's back, which was drenched in blood. His only son was a year younger than me.

"I'm out of ammunition," Joey said. "So are most of the lads."

"Fall back!" Wakefield's voice rang out loudly, clearly.

Hypnotized by the blood flowing from Adam's body into the ground, I couldn't move. Joey grabbed my arm. "Come on, Ron. There's nothing more we can do here."

The flare went out as we retreated, waves of bullets pursuing us, whistling into the night, ripping into the wet earth.

Men I laughed with, lived with and ate with for two years were dropping to the ground like their legs had been kicked out from under them. Now in total blackness, I lost sight of Joey.

"Help." There was a long gasp.

It was Jimmy Hawco from Bell Island. "Jimmy," I whispered, "how bad are you?"

"I'm hit in my legs and hand."

I pulled myself forward by the elbows and found Jimmy on his back. There was a hole through his right palm. "Don't worry." I kept my voice low. "I'll get you home."

Jimmy's chest heaved. "It's too dangerous. Save yourself."

"Can't do that," I said, sliding my hands under his armpits to sit him up. He grimaced but didn't make a sound. I knelt with my back turned to him, and he put his arms around my neck, the wounded hand hanging limp, dripping blood onto my shirt. "Hold on," I said and started for our trenches. The toes of his boots burrowed grooves in the mud. "It's not much farther, Jimmy." He tried to smother grunts of pain.

"Peter? Jimmy? Ron?" I recognized Harold: strong, hopeful. "Is anyone there?"

"Jimmy Hawco's wounded," I called.

Harold's outline appeared in the darkness. The rain continued its merciless downpour. "Peter Furlong was wounded somewhere around here," he said over the sound of rifle fire. "He'll die if he doesn't get help."

"Andy Power is hit, too," Jimmy said. "A bullet went straight through his heart. I had to leave him."

"You couldn't do anything else. He'd be proud of you," I said. Perhaps the platitude would console him.

"Get Jimmy to safety," Harold said. "I'll keep looking for the others." He vanished into the darkness.

Jimmy's arms loosened from around my neck. "Don't let go," I said. "We're almost at our lines." His body went limp. "Jimmy, try to stay awake." He slid down my back into a crumpled heap on the ground. I threw him over my shoulder, sloshed through mud, stumbled over a hole, and tripped in scattered strands of barbed wire. The rain diluted the blood seeping from the bullet holes in his trousers.

A voice came from in front of me. "Who's there?"

"Ron Marrie. Jimmy Hawco's with me. He's wounded." I hurried forward as fast as I could.

"Are Ches and Harold with you?" Cliff Hockley asked as he and his brother, Ed, came out of the trench. They lifted Jimmy from me with great care.

"Harold's gone to get Peter. I didn't see Ches. Is Joey back?"

"Yes. He's bringing some of the wounded to the casualty clearing station." Cliff checked for Jimmy's pulse. "Thank the Lord he's alive. Come on, Ed, let's get him help before it's too late."

I headed back out over no man's land and came across Joey kneeling over Andy Power. A couple of men from our unit took Andy's body back to our line. His chest was soaked in blood and his face had a sickly grey pallor.

Blood oozed from a gash in Joey's neck. "Shrapnel caught me," he said. He got safely to our line, and as I turned to go out again, more men arrived bearing the wounded. Two soldiers, each with a bullet in a leg, had an arm looped around Ches's neck and hobbled alongside him.

Captain Wakefield came behind with a man shot in the hip. He deposited the man with us and dashed away to the communications trench to report the status of the mission.

Harold Bartlett arrived next, with Peter Furlong over his shoulder, unconscious. "Looks like shrapnel grazed his forehead." Harold said, and continued on to the dressing station with Peter. It was three in the morning before Harold dragged himself to the dugout Ches had dubbed "Little Lilly's Playhouse."

Harold fell on his bunk and closed his eyes. "We're in big trouble if the Germans are that fortified all down the line. Hasn't anyone noticed their bombardment against us has only gotten heavier since the middle of June?" He hauled off his helmet and took a swig of whiskey from Fred's supply. "They're ready to bury us alive."

Ches poured a large drink for himself. "I've got a bad feeling about what's coming."

CHAPTER 8

FINAL PREPARATIONS

We returned to our billets in Louvencourt the following day, not quite sure why we'd been brought en masse to the front and then abruptly sent back.

"This goddamned weather must have something to do with it," Ches swore to no one in particular. "It rains more here than in Newfoundland, and that's saying something."

I threw my haversack down and kicked it across the bedroom floor. It struck the wall with a soft thump. "I'm fed up with the secrecy. If there's an upcoming major offensive, why keep it from the ones fighting in this war?"

"Take it easy, lad," Ches said, retrieving my haversack. "Leave the growling and complaining to someone more suited, like me."

"Listen to him, Ron. He's an expert on the subject." Gord Abbott stood in the doorway. He held an envelope out to him. "A letter for you. To brighten your day."

Ches raced across the room and swept up his brother in a bear hug. "I've missed you. We all have." He set Gord back on his feet and faked a punch to his stomach. "Gained a bit of weight, I see."

"I couldn't fool the doctors any longer, so they got rid of me."

The letter was addressed to "Ronnie." Only Joanie called me that. Fred pulled another bottle from under his pillow. "A few swallies to celebrate Gord's homecoming."

I drained my glass in one gulp and with a light hop in my step went outside, sat under a juniper tree, and pulled out two sheets of lined scribbler paper. In previous letters she'd printed, with an obvious child's hand, but this one was in cursive writing, each letter perfectly formed.

> Dear Ronnie,
>
> I miss you so much at times I can't sleep. Dad said the war shouldn't last much longer and you'll be home in no time. I don't believe that anymore because in the beginning everyone said it wouldn't last this long. Some of the soldiers who fought at Gallipoli have come home. Ronnie, I wanted to go greet them at the harbourfront but Mom wouldn't let me. She thinks she's protecting me, but I know those men wouldn't have been shipped home if they hadn't lost an arm or a leg or . . . something worse. My teacher showed us pictures of the horrible damage shrapnel can do to a face. Mom was upset but Dad said I shouldn't be protected from the realities of war. He's right.

I paused in my reading. Joanie had been eleven when I left, a little girl. Now at thirteen, she sounded so much more mature. Maybe too much so because of the war. I took a deep breath and went back to the letter.

> School is out for the summer and I'm helping Mom with the cooking because she volunteers with

the Women's Patriotic Association, knitting and sewing warm clothes for our soldiers. She showed me how to make pea soup and dumplings and I cooked it for supper last night. The dumplings were real hard but Dad said they were the best he'd ever tasted. He only said that so I wouldn't feel bad.

I haven't forgotten about your birthday on July 1. Nineteen sounds so old compared to seventeen. Mom says she's going to bake a cake like usual and celebrate even though you won't be here. I'm keeping all my presents for you, including the Christmas ones, wrapped and in your room so you can open them when you come home.

The list of soldiers missing, killed, or presumed captured are posted and Dad checks it out every day. Ronnie, do you remember Mr. Tucker, Dad's friend who works at Government House? His youngest son was killed at Gallipoli and his oldest is in a hospital in England blinded by shrapnel. Mr. Tucker came by the house yesterday. He was so sad I went to my room and cried for him. I pray every night that you, Henry, Frank, and Uncle Jack won't be badly hurt or killed.

Ronnie, maybe you can answer a question that's been on my mind lately. I don't want to talk to Mom or Dad about it, afraid they'll worry even more about you. I met a girl my age from Canada who was here with her father on business. Her brother volunteered like you did for the war and was executed last month as a coward. How can someone with two medals for bravery be a coward? Sometimes I feel the happy times are gone forever. Please come home safe. Happy birthday again. I love you.

Your sister,
Joanie

My throat hurt and I coughed to clear it, trying to keep tears from forming.

"You all right?" Harold asked. He'd approached without making a sound. "Hope you didn't get bad news from home."

"It's a letter from my little sister. She misses me." I was going to tell him about Mr. Tucker's sons but changed my mind when he became reflective. "Something's bothering you, though," I said.

"I've been mulling over how strong the Germans were on our raids. There's been other unsuccessful raids with major casualties along different sections of the German line. All the men reported they're well-fortified." Harold tossed a rock into a bush. "A Canadian bloke told me headquarters has been receiving conflicting reports about the German position." He looked off into the distance. "Do you think the negative reports are being ignored because we're considered too inexperienced?"

I tucked Joanie's letter into my pocket. "The Scottish soldiers captured prisoners who were in high spirits. That's impossible to fake if you're truly destitute."

"I have to believe our leaders are intelligent enough to know what they're doing."

Chaplain Murray approached us in slow strides. "A letter arrived this morning for Sid Tremblett. It's heartbreaking that his family wrote, unaware he'll never read it." The chaplain rubbed his face with both hands. "I'd like you both to write a few words about him. I'll send it along when I return their letter. It will give them some measure of peace."

"I'd be honoured," Harold said. As were Ches, Gord, and Fred when we asked them to add their comments.

Later that day, sixty Newfoundlanders arrived fresh from training, bringing the four companies to a total of thirty-two officers and 972 Other Ranks. My two cousins were among them, smiling like they'd won a fortune at poker. "I was beginning to think we'd spent the entire war in training," Henry said.

"Are you serious?" I asked. "You haven't been in any kind of combat?" My head spun. Was this offensive about to be their initiation?

"Not once," Frank said. "We all applauded when we were assigned here." They weren't to blame. The First Five Hundred had reacted in a similar fashion when we finally faced the enemy, although the Turks weren't the ones we'd crossed the ocean to fight. "The four Burke brothers are among this group just arriving. We heard about the steady bombing of the German lines. Will Burke, who's a captain by the way, saw stacks of empty shells piled higher than two-storey houses at the artillery site."

I sought out Will at his billet and was welcomed with a strong handshake. "Father is managing quite well without his sons at home," he said to my inquiry as to how the firm was doing. "Hettie, my sister, was thrilled with the opportunity to work with Dad. She aspires to being a lawyer and this is her chance." He looked me up and down. "It's good to see you so fit. The reports concerning Gallipoli weren't very reassuring."

"Dysentery and the weather killed as many soldiers as the enemy," I said. "Joey Baker, a friend of mine, suffered severe frostbite."

"Ron, Second-Lieutenant Sibley is a school buddy of mine. I had a chat with him this morning and he told me the impending battle along the Somme had been scheduled for June 29. The aeroplanes couldn't tell if the artillery barrage worked because of the steady rain, so it was postponed for a few days."

"Well, Captain Burke," I said. "Us lowly troops haven't heard a word."

The next morning, in the pouring rain, Second-Lieutenant Sibley, a small-framed man with smiling eyes, accompanied by Captain Wakefield, informed us that twenty-one of the men had been wounded on the raid, and three captured. Sibley's stiff posture and guarded expression left no doubt that he wasn't pleased with the outcome of his conversation with the army's commanding officer, Colonel Hadow, who had been promoted on the first of January. "We've received the 'special order' of the day," he said. "Beginning tomorrow, July 1, the Somme attack begins along the twenty-two-mile front. The British forces are occupying fourteen miles, the French eight miles."

William Burke stepped forward. "As part of the 88th British Brigade, the First Newfoundland Regiment will advance across no man's land to capture the German line in front of Beaumont Hamel. From there we'll proceed into the town and liberate it. The cavalry will ride in and clean up." He exchanged a glance with Sibley. "General Haig feels that this battle will shorten the war. If we fail, the war will go on for a long time."

Sibley sighed, but whether it was from tiredness or disgust I wasn't sure. "He believes we have the upper hand in terms of men and guns, and that the enemy will fall apart at the sight of our bravery and sheer force."

None of us showed any visible reaction as Sibley paced in front of us, his boots splashing water behind him. "Since 1916, the British army has implemented a ten-per-cent rule." He sighed again, longer, deeper. "Ten per cent of every battalion will be held back from the attack in order to rebuild the force for another assault if required. The ten per cent includes the second-in-command, one or two junior officers, some senior NCOs, and regular soldiers. You'll be paired with the Essex, Hampshire, and Worcester units."

Wakefield took a notepad from his breast pocket and called out the names of those selected from our unit, finishing with Harold, Will, and Ches. One hundred men in all.

Mumbling broke out among the chosen men and Sibley held up his hand for silence. "I understand you want to be with your buddies in the battle, but a holdback number is essential.

Your task is to clean up the dugouts we've passed through and arrange the prisoners into small groups, who will then be taken to the prisoner-of-war cage behind our lines."

Wakefield consulted his notepad again. "This is the list of equipment and supplies each of you is to carry into battle. A rifle, one hundred seventy rounds of small-arms ammunition, one iron ration, rations for the day of the assault, two sand-bags in a belt, two Mills grenades, steel helmet, smoke helmet in satchel, water bottle and haversack on back, first field dressing and identity disc, a waterproof sheet. Forty per cent of the infantry will carry shovels, ten per cent carry picks. Also, the 88th Brigade will transport sixteen hundred flares, sixty-four bundles of five-foot wooden pickets, forty-eight mauls, sixteen sledgehammers, six hundred and forty wire cutters, six hundred and forty hedging gloves, five hundred and twelve haversacks to carry the magazines for the Lewis guns, thirty-three Bangalore torpedoes."

"Captain Wakefield," I said, "how are we supposed to get out of the trench, let alone walk with that much equipment strapped to us?" I glanced around at the much shorter, lighter men. "It'll weigh almost as much as us. If we fall down, we'll have a devil of a time getting back up."

Wakefield put away his notebook. "I can't argue with your reasoning."

"Humph," Ches mumbled to me. "Seems to me the generals don't have a morsel of common sense."

As we prepared to head to the front lines, Fred produced a can of grey paint and brushes. "My job is to paint the unit's identification on all the guns taken from the Germans. The generals must be awfully confident we'll win." He threw the tin to the floor. "Wish I felt the same way."

"Before we leave," Ches said to me as Fred walked out the door, "will you write a letter for me?"

He'd finally taken me up on my offer. I opened my haversack and took out paper and a pencil. I didn't say anything as he stared out the window gathering his thoughts. "Isabelle will be surprised to get a letter from me." He smiled to himself. "Right, here goes."

> Dear Isabelle,
> Me and Gord spend our days training, marching, and digging ditches like overworked plough horses. Fishing was good preparation for over here. Gord told me he sent you a letter. He never knew, but I had the fright of my life when he got sick with dysentery. He nearly faded away to nothing, he got so thin. Your raisin tea buns and blueberry pies would fatten him up in a jiffy.
>
> Love, you know how I was against schooling for the youngsters, didn't want to hear tell of time wasted on books when chores had to be done. Fishing was good enough for me, so why not for our sons? I've seen the error of my ways, as you like to tell me whenever I'm wrong.

He chuckled to himself. "Which isn't often. Don't write that part," he said quickly as my pencil continued across the page. "The missus gets a bit testy when I say that."

"Well, well," I said, rubbing out the words. "Grumpy Ches is afraid of his wife."

"Talk to me after you're married. Now, back to the letter."

> Start little Lilly in school this September. She'll be beside herself when she finds out, and so excited to one day read for herself about them vampires she loves so much. Wish I could see her reaction. Send the boys, too, when they're old enough.

A shiver ran down my back. Ches's two sons were three and two. Was he giving his wife instructions in case he didn't survive?

Tell Mother that me and Gord are all right.

"Your father's deceased?"
"Drowned on the fishing grounds when I was ten." Ches went back to dictating the letter.

Tell the youngsters Daddy misses them something awful. Most of all, love, I miss our quiet times together.
Ches

At 9:00 p.m. we lined up in the streets, ready to begin the trek for the front lines. It had been a hot day and the sun was setting on the horizon, casting a red hue in the clouds. The villagers from the area must've somehow become aware of the coming battle and came out to see us off. Many of the women cried, and the men were visibly upset. A real spark of fear twisted in my stomach. Why the tears this time? I concentrated on the few French words I'd picked up and understood that the shouts of au revoir and bonne santé meant goodbye and good health. The villagers had grown to care for us Newfoundlanders and said they'd pray that we'd return unharmed to them. The ten per cent holdback stayed in Mailly-Maillet Wood while the rest continued the march to the support trench we'd called St. John's Road, arriving at two o'clock on the morning of July 1. Five hours of marching had left us exhausted and hungry.

We were given a final briefing on the operation by our commanding officer, Colonel Hadow, a typical English officer, sporting a moustache that I'd come to associate with British upper class. "An all-out attack by the British forces will commence at seven thirty, the big push, as it were," he said, hands clasped behind his back.

"Colonel," I said. "How many British troops are occupying the twenty-two-mile front?"

"Approximately sixty thousand men, including the Newfoundland Regiment."

I was stunned. That was double the population of St. John's.

The colonel continued. "At seven-twenty, a large mine will explode in the tunnel under Hawthorn Ridge, close to the German front line near Beaumont Hamel. Bombardment of this area will then cease. At seven twenty-eight, sixteen more mines will be exploded beneath German lines, at which time the bombardment also ceases at these points. At zero hour, seven thirty, the Royal Fusiliers will proceed to the crater at Hawthorn and capture the low-lying German Y-Ravine to our right. This will open the way to the German front lines."

Questions bounced around inside my head. Why not wait until the Royal Fusiliers left the trenches to stop the bombardment? Ten minutes was time enough for an enemy to reach the twenty-foot deep, thirty-foot wide ravine and set up weapons. That's not possible, an inner voice countered. The Germans are too weak to mount a strong counterattack.

"The South Wales Borderers will follow next. The Scottish Border Regiment will move into no man's land at eight oh five. At eight forty, signalled by the blow of a whistle, the Newfoundland Regiment, along with the Essex Battalion on your right flank, will go over the top."

"Colonel Hadow," Captain Wakefield said. "If I may take a moment to say a word to the men?"

"Yes, of course, Captain," The captain removed his hat and placed it under his arm. "The generals want you to be reassured that the Germans have almost been obliterated by the bombardment. Therefore, breaking through their lines and taking

Beaumont Hamel will be a relatively simple task. All that is required is simply to walk to the target."

Did he truly believe those words, or was this an attempt to calm our anxieties?

The colonel nodded his approval. "Well said, Captain." He addressed us once more. "Before assuming your place in the trenches, a tin triangle will be pinned to each man's haversack. When it flashes in the sunlight the artillery observers will see your position, thus enabling the artillery to fire well ahead of you."

The triangles were cut from biscuit tins, and when ours were attached, Joey and I made for the St. John's Road. "Ron," he said, "I'd rather not wear the metal sign. What happens if we're wounded and making our way back to our lines in the bright sunshine?"

I frowned. "We're easy targets for snipers."

As we sat in the trenches whiling away the hours before morning, I reflected on the events of the past weeks.

"What's on your mind?" Joey asked. His eyes were closed and I thought he'd been asleep.

"We've made two unsuccessful raids against the Germans and proven their barbed wires aren't blasted to shreds by our million shells."

"They've been bombing us, which implies they're in good shape." Joey opened his eyes. "I say we focus on getting over the top with sixty pounds of baggage weighing us down and achieving our goal."

I leaned against the sandbags, listening to the men's small talk. "Buxom Dottie can't marry us all," a soldier said with a slight stutter. Whoops and whistling rang out.

"You're all out of luck, lads," another man with strawberry blond hair said with a grin. "I'll be her man."

A man with a hooked nose puffed out his chest. "She said

she'd marry the first soldier to win a Victoria Cross. That'll be me."

"Does your missus know that?" Laughter sounded, then floated away like bubbles drifting out of sight.

I joined in the banter, although the laughter and joking didn't dispel an uneasiness hanging on like a lingering cough. My cousins had never participated in any real form of battle, and in truth they were mentally unprepared for what lay ahead. The First Five Hundred had experienced some combat in Gallipoli, yet hadn't made an all-out assault.

Joey poked me in the arm. "Worrying about what's to come expends too much energy. What will happen will happen."

CHAPTER 9

I dozed off at times during the night. Unable to remain still any longer, I pulled on my boots as the first light of morning crept over the land.

Gord Abbott stood over a boiling metal pot. "You slept more than me, lad," he said, opening a bag of tea leaves. "I've never been this close to dying before. Not even on the ice floes in a raging blizzard." Then he smiled. "I'd wager a townie like you hasn't even fished in a sparkling brook."

"You'd win the bet. To be honest I never once had the urge."

Gord spooned tea leaves into the pot. "Fishing is a way of life around the bay and a damn hard means to earn a wage. Ches's youngsters deserve the opportunity to find a better life."

"Yours, too, when you have them."

"My missus died in childbirth." Gord looked down at the ground. "As she was being born, the cord wrapped around my baby girl's neck and cut off her air. She was all blue when she was delivered."

My breath caught in my throat. "I'm awfully sorry."

"It's been three years." Gord took a photograph from his inside pocket. "This is Rosie."

A petite young woman about eighteen or nineteen smiled, her hand on her big, round stomach. Gord kissed the photo and returned it to his pocket. "There'll never be anyone else for me."

Cigarette smoke drifted into the dugout, slightly masking the musty odour of damp earth and brin sacks filled with sand. I glanced toward Joey Baker's empty bunk.

"Guess he's restless like the rest of us," Gord said.

I slid off my bunk and went outside. The last traces of a light mist lingered in the early morning air. Joey leaned against the trench wall, puffing out clouds of smoke.

"How long have you been out here?" I asked, refusing the cigarette he offered me.

"About an hour." He tapped ashes from the tip of the cigarette with his forefinger. "I'm glad this offensive will end the war." Sounds of rattling tin cups echoed out from dugouts. "We've been away from Newfoundland long enough." He took one last draw and crushed out his cigarette with the toe of his boot.

"Come on, Joey. Let's get a cup of tea while it's piping hot. Gord's brew is almost as good as my mother's."

Joey lit up another cigarette and blew out more smoke. "The field kitchen is preparing a hot meal for us. The last one before the execution. I don't have much of an appetite this morning."

"It'll be all right, Joey. We came through Gallipoli without a scratch."

Joey glanced down at his feet. "Not from the Turks, any-way." He tossed his cigarette. "We're are a sturdy people. It'll take something big to stop us." We stepped into the dugout and took the tea Gord offered us.

Fred sipped from his cup, and wiped away the tea wetting his upper lip. "I went to have a chat with some of my old buddies earlier. They all agree that our next cuppa will be in Beaumont Hamel, sitting at a proper table.

"With Buxom Dottie," Gord chimed in. We clinked our metal cups and toasted to success with the strong tea, laughing, but our laughs were drowned in the noise from the artillery shells.

Fred glanced at his chain watch. "Six twenty-five. Right on time."

A steady stream of shells zoomed overhead while we ate. My ears throbbed with the loud booms, which were more intense than rumbling thunder. The ground trembled with the blasts, so frequent and uninterrupted, and the earth undulated like waves on a choppy ocean. Rats scurried up and down the walls of the trenches, squealing, trying to escape the noise and shaking earth. Fred shouted something into my ear, but I couldn't hear him over the fierce roar. A thousand guns had to be firing at the same time to produce such a racket.

I finished my breakfast as much as the fluttering in my stomach would allow, and I watched Fred take out a bottle of rum from his haversack. "One last toddy before we go over," he said, and drank a quarter in one long gulp. He passed the bottle around with a hand steadier than a brain surgeon's. Each man licked his lips to savour every last drop, and we filed out of the dugouts and put the ladders in place against the side of the trench, waiting for the signal to go over the top.

Captain Wakefield, dressed in the uniform of a corporal so as not to be singled out as an officer by the Germans, was constantly checking his watch. The expectant look on his face was an indication that he was waiting for the mine explosion at Hawthorn Ridge. His pack contained a gas mask, ammunition pouches, a pistol, and a stick. This, in my opinion, was a dead giveaway to the enemy, since these few articles were nothing compared to that of the ordinary soldier. The Germans knew it was an officer like our captain who led his men into battle.

"Get ready for a blast like no other," he said. "Forty tons of underground explosives will go off at seven twenty." He counted backwards from five, and when he reached one, a boom rattled my eardrums. Massive amounts of earth spewed high into the air, as if ten thousand men had thrown shovels of rock and clay skyward at the same time.

Gord elbowed me, and shouted above the noise. "That blast is gonna make one hell of a crater."

A dark haze loomed on the horizon, mingling with smaller puffs of black smoke from shell explosions. Was this how the end of the world would look? "Sixteen more mines are set to go off at seven twenty-eight," I said. Right on time, more tons of earth spewed into the air in the distance.

"Right," Captain Wakefield said. He tapped his watch. "Seven thirty. Zero hour." The sun shone, eating up the mist, promising a warm summer's day.

"It's begun," Gord said. "The British chaps in the front line are climbing out of their trenches about now, charging across no man's land toward an enemy battered by days of bombardment." He paused as another thought occurred to him. "Of starvation, too, if the reports of food and water being cut off is true."

"There won't be an enemy to fight by the time we go over," a man with an oblong mole on his chin said.

One of the new arrivals, a boy no more than seventeen with blond hair, spoke up. "I've had over a year of non-stop training wasted," he said. "Until now the rats have seen more action than me." Had I looked and sounded that young when I enlisted? "This is finally my chance to fight for England."

Fred lounged against a trench ladder. "I'd say we won't have much resistance when we go over."

"I'll see how the troops are doing," Captain Wakefield said, and pushed through the soldiers, heading for the communications dugout.

Gord shoved his helmet to the back of his head. "This is the first time since me and Ches joined up that we've been apart during a fight." He looked down the length of the trench. "There are fourteen sets of brothers in the Regiment. And God knows how many cousins who are as close as brothers." He nodded to himself. "I reckon it was a good idea to assign Ches to the ten per cent holdback."

I glanced at Henry and Frank, chatting to each other to the right of me, always content with each other's company. If only one of them had been chosen for the holdback.

"Captain," Gord called as Wakefield made his way back toward us. "Any news on our progress?"

The captain didn't speak but moved aside, revealing Colonel Hadow.

I chanced a peek at my watch. Twenty minutes after eight. The men quieted down and gathered around the two officers.

The colonel stood with feet slightly apart, back straight, slapping his gloves against one hand, his face as stern as ever. Perhaps his facial muscles couldn't stretch into a smile. "I've just been advised by headquarters we're not to advance at the appointed time," he said in his crisp, upper-class English accent. "We are to remain in the trench until further notice."

"Sir," the man with the chin mole asked, "why are we staying put?"

The colonel's expression remained neutral. "No reason was given."

Fred snickered under his breath. "If commanded to fart into his tea, he'd do it without questioning why."

Gord inched closer to me. "The reason is as plain to see as a seal flapping its flippers on an ice pan. The Germans have been defeated already, so we're not needed."

No, I thought. The colonel would look pleased if that were the case.

Colonel Hadow rocked back on his heels. "Stay alert, men. I'll be watching your progress from the support trench. We need to be ready for whatever lies ahead. Captain Wakefield, come with me." The two men walked away, Hadow swinging his arm as if he were in march mode.

A sense of foreboding shot through me. Something was wrong, and not even Colonel Hadow knew what it was. The men in the trenches resumed their chatter in soft, quiet tones. No more laugher, not even a smile. Worried or not, each and every soldier would perform his duty without the slightest hesitation.

Henry and Frank strolled my way. "Ron," Frank said, "what do you suppose is going on?" He rapidly tapped a forefinger on his hip, a nervous habit he carried over from childhood.

"We're most likely not needed," the man with the chin mole interjected.

Gord hauled out his watch. "It's nine," he said. "Why haven't we received any word about a victory?"

A lull came over the men. I knew what each of them was thinking. We had trained for battle and many of us had fought at Gallipoli. Death was a shadow that loomed over every man. I'd come to terms with that possibility. The uncertainty was the toughest to bear.

"I don't suppose we're on the losing end of the battle," Gord ventured.

"How can that be?" Henry asked. "Our guns have destroyed every German dugout. Isn't that what the generals swore?"

"The captain's coming." The three words filtered down the line of soldiers.

"Men," Wakefield said, "we've been given the order to attack as soon as possible. Without the Essex Battalion on our right flank."

"Why aren't they coming for support?" I asked.

"I enquired, but an explanation wasn't offered."

"Has the German front line been captured?" Joey asked.

The captain paled ever so slightly. "I was told that the situation had not been . . ." He paused and straightened his jacket. ". . . had not been resolved as yet."

Gord's mouth gaped open. "What's that supposed to mean?"

"I'm sorry, lads. You know as much as I do at the moment. We're to go over the top from here instead of moving through the trenches to the front lines."

"Sir," Gord said, "that's awful risky. We'll have to cross two hundred and fifty yards before we even reach our own barbed wire. Then we're into no man's land."

Joey's fingers tightened around his rifle. "That won't be a problem if there aren't any Germans to stop us."

Captain Wakefield crossed his arms and surveyed his group of men. "I have the utmost faith in this regiment. Those of you who served at Gallipoli made Newfoundland and Great Britain very proud. For those who came straight from training, I believe without the slightest doubt you will show the same courage and loyalty as your fellow comrades. I have been honoured and humbled to serve as your captain." He moved to the bottom of a ladder. "We go over at the sound of my whistle."

"Ron," Joey said quietly, "you know as well as me why we can't move through the trenches."

Resolved to my fate, whatever it was to be, calmed me. "Yes, Joey. They're filled with the dead and wounded."

We helped each other put on the sixty-pound backpacks. Many of the smaller, shorter men, who were in the majority, staggered under the load before standing firm. Ten trench bridges to be brought into battle lay end to end on the trench floor. Gord and Fred stood close to the one they were assigned. "Come on, Gord," Fred said. "Let's do our duty for king and country."

Henry and Frank hoisted another trench ladder onto their

shoulders. Henry smiled at his brother. "We stay together till the end."

Captain Wakefield took out his pistol. "Fix bayonets, men."

With practiced precision we fixed our bayonets and lined up behind the ladders. "Well," Joey said with a sidelong glance at me, "this is why we came."

Henry shook my hand. "Happy birthday, Ron." He smiled, a sort of lopsided one that didn't quite meet his eyes. "See you on the other side."

"Nine-fifteen," Captain Wakefield called out. He raised the whistle to his mouth and blew.

CHAPTER 10

JULY 1

OVER THE TOP

Not a single cloud blurred the blue sky, and the sun beamed down on the warm, sultry summer morning. All faces were turned toward Captain Cyril Wakefield, the twenty-seven-year-old from one of the most respected, wealthiest St. John's families. Tall and slim, his moustache trimmed to perfection, he returned the whistle to his breast pocket and scurried up the ladder. As if pulled forward by a giant magnet, one by one, all along the trench, men climbed without hesitation for a task that would define the rest of their lives. Some blessed themselves, others whispered words only they heard. Many laboured under the weight of the haversacks, in particular Steve Gatherall. At five foot four and weighing 110 pounds, he struggled to take each rung without toppling to the side.

"Buxom Dottie or a wooden leg," many of the single men yelled as they reached the top of the trench. At the moment I didn't care for either one.

The man with the chin mole was ahead of me, and as I stepped onto the bottom rung of the ladder, his arms flew out-

ward as if greeting a loved one. He groaned and fell back, knocking into me. His chest was a mass of red and he stared unblinking
at the sky. I gaped at him, and for the first time, became aware
of the spitting of machine-gun fire. Men were flying backwards
into the trench, blood spewing out like tiny fountains from various body parts.

Thomas Quinlan, a man I'd fought beside at Gallipoli, landed at my feet, his eyes a pool of bright red blood. He moaned—a
soft, longing sound—then became quiet. All down the trench
men tumbled down the ladders like they were being shoved
back by an invisible hand.

If I went up the ladder, I'd meet the same fate. Do your duty,
my mind cautioned. I raced up the ladder, my haversack like
layers of bricks across my shoulders. My world collapsed like
a paper castle in heavy rain when I reached the top and stared
out over the open land. More men than I could count lay strewn
everywhere, some moving, others still, the crimson red of blood
the only colour common to them.

Captain Wakefield ran a few yards ahead, leading the advance, his pistol held out before him. Bullets sliced through the
air, maiming, cutting off breath, piercing flesh, bringing down
soldiers charging through a firing range with not even a dried-
out bush for protection. Shrapnel flew through the air, seeking
out healthy, pink flesh. High explosives ripped away mounds
of earth, leaving in their wake smoking holes over which men
stumbled. A bullet tore through the right arm of the man next
to me. He transferred his rifle to the left hand without slowing
his advance.

A few feet farther on, Skit and Dave Bernard ran side by
side, in perfect unison. A shell exploded in front of them and
Skit flew backwards, his arms and legs flying off in different
directions. Dave, with a confused look on his face, paused long
enough to glance down at Skit's torso. They had been insepar-

able, eleven months apart in age and almost identical. Dave ran faster, as if he was trying to outrun the machine guns and shelling . . . or perhaps the image of what was left of his brother. Bullets sank into his arms, legs, chest. Still he tried to keep going, and when he finally went down, he dragged himself along by one elbow. A final bullet to the temple and he lay motionless.

Steve Gatherall sped by Dave and tripped over a body propped up on its rifle like it was ready to take a shot. Steve caught a bullet in the shoulder as he fell. He tried to get up, but being a small man, and wounded, the weight of the backpack kept him pinned to the ground.

Henry carried a ladder to my right. He hopped over one body, then another, and stumbled several feet before regaining his balance. A bullet smacked into the end of the ladder, chipping away pieces of the wood. Several more steps and Henry stopped and looked down, disbelief on his face. The ladder slid from his shoulder, the end embedding itself in the half-dried mud. He leaned forward, then slowly crumpled to his knees, his head draped over the end of the ladder.

Frank ran back. "Get up, Henry!" He tried to pull him to his feet. "You can't stay here!"

Gord sprinted to his side. "Keep moving, Frank," he said, giving him a slight shove.

"Wait." Frank gently pulled Henry free, picked up the ladder, and ran on, his head bent low.

Shells burst all around. Smoke swelled out like budding flowers. Clay and shrapnel stung my eyes as the hail of bullets grew heavier. Fewer and fewer men darted across the brittle, barren land as they were forced to run on top of friends, family, comrades, and British soldiers from other battalions. A fit of laughter at the ridiculousness of the situation surged in the pit of my stomach, then dulled as Frank fell forward, both arms hooked in the rungs of the ladder like a scarecrow attached to a post.

My cousins were gone, erased from existence like squashed insects. Death wasn't so easy to accept. My heart thudded against my ribs. Tears clouded my vision. I stepped into a shell hole, and slipped on what looked like strings of sausages, splashing up to my waist into water and blood. A set of sightless yellowish-brown eyeballs flew past my face.

Gord grabbed my arm and dragged me to my feet. "I know it's damn hard seeing this, but you've got to keep going."

I stared at him, my brain too overcrowded with horror and death to single out one lucid thought.

"Do your duty. You're a soldier," Gord yelled.

My duty, my duty, my duty I repeated over and over in my head until I was numb, emotionless. A shell exploded in front of me and I toppled head over heels. Out of the fading smoke and charred bushes Gord ran toward me. "You all right?" I nodded and he hurried on.

My ears rang like muffled church bells as I reached our well-laid belts of wire, four layers deep, where pre-cut gaps were marked with white tape. Bodies from previous waves of soldiers clogged the holes. Captain Wakefield pulled two men away, went through, and waited for his men lining up to make it to his side. Bullets honed in on us. The white tape glowed like giant beacons for the enemy. One man got through. The next wobbled to the ground like a deflated balloon. Another soldier jumped over him. The following three collapsed. Stuck behind a line of men, I couldn't help any of them. Those closest to the gap tried to drag the dead away, only to become part of the heap. A blond boy scurried over the dead, and the man following behind was swallowed up in the smoke from a bursting shell. Another man scrambled over the mound of bodies, but his heavy pack sent him to his knees. A bullet smashed into his head as he tried to stand, sending small fragments of his skull spinning outwards. The opening in the barbed wire was clogged with my comrades, young men like me, the dream of a full life only a shattered illusion.

Colonel Hadow was watching our progress—no, lack of progress—from the support trench. Was he upset? Shocked at the loss of life? Or was he angry the mission was failing?

Men zigzagged between the lines of barbed wire to the next marked gap. Bullets flung many across the wire and their blood dripped off the metal barbs to the ground. We were like firemen running toward a fire, a fire of smoke, bullets, shrapnel, and high explosives. We were being massacred behind our own lines by a defeated, demoralized enemy. Wasn't that what the generals had proclaimed, promised, and even verified? The two men before me fell, shot multiple times. Their baby faces had never seen a razor. I pushed them out of the way, startled at how efficiently I had performed the task.

Gord followed me toward the downward slope of the battle-bruised terrain. "Oh God," I gasped. "The slaughter is worse here." Men were piled on top of each other like cod in a fish box. More dropped around me until only handfuls remained, charging onward.

"Look," Gord shouted, pointing a little to the left at the crater of a mine we'd set off.

My stomach sank. Germans occupied the rim, their machine guns spitting. "Goddamn it," I screamed.

Dave and Hank Williams crossed in front of me, carrying a ten-foot trench bridge. Hank was at the front. "Come on, Davey," he shouted. "Just a little fur—" A piece of shrapnel destroyed the space where Dave's mouth had been. Blood poured onto his chin and down his throat as he fell, pulling his brother and the ladder to the ground. Hank was the younger of the two and worshipped Dave. As I approached, Hank stood up, his jaw clenched to stop his tears, and swung the trench bridge over his shoulder as he trudged forward, head low like a caribou ready to fight for its territory.

I knew . . . we all knew none of us would stand the slightest hope of survival, yet we pushed on. To perform our duty for Colonel Hadow, for king and for country. Would that ease Aunt Elsie's grief? Or Dad's? Or anyone's?

"Jesus!" Gord cried out. "Captain Wakefield's been hit!"

He lay on his side, both hands on his abdomen, blood spraying out between his fingers. "Leave me," he gasped through gritted teeth. His face had a grey hue, and sweat beaded on his forehead.

Gord took his haversack from his back and pulled out his field bandages. "We'll get the bleeding under control, sir. Don't you worry." He pressed the white material into the wound, which leaked blood so fast it immediately turned the bandage red. "Ron, we need more."

I'd already opened my haversack and handed over my supply. A truckload of bandages wouldn't stem the flow.

Gord applied more pressure to the wound. "We'll have to take him back."

"No," the captain said. "I'll wait for the stretcher-bearers." He coughed, and blood bubbled from the corner of his mouth. "Return Beaumont Hamel to the French." He closed his eyes, as if too exhausted to keep them open. "That's an order."

"But, sir," I said. "We can't leave you . . ." My voice faded as the captain exhaled softly and his body relaxed.

Gord felt for a pulse and rose from the ground. "He's gone. You heard his last command."

The mile or so of bleak ground ahead of us was layered with even more of the fallen: some rigid, others clasping their wounds, most lying still, eyes open in sudden death. This graveyard of the unburied burned an indelible image into my brain.

The shrieks of pain all around drove me through a barrage of bullets that somehow missed me, missed Gord. Scores of the dead blocked the gaps in the German barbed wire. A shell exploded and knocked me to the ground. The weight of my haversack was a minor inconvenience in this turmoil. I hopped to my feet and ran through the smoke. Rocks of all sizes dropped on me, bouncing off my helmet with a thudding noise. A warm red liquid splashed across my cheek. It wasn't my blood. "If I wake up from this nightmare," I prayed, "please make it fade from memory."

All the trench ladders and bridges were strewn along the ground, the carriers' dead fingers gripping broken fragments. I looked around for Gord and Joey. The Danger Tree, a tangled mess of branches, was halfway down the hill. Hundreds of bodies were piled up around it, arms and legs angled out as if double-jointed. The Germans had to be using it as a reference point, mowing down men as they ran by. I had to get past it.

There was nowhere to find shelter as bullets continued to strike already dead or injured soldiers. So few of us were able-bodied, and only a handful getting close to the Germans.

Gord cut through the first layer of German barbed wire and faced rows and rows of more in front of him. Joey was nowhere in sight as I raced toward the well-hidden enemy. I wished he were beside me, a friend from home, a place I may never set foot again.

I caught up with Hank Evans, a new arrival, this his first day of battle. He'd been awfully nervous that morning and couldn't eat breakfast. At the blow of the whistle he did his duty. He was carrying twenty mills bombs around his neck. I didn't understand why a more experienced soldier hadn't been chosen. He toppled over in front of me, pain distorting his young face, blood dripping from his wounds.

He gripped my hand as I dropped down beside him. If one of those bombs were hit he'd have been blown apart. "You'll be all right," I said, removing the bombs as bullets riddled the ground around us. "Lie still. The stretcher-bearers will come for you."

I slung the bombs around my neck and ran. In an instant, my chest burned like it had been pierced with a flaming arrow. My legs felt heavy, as if sandbags were tied around them. I tried to put one foot forward, but my energy drained away like water dribbling from a bottle. My legs buckled and I fell backwards to the ground. My haversack softened the impact as I struck the earth. I was on my back, helpless, and couldn't raise my arms to remove the bombs. Gord had reached the German wire, and looked back at me, stunned. No, he was sad. He turned away and disappeared on the way to a German trench.

Were the generals prepared to send more men to a needless death? A white flare soared into the sky near the German line. I blinked from the bright sunshine. Was that the third flare? That wasn't possible. We hadn't reached our objective. My gaze strayed to our lines and saw the Essex coming out of their trenches, silhouetted against the blue sky, the most perfect targets, as were we.

I never imagined I would die this way. Young, surrounded by thousands, yet alone and far away from home. I thought I would be afraid, but I wasn't. The pain in my chest had dulled to a mild ache, each throb in rhythm with my heartbeat. Maybe if I closed my eyes I would see home, see Mom one last time. She'd be upset if I didn't say goodbye. Dad would understand the sacrifice I made for king and country. And Joanie. She'd miss me the most, I think. I opened my eyes and my breath came out as a shudder. Could I still be here among the dead and dying in this barren place? No man's land?

The sun was ribbed like a pumpkin, warming my face. Why was the rest of me cold? The earth trembled as the big guns drummed louder than the roar of a thunderstorm. Bursts of black smoke tarnished the velvet blue of the vast sky. Rocks and earth shot up, ballooned out, then rained down. Shrapnel flew overhead with a zing and cut into flesh, gnawed at chins, cheeks, and foreheads with the ferocity of starving rats. A man nearby, scarlet blood oozing from gaping holes, grabbed at what was left of his face. How do you eat without a mouth? Screams of anguish and pain tore at my soul. The black clouds were growing, dispersing into black fog. It was difficult to see through the haze.

My ears pulsated from the cries for help all around me. They were harder to bear than the steady roar of the guns. Something hit my shoulder and I tried to turn my head to look. There. My heart sang! It was Joey Baker, lying on his stomach and staring at me. Oh, God! The top of his head was gone.

The screams were closer now, more piercing. A shell pounded into the earth and the ground shook. Dirt flew up and spattered my face. My mouth was filling with clay, but I spat before swallowing too much and I coughed, with a gurgling sound. Another explosion, and a body was blown apart above me, disintegrating into splinters of bone, charred, smoking flesh, and bright red blood raining down on me. The head was intact, with shrapnel sticking out from all over the face, like a porcupine. The sweet smell of burnt flesh and urine soaked the air, suffocating me. Another explosion, and a leg with a boot attached flew past me. Explosion after explosion rocked the ground, shaking me. Clay and debris covered me, beginning to bury me in my final resting place. Men ran past me, their battle cries strong. One lad, no more than sixteen or seventeen, stared down at me. Did he recognize me? I stared back with unblinking eyes. He blessed himself and then his gaze followed his fingers as they flew away from his hand.

A crow cawed close by. A rat's tail flicked across my face.

Dream my sweet boy of chocolate bunnies in a land of candy. Okay, Mom. I closed my eyes, her soft voice singing me to sleep the way she did when I was a small child. I sighed in comfort as her hand gently caressed my cheek. The cries and screams were fading into the distance, like echoes in a long tunnel. The ground was still, the heat ebbing from my body. Peace enveloped me, softer, warmer than my grandmother's quilts. I was drifting away. All was quiet. Soon I'd be home in Newfoundland, where sun rays crown they pine-clad hills. Where Joanie was waiting with all my presents.

CHAPTER 11

Low, wailing noises penetrated a soothing calm I hadn't experienced in a long while. The sounds intensified, ever closer, more anguished. Mom's voice faded, yet lingered like the sweet fragrance of lilacs after a rain shower. My eyes flickered, squinting from the brightness. The sun was much lower in the sky and I guessed it must have been close to suppertime. I tried to sit up, but the sharp pains in my chest and arm prevented me from doing so. Something nibbled at my ankles and I kicked out, sending two rats scurrying over my legs.

Blackflies swarmed around the open wound on Joey's head. "Leave him alone," I cried, trying to swat them away. His face had turned a metallic grey and his eyes were bloodshot. "I'm sorry, Joey." A tear slipped down my cheek as I reached out and closed his eyes. All he ever wanted out of life was to become a good doctor, dedicated to the profession and to his patients.

My lips itched and burned like someone had rubbed them raw with sandpaper. I tried to lick them, but my mouth was dry, my tongue thick. Something was different, and it took a moment for me to realize that the artillery guns had stopped firing.

"Ma!" A cry cut through the air.

"I can't see!" The terror in the young voice was palpable.

"I can't feel my legs," another man screamed. "Jesus, someone help me!"

I glanced around no man's land . . . dead man's land, now. Nearby, I saw Loyola Greene. A jagged bone protruded from his upper thigh. Thick, black blood soaked the length of his leg. "Ma!" he sobbed. "I want to go home." He was one of the new arrivals, sixteen years old.

I eased my shoulder out from under Joey's head, my stomach turning at the soft splat when it hit the ground. The flies, spread out on his wound, didn't leave. Another swarm pitched on him, hungry to nest. I couldn't stop thinking they were laying eggs, which would become maggots, eating what was left of his brain. The agony in my chest burrowed deeper as I slowly turned onto my left side and leaned on my elbow. I rested a few seconds to ease the pain before pulling myself around three bodies to reach Loyola. One man's hand was black, and bloated to the size of a catcher's glove. Blackflies lined the fingertips. Yellow fluid oozed from a wide gash on his face. The stench of rotted flesh reminded me of a decayed cat I once found on the side of the road. The stink overwhelmed me.

Many dead eyes bore silent witness to my progress.

"Help me!" The plea came from a few yards to my right. A quick glance and I saw a British soldier whose legs were missing below the knees, and the ground around the stumps was a pool of fresh blood. I marvelled at the fact that he was still breathing.

"God in heaven, help me!" Another English accent from my left. Or was it behind me? I couldn't tell, the voices came from every direction.

I crawled forward, one arm dragging along the ground,

numb from the shoulder down. My chest was heavy, tight. "Loyola," I called, breathless as I neared him. I coughed and spat out pink foam.

"Ron? Ron? Is that you?" His southern shore Irish accent was unmistakable. Tears flowed down his smoke-stained face, tracing white lines on his smooth cheeks. "I'm afraid." He tried to move and screamed. His face went white under the black soot. His screams became choked sobs, and his chest rose in time with the throbbing pulse in his neck.

"Stay still," I said, and assessed his injuries with a quick glance. Clotted blood surrounded the damaged, reddish skin at the site where the bone protruded. "Your leg's broken, but you'll be all right."

He reached down to touch his wound, but I snatched his hand away. "The stretcher-bearers will be here soon. Try to rest."

"I'm thirsty." His eyelids fluttered.

"Hold on." A bullet whizzed over my head. The numbness in my arm became sharp pins and needles. I lay flat and tugged at the strap of my haversack to get it off my back. The sharp pain dug into my chest again. Sweat dripped into my eyes, and my breathing made wheezing noises. I tried to take a deep breath and almost fainted from the crushing sensation. Somehow I managed to free myself of the bombs, and panting like an over-heated dog, I gave one last tug and my haversack came loose.

I took out my water bottle. "Here you go," I said, raising Loyola's head for him to drink.

He swallowed like he had a sore throat. "Thank you," he said, lying back. "I'm much better now."

I took a small sip and looked around. Two shots rang out and hit the ground close to my elbow. Water ran out from a hole in my bottle as I covered Loyola with my arms as best I could. A single shot, then a steady burst chewed at the earth, sending rocks and dirt cascading over both of us.

I lifted my head just enough to peer around. My stomach sank to the bottom of my boots. Several yards away, a wounded man crawled on his hands and knees. The sun burned down on the tin triangle on his haversack, its reflection blinding. A rifle shot sounded and he slumped forward, yet continued to move on both elbows, both legs flopping along the ground like useless pieces of wood. Another bullet followed, piercing the tin target on his back. He collapsed and his face struck the dirt.

More movement caught my eye as wounded men struggled to reach our lines, unaware that their tin triangles betrayed them to the enemy. One by one, German snipers picked them off.

"Stay down," I tried to yell despite my parched throat. My voice was hardly audible. The noise of gunfire drowned me out.

"Ron . . . Ron." The whisper sounded breathy. It was Fred Thompson.

I stared across the sea of flesh, bone, and blood, searching, a bubble of hope rising in me that Fred wasn't too seriously injured. A hand rose into the air.

"Loyola," I said. "That's a buddy of mine. I'll see how he is and be right back." Able to put weight on my bad arm again, I started across the short distance to Fred. I passed alongside one man whose abdomen was exposed, the surrounding skin discoloured green. A little farther on I saw three strips of flesh with a knuckle attached to each one. Shards of bone about an inch long stuck up from the ground.

I had to keep moving through this graveyard of nightmares to reach Fred. His face was covered in blood, and a piece of his scalp was missing near the front of his head. "Delighted to see you, laddie," he mumbled.

"Are you badly hurt?"

He cracked a smile. "A bullet knocked me helmet off and sent me flying arse over kettle. I didn't get a scratch, so I got back up and found my rifle. My helmet was too twisted out of shape to wear."

"What happened to your head?"

"Shrapnel." He gingerly touched the open wound. "It'll take more than a German to stop me."

I hauled a handkerchief from my pocket and wiped blood from his face. Shrapnel about half an inch long was embedded in his forehead just above the right eye. "Can you move?" I asked.

His hand went to his side, and I saw that his pants were wet with blood. "Caught a bullet in the hip." He grimaced. "The shrapnel grazed me in the forehead as I went down. I'm one lucky son of a bitch."

Three shots fired in quick succession, and I watched three men sink to the ground.

Fred balled his hands into fists. "The heartless goddamned cowards are shooting our wounded men like they're wild animals to be put out of their misery."

"Would we do any different?"

Fred made to sit up, and dropped back down amidst a spray of bullets. They spattered the ground at his feet.

"We'll have to wait until it's dark before we move," I said. "It'll be a while before help gets to us."

"Do you think the ten per cent holdback troops are out here?"

"I don't believe anyone in their right mind would've sent them out after this colossal failure."

"Take a gander at the carnage," Fred said through clenched teeth. "You really think the generals are in their right minds?"

The shrieks of pain, cries for mothers, and pleas for help intensified. Fred squeezed his eyes shut. "Sweet Jesus, please help them."

The sun lazed about on the horizon, the sky above it streaked with crimson. I didn't have the inclination to admire its beauty. I took a sip from Fred's water bottle. "I'll check the men around here, see if any need water."

"I'll help." Fred groaned, his face flushed.

"Your hip will start bleeding again if you move. Stay put."

He looked at my bloodstained chest. "You take care as well."

I found one soldier lying on top of another and assumed the bullet went through the first and into the second. Shrapnel had cut away the ear and the side of another man's head. The skin around the injury was charred and smelled like burnt liver. White specks filled the hole. I stifled a gag and moved to another soldier. His lips were gone, his teeth scattered on the ground in front of him. His bowels had given way at the time of death, and the smell was thick in the air.

I lowered my head into my hands and cried for the dead, for their loved ones, and for myself.

"That's enough for now," Fred said softly. "It'll be dark in an hour or so. You should rest."

"Time for that later," I said, and crawled back to Loyola. There was fresh blood around the protruding bone. His face was paler, his pulse slower, and his breathing shallower. "The pain's not so bad anymore."

"That's grand," I said.

Loyola looked at me, his youthful face serene, the skin waxen like a store mannequin. "I had the most lovely dream," he said. "Me, my baby brother Ray, and Dad were fishing for salmon on the Exploits River. We go every year, but I never catch one. Ray does, and he always teases me about it." His body jerked as if someone had kicked it. "This time I reeled in a mighty big one. Ray and Dad cheered me on. Ron, it was like I was really with them." He closed his eyes, and with a soft smile on his lips, he gasped. A rush of air escaped as both hands slipped to the ground.

"Loyola! Loyola!" I shook him. "Wake up!"

"Is he gone?" Fred's voice floated across the short distance.

I checked his neck for a pulse. "Yes. He lost too much blood." Each breath I took whistled louder, the pressure on my chest stronger. Maybe I'd die soon.

"Hang on, lad. We'll get out of this mess."

"Loyola might have lived if he'd been found sooner and treated." I crawled the few feet back to Fred and lay beside him.

"Ron." A hand shook my shoulder. "Wake up. It's dark. Now's our chance to move."

I opened my eyes to a sky shimmering with silver stars. The constellations fascinated me. I looked for the Big Dipper.

"Ron." Fred spoke a shade louder, pointing to the soldier hugging the ground beside him. "This is Captain Cyrus Reynolds from the Essex Regiment."

The British captain, a medium-built, dark-haired man in his early thirties, nodded to me. "What a right bloody mess. Good to see some of you Newfoundlanders alive."

Groggy, disoriented, I stared at him.

"A bloody massacre is more like it," Fred said.

"I'm sorry you blokes didn't have our support." Reynolds touched a large bruise over his eye, bloodshot and nearly swollen shut. A bloodied bandage dried to a rusty brown covered his right hand. The ring and pinky fingers were gone. "Our colonel requested permission to clear the trenches of dead bodies in order to get to the front lines."

"Christ," Fred said, "Hadow should've done the same for us. Most of us were shot down behind our own lines."

"Some of my men realized this was a lost cause and didn't want to go over." Reynolds sighed. "They weren't cowards, you understand. Just men who knew when a situation was hopeless. We had two options. Refuse to go over and get shot as cowards, or die in battle. Needless to say, we opted for the latter."

"Captain Reynolds," I said. "Did any of your men reach the Germans?"

"The few who did were either killed or captured." He held out his bandaged hand. "Shrapnel blew my pistol away, along with my fingers. Another piece hit my eye, and that's the last I remember. When I came to I couldn't see out of it."

Howls of pain grew louder in the absence of shelling and gunfire. The captain looked down at Fred's hip. "You're bleeding again," he said. "We'd better get you back. The darkness will give us some protection."

"Thank you, sir, but Ron's wound is more serious."

"I can move on my own. You can't."

"Fred," Reynolds said, using an officer's tone, "you've lost too much blood already. You're coming with me."

Fred paled considerably as I helped him get into position on the captain's back. With his arms wrapped around Reynolds's neck, he smiled at me. "See you soon, Ron."

The Essex captain crawled away on hands and knees, Fred hanging on, his bad leg slightly out to the side. He looked back at me, an apologetic expression on his face. I waved as loneliness stole over me.

A light cloud slipped across the moon, allowing just enough light for me to perceive the shadowy forms of Reynolds and Fred in the distance. Other dark shapes moved, deformed creature with only heads and shoulders, creeping over the ground. How many of those who make it would live the rest of their lives physically or mentally shattered by what they'd suffered and witnessed on this battlefield?

I looked down at Loyola. He looked serene and relaxed, the anguished lines of pain and terror gone from his face. A breeze blew, chilling me despite the warm night. Sweat dripped into my eyes and I shivered, hot and cold at the same time. I crept forward, trying to keep Captain Reynolds and Fred in sight, but sharp knives stabbed into my chest and I had to stop and rest.

A flare from the German line illuminated the sky, followed by a renewed rat-a-tat-tat drill of machine-gun fire. Bullets riddled the ground, throwing rocks and dirt over my head. I peered through the debris to see if Reynolds and Fred had been hit. Reynolds pushed over the crest of a hill with Fred clinging to him, Fred's good leg pushing into the ground. I remained still, one arm over my head, and waited for the flare to burn out. More bullets zeroed in on me, cutting instead into soldiers who no longer felt pain. I tried to hold my breath against the pain tearing at my chest.

No one should depart this earth on his birthday, least of all a nineteen-year-old. Joey Baker's vacant eyes sprang into my mind. He was nineteen and gone. The flare eventually fizzled out, the guns quietened. A cloak of darkness veiled the land, and for an instant I recalled summer nights in St. John's. The memories gave me the strength to press on. I got to my knees and crawled, pausing every few yards to listen for the pop of a flare. I crawled over dead bodies, mostly British soldiers I didn't know or had only seen in passing. The smell of decay assaulted my nose. Bloated, blackened faces stared up at me, some younger than me, many more not much older. Rats gnawed on exposed flesh.

The crackle of a flare alerted me and I flattened to the ground. Random sniper shots struck swollen corpses and made them twitch. I heard a moan and saw a bullet enter the back of an Essex soldier's head, another life stripped away. He'd soon decompose into an unrecognizable blob under tomorrow's hot sun, food for the insects and rats.

The flare dimmed and went out. The pain in my chest knifed all the way to my back as I set off. Men sang out for loved ones, desperate calls for people who couldn't hear them.

"Ron." Another hoarse whisper in the breeze.

It had to be the imagination of my fevered brain . . . or a ghost. He couldn't have survived. Those soldiers from Britain and the Dominion would forever haunt no man's land, their ethereal cries resounding in the night.

"Ron." The disembodied whisper was hoarser. A hand slid along the dirt and debris to touch my arm, the fingers bloodied. "I'm some glad you're all right."

"Frank? Is that you?" I crawled closer. His lips were dried and cracked, his face sunburnt. Broken blisters formed scabs on his lower lip. "Henry is dead," he cried softly.

"I know." My eyes went to the wound in his stomach. Dried blood had congealed on the bandage wrapped around his waist. His left knee was expose to the bone. "I thought you were, too."

"Tell Ma I'm sorry."

Anger surged inside me. "You can tell her yourself. I'm getting you to our lines."

"No, Ron." He pushed my hand away. "It's too risky. One of us educated boys has to survive."

Another flash of light. I ducked, placing a protective arm over Frank.

Frank's voice quivered. "The soldier next to me got hit in the last flare. He'd been wounded in the foot but stayed to tend my wound." The soldier, about thirty, lay on his side, a bullet straight through the back into his heart. "His name was Alphonsus Tiddleford," Frank smiled a tired, sad smile. "Quite the name, don't you think? He was a train engineer from London and showed me a photo of his wife and four children." A short burst of rifle fire near the German line interrupted his words. "Ron, it's my fault he's dead." Tears cascaded down his face. Another flare poured its light over the land before the previous one had faded.

"We can't stay here," I said. "We'll find refuge in one of the craters."

"Please, Ron. You'll make too easy a target with me."

"We'll move as soon as the flare goes out. Arguing will only delay us."

"Ron, Alphonsus has a letter from his wife in his jacket pocket. The address is written on the envelope. I want her to know he saved my life."

I quickly rummaged through a pocket, found the letter neatly folded in two, and placed it in my pocket. "Frank," I said quietly, kneeling beside him. "Ready to go home?"

He nodded.

CHAPTER 12

NO MAN'S LAND

The flare petered out as I took one last glance up the hill. It would be light in a few hours, with no chance of getting back to our lines. I hauled out the water sheet from Frank's haversack and spread it out, tucking the end of one side under him. He rose up onto his elbows and cried out in pain. "Sorry," he gasped, making another attempt to shuffle onto the sheet. Fresh blood soaked through the bandage around his stomach.

"Lie back," I said. "Let me pull you onto the sheet."

"Ron, you're wounded as well. And look at your arm. It's hanging limp."

"One arm will do." I took short breaths to lessen the piercing stabs in my chest.

Frank grabbed my hand. "Stop. Your chest wound is serious. Too much exertion might kill you."

"I'm not leaving you, so shut up and help me." I grabbed him under one arm and pulled. His body tensed, but he didn't utter a sound. There hadn't been a flare for a while. Maybe the Germans had finally run out. Sweat dripped into my eyes and

I pulled again until Frank's upper body was on the sheet. The stars and moon were fading. Daylight wasn't far away. I crawled around Frank and lifted one leg at a time onto the sheet.

Ches and Harold hurried toward us, their bodies low to the ground. I couldn't believe my eyes. "Ron," Ches said, "we thought you were killed."

"Me too, at first."

"Jesus," Ches said, looking at my chest. "You've been shot. How bad is it?"

I opened my mouth to answer, but coughed and spat out blood instead. "Did Fred Thompson make it back?"

"Yes," Ches said. "The British bloke who brought him in was hit below the knee by a sniper, but it didn't cause any serious damage."

Harold knelt beside Frank. "I'm sorry about Henry."

"You saw him?"

"Yes." Harold glanced at me. "Your uncle Jack brought him in this morning."

"Thank God, Jack is alive. I was afraid he'd be lost and rot in this cursed land."

Frank wiped a tear away from his cheek. "I wish Henry could be buried at home. Ma will be awful upset she won't get to visit his grave every day."

"She won't be the only mother with no grave to visit," I murmured.

Frank let out a long breath, almost as if he was shedding his sadness. "Is General Haig satisfied with our efforts?"

Harold and I exchanged a look. "That's what our boys asked," Harold said, "as they dragged themselves, shot up and bleeding, back to the trenches."

Ches gave me his water bottle. "I don't give a damn if he is or isn't. I figured something was wrong when the holdback crew weren't called up to the front. A good source informed us that the few survivors from the first wave reported the Germans were well-fortified and blasting them into eternity. Add to that the huge number of wounded who'd returned."

I drank slowly. "Then why were we sent over?"

"My guess is Haig either didn't believe it or didn't care. He wanted the Germans beaten at any cost."

Harold unscrewed the cork from his water bottle and passed it to Frank. "You're dehydrated. Drink this, slow sips."

I coughed up more blood and wiped it away with my shirt sleeve. "We charged into a steady hail of bullets and bombs. Most of us were mowed down at our own lines."

"I know," Harold said. "The stretcher-bearers have been out all day bringing in the dead and wounded."

Harold wrapped Frank's knee with extra dressing, taking care not to wind it too tight. "If that wasn't bad enough, Colonel Hadow was ordered to round up as many men as he could and send them into battle again."

My mouth dropped open. "It was a slaughterhouse out here. He must've seen that for himself!"

Ches shook his head. "We all know the colonel doesn't question orders." He lifted Frank more securely onto the water sheet. "Why should he? His life wasn't on the line. Thank God a sane officer overrode the order. He'd witnessed the assault just like Hadow and said there'd been enough senseless deaths for one day."

Blood seeped up into my mouth, the taste like old metal. The wheezing had become more pronounced. "Ches, Gord reached the German trench just as I got shot. That's all I know."

"Then he's either dead or taken prisoner." He cleared his throat. "Enough talking. We got to get you boys back."

A man close by moved an arm and Harold scurried over to him. "It's Rick Carter," he said over his shoulder. "Fred will be glad to hear he's alive."

Rick groaned and opened his eyes. "What took you fellas so

long?" He smiled through cracked and blistered lips. Blood had congealed at the corners. "My bloody hip is killing me."

Harold smiled back. "We saved the grumpy men for last."

The first light of dawn sneaked through the clouds. "We have to get going," I said. "The Germans are crack shots, and if we linger much longer they'll kill us."

Ches caught hold of the water sheet. "Ron," he said, "can you make it on your own?"

"Yes." I noticed yellowish green fluid leaking through Frank's bandaged knee. "Get Frank and Rick out of here. They won't survive another day in the heat and sun."

Ches pulled the water sheet, dragging Frank away, while Harold carried Rick on his back. I followed, my chest on fire with the slightest exertion. The distance between us grew. I fought off waves of exhaustion and dizziness until I couldn't move a muscle. My breathing seemed to grow louder than a foghorn, and I slowed to rest a minute.

The back of my neck burned, rousing me. I lifted my head to the dazzling sun. Daylight! My heart lurched. I'd been unconscious for hours. The sun reflected off the tin badge of a soldier to my right as he pulled himself forward. One shot rang out and he stopped moving. Three bullets riddled the ground, so close to me dirt sprayed my face. Machine-gun fire ripped above my head.

The Danger Tree was yards away, and I saw three pairs of men carrying stretchers. Each placed a soldier on a stretcher, as if oblivious to the bullets buzzing around them like angry bees. One by one they disappeared over the crest of the hill. Another group of stretcher-bearers arrived. More bullets rang out, then the ground shook and spewed out black smoke. A single scream and one of the stretcher-bearers rose into the air, as if pulled up by an invisible rope. His helmet rolled down the incline and came to rest in front of me.

More explosions and dirt pounded my back. The stretcher-bearers carried their burdens away. If I remained here, the next explosion or the one after that would surely strike me. A crater was my only hope. I gathered every reserve of strength, looked around, and spotted one. Time stood still as I covered the many yards, slower than a worm in a foot of snow. My heart banged and my lungs refused to expand, forbidding air to enter. Exhaustion sinking into every muscle, I lay my face against the dry earth and closed my eyes.

The next thing I knew, a hand grabbed me by the back of my jacket. I gasped, overcome with the stabbing in my chest. I didn't have the energy to look up. I was pulled over the ground a few feet, then dipped downward, and pulled some more. A gentle hand turned me over onto my back.

"Ron, open your eyes."

A gurgling noise filled my ears.

"Ron, look at me." The voice, vaguely familiar, was calm yet conveyed a sense of urgency.

I opened my eyes and tried to talk, but only managed a rattle. Uncle Jack knelt over me, his hand on my chest. He looked so much older, wearier.

"Ron, listen to me. Your chest cavity is filling with blood. I have to release the pressure."

Blood pumped at my temples and I was light-headed. Jack took a knife and rubber tubing from his haversack. "I have to cut into your chest."

I couldn't swallow, couldn't utter a word. I strained to nod as a sign that I trusted him.

Jack opened my jacket and shirt in one quick movement, gripped the knife firmly, and cut. I would have screamed if I'd had enough air in my lungs. Red liquid squirted out through the tube, slowed, then stopped. My chest expanded with the influx of air.

"You'll be all right now," Jack said, and sat back on his heels. "You gave me quite the scare."

The world faded out.

The sun was high in the sky when I awoke. "Take it easy," Jack said, helping me sit up. He took my pulse. "You've been unconscious for the better part of the day." My chest was wrapped in bandages, with a single spot of blood over the bullet wound.

I looked around the huge crater, which was at least five metres deep and fifteen on the round. A soldier, possibly my age or younger, crouched against the side opposite me, shaking, staring around with a confused look on his face. He didn't notice we were there.

"He's from the first wave of British soldiers," Jack said.

"What's wrong with him?"

Jack removed his helmet and ran a hand through his light hair, streaked with dried blood. "I've seen men react like that before."

"He's afraid?" I didn't like the word coward.

"That couldn't be further from the truth. That soldier risked his life to save two men this morning despite shells exploding around him. His mind is shattered." Jack shrugged. "Maybe it's a combination of events. The incessant noise from the guns, maybe he's seen too much carnage and destruction. Only he knows the true cause. But being afraid isn't why he's here trembling like a frightened child."

"Will he be all right?"

"Every time I tried to talk to him he shrank away." Jack put his helmet back on. "I hope these men become normal again." He rubbed his temples as if he had a pounding headache. "This battle has been one enormous disaster. At least twenty thousand dead and forty thousand wounded or missing."

"The Germans were more than ready," I said. "Someone at the top made a mistake."

"We started bringing in the injured right away despite the constant shelling." He squeezed his eyes shut, forming wrinkles at the sides. "The doctors have never seen such atrocious injuries before."

"Jack, how did you end up in the crater?"

"A shell exploded, killing the stretcher-bearer and knocking me out." I noticed the gash over his right eyebrow. "When I came to, that poor boy was wandering around in circles, calling for someone named Eric. A flare went off and I managed to spot him. He kept pushing me away. I had to knock him out and carry him over my shoulder to get him here."

"Eric's probably a good buddy from home . . . or his brother."

Jack lowered his voice. "Eric is his identical twin. I passed his mangled body on the way here." He glanced at the soldier. "He was nearly decapitated."

"Henry is dead."

"I know."

There was no time to dwell on it. The young man jumped to his feet, about to leave the crater. He had a wild look in his eyes. "Stay down, Eric," he cried, as he ran around the crater. "Eric! I can't find you!"

Jack cautiously approached the soldier. "It's all right," he said softly. "Eric's waiting for you in the dugout."

The boy stood still, his eyes blank as Jack led him back and sat him down.

I coughed and my chest felt like it had exploded. A fresh patch of blood spread across the bandage.

Jack scrambled over to me. "I can't risk moving you. And I don't want to leave that poor boy alone."

"It'll be too dangerous to try and rescue us in daylight," I said.

Jack slid down next to me. "Too many are going to die from their wounds and loss of blood stranded out here."

His gaze flickered to my chest. I would join those ranks if help didn't come soon.

A shadow appeared at the rim of the crater. "Ron, you plan on staying down there for the rest of the war?" Ches lay on his stomach, grinning down at us. "Anyone need a stretcher?"

Johnny Rendell, one of the guards who'd let us slip out of Edinburgh Castle after curfew, appeared next to Ches. He spoke, but the blast of artillery guns smothered his words. Rocks and dirt tumbled down into the crater.

"Ron needs assistance getting out," Jack said. "A sudden, awkward move and he'll bleed out or his lung will collapse."

Ches and Johnny Rendell helped me to my feet. I coughed, an uncontrollable hacking that tore at me from the inside out. The bandage reddened even more.

"Get him back as quick as you can," Jack said, and turned to the British soldier. "I'll watch out for this fellow."

"What's the matter with him?" Johnny asked.

"I believe he saw his twin brother blown to bits. Only the head was untouched."

"Christ," Ches said, swallowing hard. His Adam's apple bobbed up and down.

The boy refused to move and shoved Jack away.

"Eric's waiting for you," Jack said softly. "We need to hurry."

He looked up at Jack, a semblance of clarity in his eyes. "Eric won't let me go anywhere without him. He joined up because I did."

Ches's Adam's apple bobbed faster.

"What's your name?" Jack said.

"Evan." The cloud of confusion lifted for a brief moment.

"All right, Evan. We have to stay low so the Germans can't see us." They crawled up the side and slipped over the top.

"Ron," Johnny said, as he and Ches helped me climb out of the crater. "Your uncle Jack came looking for you yesterday. He'd brought in at least a dozen wounded and kept going out to find you."

They laid me on the stretcher. I was relieved they weren't wearing their haversacks with the shiny tin badges. Artillery fire rocked the ground in short bursts.

"There's Harold," I called over the rattle of machine-gun fire. He ran a few yards ahead with a soldier draped around his back. A little farther on, Captain Will Burke carried a man slung over his shoulder.

"Every one of our captains who went over the top yesterday is dead, wounded, or missing," Johnny said. "Captain Wakefield was the finest man I ever knew."

"Me and Gord did our best to save him," I said.

A blast to the left of us rattled the ground. John, in the lead, was thrown off his feet. I grabbed the sides of the stretcher and hung on. John picked himself up, grabbed his end of stretcher, and sprinted over a dead body, with Ches keeping pace.

The outer belts of our barbed wire came into view, and without a second's hesitation John and Ches bore me through the zigzag paths to the trench. Inside a dugout, Jack sat with Evan, talking to him in quiet tones.

The number of stretchers laid on the ground was staggering. The moans and groans from the men placed on them distressed me more than the heaviest artillery. Bandages covered eyes, ears, noses, stumps of legs, arms, and empty shoulder sockets. Another sound rose above the rest—the sound of saws cutting through bone. I had descended into hell.

A doctor approached stretcher, and knelt down, his once-white apron stained red and yellow. "Let's take a look, young fellow," he said. A British upper-class, polished accent. He was tall, straight-backed, with a warm smile that naturally put an anxious patient at ease. Did he save that smile for those about to die?

He unwound my bandage and threw it aside. "Hmm," he said. "Whoever patched you up did excellent work." He took a medical instrument that looked like a pair of pliers out of his pocket and gently probed the wound. It's astonishing the amount of pain one learns to endure. "The bullet's still in there," he said.

An assistant rushed over. "Dr. Melville, that man over there needs help now," he said, motioning with his head. A soldier lay on a stretcher, blood gushing from his groin. Dr. Melville darted to him and applied pressure to the wound. I shut my eyes, refusing to watch the life drain from the soldier's face. I drifted into unconsciousness, weightless, the scene before me dimming to black. I didn't fight against it. Hell was an ugly place I had to escape from.

"Ron, wake up. I've brought you something to eat."

I opened my eyes, still surprised to be on the ground outside the dressing station. The dark sky shone with stars. "What time is it?"

Harold towered over me. "Nine o'clock." He laid a plate of food aside and put a haversack under my head. "You've been asleep for hours. Good thing, too. The doctor removed the bullet that nicked your lung as well as shrapnel from your shoulder."

Next to me was a large patch of blood that darkened the ground where the man with the damaged groin had lain. Harold followed my gaze. "He's still alive. Your uncle Jack said Dr. Melville is an excellent surgeon. The most critical cases were taken to the field hospital. You may have to wait here a few days."

The heavy circles under Harold's eyes accentuated his tiredness. "You should be up and around in a month or so."

"How many of the regiment made it?"

Harold handed me the plate of food. "Sixty-eight answered the roll call this morning. We've brought in over two hundred injured. Seven died later from their wounds." He sat on the ground and hugged his knees. "Rescues are safer at night. I've been ordered to rest for a few hours."

Harold rested his face in his hands. "The ten per cent hold-back left Mailly-Maillet Wood at six-thirty. We wanted to get to St. John's Road to see you all before you went over the top, but were delayed until after nine without being given a reason. We found the communications trenches clogged with wounded soldiers, most of them on stretchers. It took us hours to get through. Anyone with half a brain knew we were on the losing side of this 'big push.' Hadow ordered us back to our units, a tell-tale confirmation that we were right. Artillery shelling was so heavy, a quarter of us were killed."

I was about to comment when Jack arrived. "How's Evan?" I asked.

"You'll never believe this, but his father is Lord Emery Standing. General Standing, I should say. He's ordered Evan on the next ship to England to recuperate."

"Do you think he will go?"

"He was more coherent and talkative when he left. General Standing is convinced a few weeks' rest will do the trick." Jack rubbed the bridge of his nose. "He'll need more than rest to mend his mind."

CHAPTER 13

DRESSING STATION

I dozed and woke with a start, anticipating the next bullet or shell to hit me. "Ches? Harold? Where are you?" I stared around, groggy. Flickers of light shone down from the night sky. My breathing slowed as realization dawned that I wasn't in no man's land. However, the cries and screams of pain and distress were still all around me. A warm breeze blew across my face and I relaxed somewhat, taking in my surroundings.

The dressing station was comprised of a large tent structure supported by wooden poles. I could see the cots that lined the inside, and lanterns containing candles hung from the wooden frames. Medical supplies lay on a long table. Once a doctor treated a soldier's injuries and stabilized him, the soldier was taken outside on a stretcher and placed on the ground among the others with me, waiting for evacuation to a field hospital for further treatment or recovery.

I faced the tent opening and observed the medical staff inside rushing from cot to cot, the constant flow of stretchers carrying wounded men, some injuries more severe than the last. A nurse tended to a young soldier, holding his hand as he shiv-

ered while the blood drained from a severed leg. She smoothed
hair from his forehead and leaned in close, whispering what
must have been words of comfort to the dying youth. She stood
back and closed his eyes, and as she turned away I saw tears
flowing down her cheeks. She hastily brushed them away with a
bloodied hand.

A soldier carried a young red-haired man on his back into
the tent and laid him on a cot. The young man's right foot was
bare, the toes and upper portion blackened. He tossed and
turned, crying out, delirious. "Infection has set in," Dr. Melville
said. "The foot may eventually need to be amputated to save his
life."

I tried to go back to sleep through the agonizing screams,
visions of shattered bodies, and the smell of decayed flesh, rem-
nants of what and who these soldiers once were. The medical
staff worked for hours, doing their best to stave off death. Row
upon row of stretchers covered every inch of available land. For
those of us outside the tent there was no rain to complicate our
conditions or make them worse.

A young nurse with tired eyes wheeled a small trolley covered with a bloody sheet out of the tented area. Three fingers
stuck out over the edge. "Are . . . are they the amputated parts?"
I asked.

The nurse slowed and looked my way. "Afraid so."

"Where are you taking them?"

For a moment I thought she hadn't heard me. "We burn
them in the incinerator."

I imagined her tossing human parts to be burned like wood
or coal.

"I'm sorry," she said, and wheeled the trolley past me.

Voices carried from the tented area. "I hate to say this,"
Melville, the doctor who had treated me, said to a British
captain, "but we're going to have to finish burying the dead

right away." He dragged his bloodied hands down the front of his soiled apron. "We can't risk disease from decomposing bodies."

The captain, an older man with a ruddy complexion, tapped his foot on the ground. "We've buried as many men as possible in the craters. We'll have to dig graves."

Melville didn't have time to agree or disagree, for another load of wounded arrived. The captain left to order a detail to carry out the gruesome task of organizing a burial detail. About forty men with picks and shovels walked between the rows of stretchers and proceeded to an area about ten yards from the dressing station. A quiet settled over them as they swung at the ground with a soft, plunking sound, breaking apart the chalky earth and shovelling it aside. I didn't need to see their faces to understand the emotions twisting like a rope coiling inside their chests.

I watched the grave diggers sink lower and lower. The damp, musty smell was like sweet perfume compared to the stench of newly rotting corpses. The clay piled up on the sides, and I thought about what the world had evolved into, what my new norm had become. Men killed en masse. Men buried en masse with no loved ones to witness their final departure or visualize the final resting place.

The soldiers continued to work in silence, in eerie reverence for the daunting task that others might have to perform for them. I saw picks and shovels fly out of a hole, the first mass grave completed. The men climbed out and walked toward the dressing station, tying handkerchiefs around their noses and mouths. Melville directed them to an area on my right. Every conscious man on the stretchers followed them with their eyes as they transported the dead, stopping only long enough to remove their identification tags, the one piece of evidence these soldiers had perished in the line of duty.

Harold walked briskly toward me, slowing when he noticed what was in progress. "I never want to be part of a burial detail," he said, his eyes glued to the procession of bodies.

A shiver ran through me. "Buried in a mass grave scares me more than dying. Thank God Frank's not here to see this." He'd been evacuated from the field hospital earlier today. "I can't believe this is where Henry . . ."

Harold sat down beside my stretcher, his arms loose at his sides. "It's tough. At least poor Lucy was honoured with a proper funeral." It was the first time he'd mentioned his sister's name since the day he'd returned from compassionate leave. "My family can visit her any time."

"Has there been word about Gord?"

"No. There's thousands more unaccounted for. I want to get back out there and help the stretcher-bearers. It'll be days before we bring everyone in." He stood up. "We've been ordered to retrieve all the weapons we can."

"Is Ches all right?"

"He's been bringing in wounded, but he'll keep looking for Gord while he's able." Harold turned to leave, but hesitated. "You're never the same when someone you love is killed. Especially when you have to leave them behind."

The burials continued throughout the night, with people of all religious denominations laid together, with chaplains presiding over brief services. I closed my eyes in disbelief. I was still alive. Hundreds of thousands of soldiers had left the trench on July 1. Too many had died. Was it simple luck or a more deliberate act of fate that I had survived?

The burial detail took away more bodies and register more names, ages, units, and places of burial. I turned my back, not wanting to witness any more soldiers from England, Scotland, Wales, Ireland, and Newfoundland going to the overcrowded graveyard.

"Sorry about this," a strong Scottish brogue said.

Two soldiers carried Henry's body on a stretcher. The hole in his chest was black, his face an awful shade of grey-blue.

The soldier spoke again. "I was told this boy was a relative of yours."

This was my life now, witnessing deaths of the young on a grand scale, their burials on a grand scale. Henry was one of those. And Joey. If I lived long enough, I'd see more. "Thank you. He was my cousin. Could I have his Cross and chain?"

They laid Henry down beside me as gently as possible. His head rolled in my direction. One of them opened the top button of Henry's shirt and removed the chain. "Here you go, young lad. His mother will appreciate having that."

"She would," I said quietly, closing my fingers around the Cross and chain.

"It's bloody hard," the man occupying the stretcher across from me said. "Yesterday morning I lost over ten blokes I grew up with." He glanced down at his blanket, where there was the imprint of only one leg. His gazed slowly strayed back to me. "I used to be a professional footballer." He sucked in his breath. "Guess I'm the lucky one. It's bloody odd how I still feel my toes." He gave a harsh laugh. "I can even wiggle them."

Joey would've been able to explain that phenomenon.

He grabbed the edge of his blanket and crumpled it between his fingers. His knuckles were white. "All my football mates from my home town were in the same unit. What a stupid idea, to put us all in the same company to be slaughtered together."

"I suppose that's how things are done."

The British soldier loosened his grip on the blanket. "The war's over for me." He pointed to my chest. "You'll be fit in no time and back at it."

"I guess so. The war's lasted longer than anyone expected."

The soldier closed his eyes. "I'm bone tired. Wish I could sleep."

The tap, tap of a hammer drew my attention to the graves, where rows of wooden Crosses were being hammered into the ground. Chaplain Murray stood to the side, holding a prayer book, as soldiers shovelled clay onto the most recently buried. I had to get over there. I rose up on my elbows, and my chest throbbed with pain as I attempted to stand.

Chaplain Murray rushed over. "Take it easy, Ron. You'll start bleeding again."

"I want to be able to tell my aunt I was at Henry's burial."

"Fine, fine." The chaplain got me to my feet and, with an arm around my waist, guided me to the gravesite.

We stood side by side, my hand on his shoulder for support. "Joey was brought in while you were sleeping," he said. "Ches and Harold already paid their last respects." Chaplain Murray indicated a bugle in the earth two rows over. "He's with fellow Newfoundlanders."

The full moon and stars were at their brightest. A lovely night for a walk. The plat, plat of clay filling the grave went on and on. I leaned into the chaplain to stay on my feet. "Joey was an only child," I said, as if that made any difference to his passing.

"He told me." One corner of the chaplain's mouth tilted up ever so slightly. "He nearly drove me crazy demanding I remove my boots to check for trench foot."

The last heap of clay landed and the soldier patted down the earth with the back of his shovel. "This is the worst part of the war." He sighed, wiped sweat from his forehead with the sleeve of his shirt, and went on to start another grave.

Chaplain Murray opened his prayer book and recited words that I couldn't focus on, no matter how hard I tried to concentrate. My mind sped back to my school days, to one particular incident involving Joey and Henry. A week before final exams for grade ten, Henry, as was his practice, and without confiding in anyone, had decided to play a trick on Mr. Snooker, our science and math teacher. Mr. Snooker was the sort of man who wore wire spectacles, a suit, and bow tie, and he called each student by Mr. So and So, never by our first names. Every lunchtime he'd walk the same route around the grounds of St. Bonaventure, his nose in a Sherlock Holmes book.

A wide, luscious lawn spanned the front of the three-storey concrete building inside a wrought-iron fence. One morning before any students or teachers had arrived at the school, Henry dug a hole a foot wide and a foot deep in the lawn midway along Mr. Snooker's route and filled it with loose grass. Mr. Snooker stepped into it and fell over, as Henry had planned. The teacher hobbled back into the school on his badly broken foot. Henry had played one too many silly pranks on his teacher and had been warned that one more incident of any kind would result in expulsion. Joey confessed in order to save Henry, but Henry willingly accepted the blame, despite Joey's insistence he was the guilty party. Heartfelt concern for Mr. Snooker's condition put an abrupt end to Henry's career of stupid pranks. To everyone's surprise, Mr. Snooker spoke on Henry's behalf, resulting in a mere two-week suspension.

"May they rest in peace."

The words brought me back to the present.

"Chaplain, how can those men rest in peace?" Machine guns rattled in the distance. "A shell might well blow those graves and bodies to bits."

Murray closed the prayer book before looking me straight in the eyes. "I agree that this gesture of human decency may be a ..." He paused as if searching for the right term. "... a senseless endeavour. I believe every man buried here would appreciate and thank us for the dignity we afforded them, even if it's all literally blown apart later."

I hung my head. "I didn't mean to . . ."

"No harm done, Ron. There are occasions when we must question our faith. Events like this test my own beliefs that we're doing the right thing by engaging in this war."

Chaplain Murray walked me back. Sweat drenched my shirt. "You've been on your feet too long." He settled me down on my stretcher. "Rest. That's an order, son." He looked toward the gravesite. "I've too many more men to preside over."

The bandage on my chest leaked fresh blood. I lightly touched the spot. There was no point in calling anyone to check the wound. The medical team had enough to deal with.

Soldiers trudged in with wounded on their backs, on stretchers, while others limped in on their own. "We have to make room for more," the doctor bellowed. He'd been on his feet since I was brought in, and I marvelled at his will to keep going, to treat ugly, gaping wounds that would've sent any man scurrying away, sick to his stomach.

Two men brought a young soldier into the tent and placed him on a cot. The soldier's left ear and eye were missing, and blood gushed from the stump where his arm had been blown off. The doctor worked to staunch the flow of blood while a nurse wrapped the side of his head. Even in his unconscious state, the young soldier whimpered.

One of the two soldiers who'd brought him stood to the side. He wrung his hands and from time to time wiped a tear from his face. "Doctor, will Patrick make it?" he asked, in a strong Irish accent.

The doctor continued working on the young soldier. "If we get him to the hospital in time, he has a chance." He gave an apologetic smile. "You know him?"

"He's my younger brother."

I looked away as the soldier went to his brother. He deserved the dignity of saying goodbye in private. I stared up at the stars and tried to envision myself back home in my room, gazing through my curtained window. I yawned. The twinkling stars hypnotized me and my eyelids fluttered and closed.

I stood by the Danger Tree in no man's land, in broad daylight, enshrouded by a white mist. The land was a mess of craters and churned-up earth, blackened by pools of dried, clotted blood. Rain poured down, but the white mist protected me like an oversized umbrella. The surface of the ground suddenly started undulating, accompanied by a squeaking noise which grew louder. I leaned forward to get a better look and staggered back. Hundreds of rats scurried up the hill, running around and around in the white mist. A large grey rodent stopped and stared up at me. A human nose stuck out from its mouth.

My chest tightened and squeezed away my breath. I kicked at the mist, trying to break through. The more I kicked, the thicker it became. Something sharp and wet grabbed onto both my arms. "Oh God!" I screamed. "They're going to eat me alive!"

"Ron, wake up." Harold's voice, anxious, hollow, a long way off.

The rats gnawed through the mist, their whiskers twitching, their black eyes on me. One broke through and pounced, its sharp teeth sinking into my neck. I screamed. Another and another, scampering over each other to get at me.

"Ron, lad. You're having a nightmare." Ches's voice, gentle.

I wheezed. My temples throbbed.

"Ron!" Ches yelled. "Snap out of it."

The mist evaporated. My eyes opened and my heart banged in my chest. I'd kicked off my blanket; Harold draped it back over me.

"That was some nightmare, Ron."

"Where's Jack?" I longed to see him. "Is he all right?"

"He's gone back to his unit to help with the wounded," Ches said. "The doctors and nurses are overwhelmed."

A horse neighed close by. Dr. Melville stood next to it with two men and pointed in my direction.

"About bloody time you get proper treatment at a hospital," Ches said. "I was beginning to think the horses and mules had priority over us."

I would've laughed but my chest hurt too much.

A horse and cart were used to carry coffins to the graveyard in St. John's. That thought plagued me as the stretcher-bearers hoisted me onto the cart.

CHAPTER 14

The days passed quickly volunteering with the Women's Patriotic Association, every hour occupied with working to keep the soldiers warm and as comfortable as possible under the circumstances. Last May the women shipped overseas forty cases stocked with shirts, socks, scarves, and mittens with a trigger finger to enable the soldiers to use their rifles. The nights were hard to bear, stretching to eternity since Anne's brother Jack, and son Ron, went to fight in the war. Tonight was no exception. Tom slept after he worked all day unloading the cargo ships, which were fewer and fewer since last year. He dropped off to sleep an hour ago.

It was the middle of July and the second birthday Ron had been away. The news about the war hadn't been encouraging, as there was little progress on either side. Tom called it a stalemate. If it continued, the war would only end when there weren't any men left to fight.

A strong breeze blew through the open window, but gave Anne no relief from the hot, humid weather. The lace curtains fluttered like clothes on a line hung out to dry. The sun was rising over the South Side Hills, turning the sky over the Narrows an expanse of crimson red. She lingered in bed a while longer, thinking about her day ahead, and got up at seven to start breakfast. The pancakes were sizzling in the bacon fat when Tom and Joanie came down the stairs. Tom's restless night showed in the fine lines around his eyes. Joanie darted into the kitchen, while Tom went to the front door for the morning paper. Anne buttered crisp toast, almost burnt, the way her family preferred it. Once tea was poured for each of them, she sat down.

"The paper's late?" Anne called when Tom hadn't come in to breakfast.

He didn't answer, and she called to him once more. When he still didn't respond, she stood up to go see what was delaying him. As she did, Tom came into the kitchen, the paper loose between his fingers, his face white. Joanie cut up her pancakes and didn't notice. Anne fell back into her chair as Tom pulled out his glasses without uttering a single word and laid the paper on the table.

Joanie looked up. "Dad, you look funny. What's the matter?"

"Joanie, love, there's news from France."

"News from France," Anne repeated. "What do you mean?"

Joanie cranked her head to one side to get a better look at the paper. "Beaumont Hamel," she read out loud. "Where's that?"

"In France along the Somme River," Tom said. "The Newfoundland Regiment fought a battle there two weeks ago."

Anne's breath stopped. "What happened?"

Tom lowered his eyes to the paper. Anne wasn't sure he'd heard or even understood the question.

Joanie's fork dropped to the plate with a loud clang. "Dad, why didn't you answer Mom?" She tugged on his arm. "Dad, you're scaring me."

· Tom squeezed her hand. "The Newfoundland Regiment was part of a major offensive against the German front lines outside the town of Beaumont Hamel. Over eight hundred of our men went into battle." He paused, and the hand resting on the paper shook. "Sixty-eight answered roll call the next morning."

"Jesus Christ," Anne whispered, then blessed herself. She felt sick to her stomach. "Are the names of the dead listed?"

"I couldn't bring myself to read them."

Joanie erupted into tears. "Is Ronnie dead?" She tried to grab the paper. "What about Frank and Henry?"

Tom turned the paper toward his wife. Rows of names filled the page, and she scanned down the columns. "Oh my God, Joey Baker was killed."

Joanie's tears tumbled onto the table. "He enlisted the first night with Ronnie."

"Harold's name isn't here." Anne ran her finger down the list. "Neither are Frank or Henry's." She skipped to the names beginning with M. "Ron's not mentioned," she said, on the verge of throwing up.

Joanie jumped up from her chair and stood next to her mother, and stared at the paper. "That's not anywhere near eight hundred names. Ronnie might be dead and they haven't found his body yet." She started bawling, and her shoulders shook with the loud sobs.

Tom smoothed down the side of her hair. "Joanie." Her eyes were red, her cheeks splotchy. "It's a good sign Ron's name isn't on the list. Promise me you'll hold on to that for now."

She hiccuped. "I'll try, Dad."

"Ron would want us to be strong and believe he's alive."

Anne couldn't move. It was as if she were chained to the chair.

Tom reached for her hand. "Anne, you need to hold onto that thought, too."

The family ate in silence, trying to absorb the reality of the enormous death toll. They were thankful their loved ones weren't listed among them. Tomorrow could be different.

"I don't want to go to Bowring Park today," Joanie said. "Harold's sister won't mind."

"Sweetie," Tom said, "you promised those girls to take them to the park. Don't break your word." She left with the bologna sandwiches Anne had packed for each of the three girls for the hour-long walk to the park.

Tom read through all the names and left the paper open on the table. "I'd better get to work."

His wife followed him to the front door. "Jack's with the British army. Would his name—"

Tom cut her off. "No." He hesitated, his hand on the door-knob. The first cargo ship in three months was due this morning. He pulled his salt and pepper cap from his pants pocket and slowly put it on his head. The peak hung down over his right eye. "I recognized three of the names in the paper."

"Sons of men you work with?" Anne kissed his cheek. "I don't mind if you stay home. It'll be awful to see the fathers—"

He placed a finger gently on her lips. "We have to be strong for each other."

Alone, Anne lay down on the sofa and thought about Ron, her nephews Frank and Henry Corcoran, and Harold Bartlett. Harold's mother had suffered the death of one child. Could she bear the death of another? More than 700 young men dead or wounded. She cried for those lives that would never go on, for the loved ones who'd never hold them again.

The horse-shaped clock on the mantel ticked through her tears. She stood up and dried her eyes with the tail of her apron. "Enough of this foolishness," Anne said to her reflection in the mirror. "There's work to be done."

She tore the newspaper to shreds and stuffed the bits into the stove to burn. If only the flames could burn away the fact that the men were dead. On her way to the pantry to check for potatoes, she remembered she'd run out the day before. An involuntary sigh escaped. Anne whipped off her apron, took her purse from the hook on the back of the kitchen door, and made her way to Williams Grocer.

The street was empty, which was unusual for eleven o'clock. No children skipped rope or played hopscotch, no cars chugged up and down the street. Anne jumped when a tin can rattled on the sidewalk in front of her.

She reached the grocery store and stepped back, her body trembling all over. The interior was dulled and the door was locked. A sign hung in the window. The big black words screamed at her.

CLOSED DUE TO DEATH IN THE FAMILY

Mr. Williams's four sons were fighting in the war. Boys she had known since birth. Had more than one died? Anne's legs buckled and she leaned against the store. For the first time since Mrs. Williams's death from a heart attack five years earlier, Anne was glad she wasn't alive. She went home, prepared a bologna sandwich for Tom, and left him a note to let him know where she had gone.

She hurried through the streets to Government House for the afternoon meeting of the Women's Patriotic Association. Everywhere she looked, someone held a newspaper, people gathered in groups, shock and disbelief carved on their faces. Despite the sun's brilliant glow, the city was locked inside a dark cloud. Children sat on doorsteps, resting quietly while others sobbed in their mothers' arms. The bereaved comforting the bereaved. Anne passed the butcher shop and stopped cold. Another sign glared at her.

CLOSED DUE TO DEATH IN THE FAMILY

Mr. Wheeler had one son.

Anne reached Government House and dashed up the steps like someone was chasing her. Inside, several men clustered in a corner looking at a newspaper. She could have brought in a rifle and neither one would have noticed. There were no friendly smiles or polite hellos. One of the clustered men slumped against the wall and slid down to the floor. A security guard said, "I'm terribly sorry, Lewis," and helped him to his feet.

It wasn't right for a small nation to lose 700 young men, dead or wounded, cut down in one day. Anne ran down the corridor to the drawing room.

Mrs. Burke sat at the head table and wiped her eyes with a linen handkerchief. She made no sound. A sweep of the room showed that at least one third of the members were absent. Anne walked toward Mrs. Burke, passing by tables where women sat in solemn quietude, stiff like stone statues, their gazes empty, their faces grey.

As she pulled out the chair next to Mrs. Burke, the older lady smiled at her, a solemn, lonely smile. She thanked Anne for coming and stood up to address the volunteers. "Ladies." Her voice was thick. "Newfoundland has been dealt a tragic blow." Tears flowed down her cheeks and gathered on her chin, which she dabbed with her soaked handkerchief.

The truth of Mrs. Burke's situation hit Anne harder than a kick in the stomach, and her hand flew to her mouth.

"Ted was killed on the first of July." Mrs. Burke squeezed her eyes shut to gather strength. "Many ladies of the WPA have suffered losses as well." She glanced from table to table. "We must find the courage to continue our good work for the remaining men who witnessed the slaughter of their comrades."

Anne passed her a dry handkerchief, which Mrs. Burke accepted with a gracious nod.

She picked up an envelope from the table. "Mr. Burke and

I received this letter in the mail this morning from a British officer who was very complimentary." She pulled out a sheet of cream-coloured paper, and read aloud.

"Dear Mr. and Mrs. Burke. I wish to convey my deepest sympathies on the untimely death of your son, Ted. The Newfoundland Regiment fought a valiant battle, and as a British subject I am proud of your son and proud of your nation's loyalty to King George V. My men and I have had the privilege of fighting alongside the First Newfoundland Regiment on many occasions. They have proven themselves disciplined soldiers and honourable men.

"My wife and I have also lost a son to this war and understand your pain and grief. It is my wish that you find a measure of peace in the fact your son died in defence of a country he cherished as much as his own. May God be with you always. Lieutenant-Colonel Arnold Winkerton, Essex Battalion."

More letters of condolence arrived from British officers. Mr. Williams received one and allowed Anne to read it. The letter was as heartfelt as one Arnold Winkerton had written.

"Mrs. Marrie," said Mr. Williams, "my son Alfred would be pleased to know I got this letter and I know he'd not want me to regret his decision to go overseas."

At twenty-four, Alfred was his oldest son, and had married one month before enlisting. Anne doubted whether Alfred's widow, at twenty, would agree with that assessment.

Every day a new list of the dead appeared in the paper. A week later, Mr. Williams read that another son, Michael, had also died. Anne came across him sitting on a bench in Bowring park. "Alfred and Mike loved walking here."

She sat beside him. "I can't imagine how you feel."

Never a heavy man, he'd lost weight and his sunken cheeks made him look much older than his fifty years. "It's like waking up to realize you've stepped into a living night-mare with no end."

Dark clouds had settled over the entire island, which not even a ray of sunshine could penetrate.

On the twenty-first of July, Tom came home from work with the *Evening Telegram*, which he rarely read, even though it was considered the "people's paper."

"General Douglas Haig, the Commander-In-Chief of the British Forces, has praised the Newfoundland Regiment." He stood in the middle of the kitchen and read.

"Newfoundland may well feel proud of her sons. The hero-ism and devotion to duty they displayed on the first of July has never been surpassed. Please convey my deepest sympathy, and that of the whole of our armies in France, on the loss of the brave officers and men who have fallen for the Empire and our admiration of their heroic conduct. Their efforts contributed to our success, and their example will live."

Tom opened the grate of the stove and shoved the *Evening Telegram* down into the hole. "Their example will live," he said. "The men didn't."

CHAPTER 15

The journey by horse and cart lasted for hours, travelling over bumps that shook me until I was nauseous. Across endless miles we bounced over land which had been blasted in recent fighting. Holes concealed by water nearly cracked the front wheels more times than I cared to remember. The cart rocked, struggling through knee-deep mud, tilting and almost tipping over several times; the horses' nostrils flared with the effort, as they struggled to keep their footing and move beyond the obstacles. Even at night, the early July heat drained all my energy. Flies hovered, hungry for the taste of my blood. Late into the night, sleep still evaded me. The last hidden hole jerked me so violently the wound in my chest came open. I bit my lip to keep from howling with pain. I must have lost consciousness, for when I awoke we'd reached the semblance of a road, where I was loaded onto a motorized ambulance. The trip had exhausted me more than the twenty-mile marches I'd taken so many times since coming overseas.

An ambulance transported me to the casualty clearing station at the railhead, arriving at dawn on the fifth of July. Every cot was occupied with the wounded, all destined for a hospital. A young doctor with a face full of freckles, not much older than Jack, checked my injury. "A clean bandage will set you right until you get proper care," he said.

I nodded, saving my breath.

The doctor smiled. "Hang on a little longer, soldier."

Near noon, dozens of us were loaded onto the train and set out for the hospital at Rouen. I caught a few snatches of sleep during the many hours along the way, and woke again as I was transported by ambulance to the hospital. Sweat rolled into my eyes and I felt like I'd been placed in the middle of a burning room. My wound had become infected, and I was immediately rushed into surgery. I didn't come to for twenty-four hours. The doctors were amazed I had survived the injury, not to mention the long, three-day wait for further treatment, which could have resulted in a collapsed lung. My shoulder displayed signs of early gangrene, which they cleaned out.

Two days later, another ambulance drove me to a second hospital train, bound for Havre. From there I was put aboard a hospital ship for Southampton. My seasickness returned with a vengeance the first hour out. I was convinced I threw up most of my insides. Endless hours passed not being able to keep down water, and at times I felt that life in the trenches was preferable.

"It won't be much longer," a tall British captain in his mid-forties said. He wore a patch over his left eye. "The pretty nurses will have you on your feet in no time." He sat down beside me and lit up a cigar. My gaze lingered on the patch. "I was a surgeon." He tossed the cigar overboard, then straightened his shoulders. "Not to worry. I'll consult and set up a general practice." I wondered who he was trying to convince.

From Southampton, I journeyed to the Second London

General Hospital, situated at St. Mark's College, Chelsea, another two hours by train. The main hospitals were full to overflowing. Thankfully, I fell into a deep sleep. Upon arrival, my torn stitches were repaired and I was given morphine for the pain.

For the rest of the week I drifted in and out of sleep. Midway through the second week I was able to sit up, thrilled to not need a nurse to feed me. By the third week I had graduated to walking up and down the ward with the help of an orderly. Three pieces of shrapnel had torn the muscles in my shoulder, which hindered my recovery more than the lung injury.

My cousin, Frank, had been sent to the First London General Hospital. One of the nurses who made inquiries for me reported that the doctors were pleased with his progress. He was slated to leave for home in a few days.

The wards, containing 260 beds, were different sizes and spread out on the first and second floors. The third floor housed the nurses' sleeping quarters, sitting room, and dining room. The kitchens were relegated to the basements. One sunny morning I decided to take a walk outside on the large lawns. The wall on the west side of the grounds had been partially demolished to give better access to Chelsea's railway platform. This provided the shortest route for patients arriving on the hospital train.

In early August I developed a cough along with a fever and came down with pneumonia. My regiment was never far from my thoughts, and bedridden once more, the ever-nagging fear I might never see any of them again intensified. Either they would die in battle or the pneumonia would take me.

I learned that a ceremony had taken place to present medals to the widows of the British soldiers who died on July 1. Nurse Abigail, short and plump, with a permanent smile told me about it. "It was a magnificent sight," she said, as she placed a wet cloth on my forehead. "A band played while the generals presented the medals. The women were so proud of their husbands."

Every inch of my head ached. "Twenty thousand medals is a lot," I mumbled. "What about the forty thousand wounded?"

The nurse's expression convinced me she thought I was delirious. "The number of dead and wounded wasn't listed in the newspapers," she said. "I'm sure it wasn't anywhere near that many."

Too tired to speak anymore, I didn't object. Of course, announcing a death toll of that magnitude during one single day of fighting would demoralize the nation.

I came to know the two patients on either side of me quite well. Pete Hall was a Canadian soldier and carpenter from Alberta. Cliff Kavanagh was a butcher from York, in northern England, who boasted his home was one of the best-preserved medieval cities in the whole of Europe, retaining its tiny winding cobble lanes and the massive Gothic cathedral of York Minster. He'd been shot in both thighs and deafened by constant shelling, but he was gradually regaining his hearing. The ringing in his ears persisted for another few days. Half his unit had been killed in the first wave on July 1. "I joined because of the Pals battalions," he shouted, unaware he was doing so, "which promised all the men from our town would serve out the war together. It was comforting to know your blokes would fight alongside you."

Pete settled back against his pillows. "Has to be devastating for the town when over half were killed." He raised his right arm, then switched to the other and scratched his chin. His right hand had been blown off when a bomb landed in his trench. "The goddamned Germans are nothing but savages."

Cliff was reflective. "I used to think that, too."

Pete glared at him. "Used to? What the hell does that mean?"

"My battalion covered the Mash Valley–Sausage Valley sector of the Somme front. For two days the Germans allowed our stretcher-bearers to collect the wounded all the way to their third trench—where they found me—without firing a single shot."

One sunny morning the stomp, stomp of marching boots sounded outside the window. An orderly led a line of seven Canadian soldiers, each with a hand on the shoulder of the man in front. It was obvious they were blind. The orderly crossed over the lawn to the sidewalk.

"They're from my unit," Pete said. "Mustard gas got them. They're scheduled to return to Canada tomorrow." He glanced down at his missing hand. "Guess I'm the lucky one."

I was transfixed by the blind soldiers marching with vigour, with pride in their steps. "Is anyone lucky in this war?"

"You fellas certainly weren't," Pete said. "I heard the Newfoundland Battalion was all but wiped out."

"Sixty-eight out of more than eight hundred answered roll call the next day."

Cliff's face took on a stone-cold appearance. "Another horrible example of Pals battalions gone wrong."

Pete turned onto his side. "Cliff, I've noticed you British soldiers all but get down on bended knees in front of your generals, who I might add, expect that from you." He glanced to me. "You fellas do the same?"

"Not everyone," I said quietly, thinking about Ches.

"Good to hear," Pete said. "The British are in charge of battle strategy and pass orders down to Canadian generals. We respect the rank, yet see our generals as ordinary men like us, not some knight, earl, or fancy lord. They treat us with the same respect and are visible in the trenches. They are actually concerned for us." He looked past me to Cliff. "Can the same be said of General Haig?"

I knew what Ches would have said to that.

Cliff and Pete were discharged two weeks later. Cliff returned to his regiment, and Pete shipped home to Canada. The men had barely left the hospital when their beds were taken by two Australian soldiers, one with a serious head wound, and in a coma, the other suffering from severe mustard gas inhalation. One side of his chest and neck was covered in red, oozing sores inflicted by the gas.

Nurse Abigail confided to me that the man with the head injury, was expected to die without gaining consciousness. That night I opened my eyes to see him staring at me. "Where am I, mate?" he asked in a hoarse voice.

The nurse scurried to him, the biggest smile on her face I'd ever seen. "It's so uplifting when a patient beats the odds."

She looked at the gassed soldier, whose health had gone downhill and who was now semi-conscious. His chest slowly rose and lowered again, his breathing loud, wheezing as his damaged lungs failed to take in enough oxygen. I watched him through the night; each breath he took seemed more difficult than the last. The moon shone on his face, and I could see his lips were pale blue. I threw off my covers and sat on the chair beside his bed.

He opened his eyes. "Ron," he gasped. "No one . . . deserves . . . to die . . . alone."

I reached for his hand. "You're not alone, Bill."

He smiled and closed his eyes. For twenty minutes I talked to him about Newfoundland, describing snowy winters and skating on frozen ponds. "It's thrilling to glide over the smooth ice, the wind in your . . ." His grip slackened and his chest stopped moving.

Nurse Abigail tiptoed to my side. "Thank you, Ron. I'll write his parents and tell them about your kindness to their son."

In mid-August I received a letter from Joanie. I'd made a full recovery from pneumonia and was able to raise my arm waist-high without blacking out from pain. The familiar handwriting lifted my spirits. I was excited to hear news from home.

It was dated July 29.

> Dear Ronnie,
>
> The Prime Minister learned about the awful Beaumont Hamel tragedy a few weeks ago from a General de Lisle. The whole country is trying to take it all in, to accept those men are never coming home. This is what he said about the Newfoundland Regiment. "It was a magnificent display of trained and disciplined valour, and its assault only failed of success because dead men can advance no farther."
>
> Ronnie, it startled me that he described men going into battle to their deaths as a magnificent display. Is this how all British generals think? Courageous would have been a more accurate and appropriate word.
>
> The sealing disaster with seventy-eight deaths was shocking, tragic enough. The massive losses at Beaumont Hamel have plunged the entire island into deep mourning. Every day more names of the dead are posted in the newspapers. Clergymen spend all their time visiting the grieving families. Mom says a prayer before checking the list. I can't breathe until I know your name isn't there.
>
> Henry's name hasn't been listed, but we know he died. Aunt Elsie got back a letter she wrote to him with DEAD written in big red letters on the front. She screamed and screamed. Dad calmed her down and sat with her for hours. Ronnie, it was cruel for her to find

out that way. I'll never see him again or hear him tease Aunt Elsie about her floppy hats, but my heart hurt so bad I can't cry. Isn't that funny?

Mr. Meeker's barbershop is closed today. His two sons' names were listed in the *Daily News* yesterday. I went with Dad to pay our respects. Mom couldn't bring herself to go. Ronnie, I'd never seen a grown man cry before. Despite what happened, men continue to enlist. Dad's still involved, though he's not nearly as enthusiastic as before.

Aunt Elsie and Mom have become great friends with Harold's mother. I think Mrs. Bartlett will help Aunt Elsie cope with her grief. Poor Frank.

Ronnie, I love you always. Please come home safe.

Joanie

Joanie had hidden her greatest fear until the very end. She was scared that she'd written to a dead man. I wrote back immediately to assure her and my parents that Frank and I were still alive, though Frank had been injured and was on his way home for recuperation. Fearful the papers would list the survivors as seriously wounded, I explained my injuries, making light of them, and said I was due to return to active duty any day. Not quite the truth, though a lie I could happily live with.

Early September I received an unexpected visitor one night after supper. Chaplain Murray had been given leave to attend the funeral of a priest he'd known since their days in the seminary. He'd been wounded by a sniper and died two weeks later. The chaplain pulled a chair up to my bed. "I'm pleased to see you looking so well."

"How is everyone?" I asked before he had the chance to say another word.

"The regiment was sent back into reserve at Englebelmer

on July 6. The hundred or so of us left, that is," Murray added after a slight pause. "The town was all but destroyed by
heavy artillery. The bombing continued after we arrived, so
we sought shelter in the ruined houses." He removed his hat
and placed it on the foot of my bed, then stared down at the
floor, a habit of which I'd become weary. I braced myself to
hear the worst.

"Johnny Rendell and Fred Thompson took advantage of a
lull in the shelling to stretch their legs one night. A shell exploded in front of them as they turned a corner. Fred was dazed, but
Johnny was literally blown to pieces. To protect us, we were sent
farther back to a camp in Mailly-Maillet Wood." The chaplain
shook his head. "It was too late for Rendell. Fred took it awfully
bad. He's consoled somewhat that Rick's back in Newfoundland.
After ten long days of existing in tents, we were sent to billets in
Acheux."

"Where are the men now?"

"At the end of July we were loaded onto a train and travelled
north to Ypres in Belgium. A hundred and thirty new recruits
had arrived from home July 11." Chaplin Murray became quiet.

"What's the matter?" I asked after a prolonged silence.

"I believe Major Forbes-Robertson, who's in charge of training, is pushing the men too hard. He's set parade hours from five
thirty in the morning to seven thirty at night. Many of the officers, particularly Captain Will Burke, agree it's overly harsh,
unfair, and have stated so. The men deserve time to mourn their
family and friends lost at Beaumont Hamel."

"Maybe that's the whole point," I said. "The major doesn't
want them to focus on that. Still, they must resent him. I'd wager
Ches has expressed his opinion."

"Indeed, and to tell the truth, I agree. The men are exhausted
physically and emotionally. They deserve some real rest time."

The patient three beds down coughed, choking as he tried

in vain to catch his breath. Nurse Abigail ran to him with comforting words. "He survived a gas attack," I said to Chaplain Murray. "If you call that survival."

The chaplain blessed himself. "We came under gas attack last month for the first time. The white cloud was first spotted low to the ground. The wind carried it toward us, rising up like a living thing as it drew nearer."

I sat forward, my mouth open.

"No need to worry. The order was given to put on gas masks, which fortunately prevented any injuries or casualties."

I'd seen the canisters of liquid mustard gas, which once exposed to the air became gaseous. "Too bad the wind didn't change and blow it back on the enemy."

Chaplain Murray folded his hands together as if about to pray. "The value of human life is diminishing with every passing day in this war."

CHAPTER 16

RETURN TO FRANCE

On October 7, I was given a clean bill of health and sent back to France. En route, I learned the Allied forces had advanced a mere eighteen kilometres on the Somme. On average, about 4,000 men had died each day of fighting. I arrived at Flers, fifteen kilometres southwest of Gueudecourt. I ran across Ches and Harold sitting on the front porch of a house on the outskirts of town. A third soldier, unknown to me, sat with them, and without a doubt a new recruit sent to raise the number of our battalion to 1,000 men. He had a dark complexion, a black tan, and dark brown eyes.

"Well, well," Ches said. "Look who decided to pay us a visit." He relieved me of my haversack. "It's good to have you back."

"What have you all been up to since I left?" I deliberately avoided mentioning Gord's name.

Ches rolled his eyes. "Marching, training, and more marching."

"That's right," Harold said, paling slightly. "The men in charge think we need time to recuperate from our heavy losses."

"Ron," Ches said. "You can ask. I know. Gord was never found." He stared over at the oak trees lining the side of the road, their leaves a striking orange and red, the colours of early autumn. "I won't believe he's dead until I see his body for myself."

The dark-complexioned soldier glanced at me, then quickly looked away. I wasn't sure if he was Eskimo, and I put his age in the mid-twenties. Short in stature, he was muscular and stood straight, as if at attention. He had a friendly, quiet look about him. "This is John Shiwak," Harold said. "The first Eskimo in our regiment. He got here a few weeks after you were evacuated to England."

"Ronald Marrie," I said, shaking his hand. His grip was firm. "Where are you from?"

"Rigolet, Labrador," he said, a little above a whisper.

Ches cocked an eyebrow at him. "He's the best scout and sharpshooter I've ever come across."

"It becomes second nature when you do both for a living."

"Ron, I'll show you around," Harold said. "There's been a lot of new recruits lately." We were seasoned veterans compared to the boys and men who'd come straight to the front after months of training. In a way I had come home, to the men I'd served with since the beginning of the war.

John Shiwak was the first Eskimo I'd ever met, and I was delighted to share a billet with him. I looked forward to learning about his culture.

The next morning Captain Will Burke, Wakefield's replacement, assembled "A" Company to brief us on the day's activity. "Ron, Father was pleased to hear you made a full recovery."

"Thank you, sir. It's taken a while."

Captain Burke addressed the men. "Captain Wakefield was a personal friend. I'm sure you'll all agree he was a good man and exceptional leader."

"One of the finest," Fred said.

The captain walked a few paces back and forth in front of us. "The battle of Beaumont Hamel took a heavy toll on the regiment in more ways than the death of our comrades." He stopped moving. "Two of my brothers were lost. We must again become engaged in this war with renewed enthusiasm, to avenge the loss of all our friends. Which is why I've assembled you together. We're going back into action."

"High time," Ches said. "Any more recuperation and I'll go crazy." Mutters of agreement came from all around. Despite the display of exuberance, there was an air of apprehension from the recent arrivals.

"We leave for the front line, which is near the town of Gueudecourt, today. On the twelfth, the Newfoundland Regiment will advance, with the Essex on the left flank, for the heavily fortified trench named Hilt Trench, four hundred metres beyond our front lines. Once that trench is captured, both regiments will move another four hundred metres to the German's second line, called Grease Trench. We'll be using the new military tactic called the creeping barrage." The captain opened a large sheet of paper the size of a school blackboard. Lines drawn at equal distances from each other criss-crossed the paper. "The artillery will fire, then aim ahead fifty metres every minute before firing again." He placed a finger on certain lines as he explained. "You men will follow forty-six metres behind each barrage. The blown-up earth and smoke produced will cover your advancement with the enemy no wiser you're closing in on them. 'A' and 'B' Companies will move out first, followed by 'C' and 'D' Companies."

"Sir," Harold said. "I'm a little concerned. If we advance too quickly we may be trapped by our own artillery."

"Which is why we need to pay careful attention to how swiftly we advance."

As we headed out, Harold marched alongside me. "You're keeping pace pretty good," he said. "Your chest or shoulder giving you any problems?"

"No. I was worried the months of convalescence might've made me soft and out of shape."

Grassy hillsides and luscious trees were interspersed among woods turned into sticks and soil stripped of any life. By nightfall we were settled in the front line trench along the northern outskirts of Gueudecourt. The march had indeed tired me more than usual, and I was able to rest for a few hours.

A few minutes after two o'clock in the morning, the order quietly passed down the line for men to fix bayonets and take care not to show them over the top of the trench. At 2:45, a shell landed a hundred yards out in no man's land. A veil of smoke before us, "A" and "B" Companies moved over the parapets, "C" and "D" Companies following behind several minutes later. Back in action, it was like I'd never been away. The captains for each company kept a check on their watches and the blasting ahead, which hit every fifty metres. A moment of silence and the artillery recommenced another fifty metres farther on, while we remained fifty metres behind the last blast. "A" and "B" Companies moved ahead as planned.

The newer recruits from both "C" and "D" Companies reached us and ran ahead. "Christ, what are you doing?" Ches growled deep in his throat.

"Slow down," Captain Burke ordered. "You'll get caught in the barrage."

Whether his voice was lost in the noise or they were too confused or excited to hear him, they dashed farther ahead. An incoming bomb impacted the earth. Shrapnel flew off in every direction, sending men and weapons spinning upwards.

"We can't turn back," Burke called. "Keep going!"

Handfuls of the fallen were spread out on the ground like broken branches as we kept forging ahead. Shells whistled toward us. "The Germans are firing at us," Harold shouted. More men fell, some from a direct hit, while others were blown back by the force of a shell. The smoke from our artillery hindered the Germans' use of their machine guns—a small measure of good fortune for us.

Hilt Trench, our first objective, was a few yards away with not much barbed wire to impede our progress. Harold, Ches, and Fred threw hand bombs and John Shiwak picked off soldiers with deadly accuracy. Germans rushed out of the trench, and for the briefest second I was somewhat nervous to realize this would be my first hand-to-hand battle with the enemy.

Ches thrust his bayonet into a soldier's stomach, while another came at me. I plunged mine deep into his chest. I heard a squelch as the blade pierced the skin and dug into organs. He dropped to his knees and stared up at me, horror and pain in his eyes. Another enemy hurled himself at me, and with no time to reflect on the life I'd just taken, I pulled out the bayonet and plunged it into another human being. John's precise shooting felled several soldiers, before they got close enough for hand-to-hand combat with bayonets.

Cries and yells arose from both attackers and defenders; it was impossible to distinguish one from other. From the corner of my eye I saw Ches go down, a bayonet inches from his chest, ready to cleave into his body. In one brisk movement I turned and thrust my bayonet into the German's back. He spun around in shock, his eyes, bluer than the sky, dulled. Blood spurted from his mouth. Ches rolled out of the way as the German fell to the ground. His dead eyes stared up at me.

Ches sprang to his feet just as another bayonet veered for him. A rifle shot rang out, and the German went down. "Thank you, John," Ches called. Shiwak nodded and aimed his rifle at another enemy.

Harold and Fred threw more bombs into the trench. As the dirt and smoke cleared, Germans emerged, hands held high above their heads. Bodies were sprawled all around—us and theirs. "A fine job," Captain Burke said. "We've secured our section of Hilt Trench in twenty-five minutes." He scanned the dead and injured, then spun on his heel to face us. "All right, men, let's move on to Grease Trench."

Wounded Newfoundland soldiers escorted the prisoners back to the allied line.

"Four hundred metres more to go," Harold said. "This creeping barrage isn't such a bad idea."

"You can say that again," Fred said. "Too bad the manoeuvre wasn't used at Beaumont Hamel."

On the next fifty-metre advance, machine-gun fire cut into the regiment from the front and left. Out in the open, man after man was hit, until half of us were either dead or wounded.

Harold crawled over to me. "The Essex unit must've been attacked before they could reach us," he said. "We're vulnerable on the left flank."

"Pull back to Hilt Trench," Burke ordered. The captain of "D" Company followed suit. The captains of "B" and "C" Companies had been killed. As we retreated, Captain Burke received a message stating the Essex unit had met a counterattack from the Germans and had been forced back to Gueudecourt. He commanded us to slip into the unoccupied portion of Hilt Trench. "An enemy attack is inevitable," he said. We dug in like ants into the chalky ground to build new firing steps and protective mounds between us and the Germans, who were a little ways off to our left.

"There's at least five hundred," Fred shouted as they came at us in the afternoon.

We held them off for hours with our rifles and Lewis guns. Harold nicked a German's helmet, knocking it from his head. "I hope we don't run out of ammunition before relief arrives."

Ches shouldered up next to him. "We have bayonets."

Day dissolved into night, and the relentless exchange of bullets continued from both sides. Ches reloaded his rifle. "They won't slaughter us so easily like they did at Beaumont Hamel. This time we have a fighting chance."

Fred didn't take his eyes off the enemy. "I still would appreciate help from reinforcements." Nighttime in no man's land when the moon and stars were absent resulted in total blackness, where even the whites of a man's eyes weren't visible. John Shiwak was the only person among us who could make out specific forms.

Reinforcements arrived at nine o'clock, and the fighting raged on into early morning. Captain Burke received word at 3:00 a.m. that we were relieved. He led us out of Hilt Trench, and we marched two kilometres to the support trench behind Gueudecourt for much-needed food and sleep. I never got used to losing men, and this time out had cost us dearly: 120 killed, 119 wounded.

The next day Captain Burke returned from speaking to his commander with a message from headquarters. "Congratulations," he said. "The Newfoundland Regiment has the honour and distinction to be the only unit to capture and hold an objective in this campaign."

Fred puffed out his chest. "That sure is something to write home about."

"With the losses we've suffered," Captain Burke said, "the regiment will be out of any major fighting for the foreseeable future. We'll remain in the area for two months to help relieve other units when needed." He rubbed his bloodshot eyes, which were slightly watery from the dust and dirt. "Then a month of well-deserved rest."

During this time I came to know John Shiwak, as a man and as a Labradorian. He was exceptionally quiet and shy. Chosen to be a sniper because of his skills, he was often away for hours at a time. One day after he came back from a ten-hour stint of sniper duty, I sat on a sandbag next to him while he ate. He was never one to start a conversation, so I engaged him. "I tried sniping once and didn't like it. It bothered me that—"

Ches wandered in, smoking a cigarette. "Don't let me interrupt your conversation."

"Sniping is like watching for seals," John said. "The patience to wait for hours is vital to catching your prey. Sneaking a kill on a human being isn't pleasant. I believe it will help end the war sooner."

"I never thought about it like that before."

Ches offered John a cigarette. He politely refused. "You have a really accurate aim. The best I've seen over here."

John blushed. "Thank you. Many of my people are swatchers. It's a way of life for the Inuit."

Ches nodded. "Regardless, you're damn good." I'd never heard the expression before and was about to say so when Ches spoke up. "A swatcher is someone who can shoot a seal in open water when it sticks its head above the surface to breathe."

Captain Burke told me John had once caught a silver fox and sold the skin to the Hudson's Bay Company for $469.

"Yes," John said when I mentioned it. "I went to St. John's to buy clothes." He blushed darker. "I like fancy garments."

CHAPTER 17

1917

When Christmas rolled around we went to a small village to celebrate with the locals and enjoy their hospitality. I'd fashioned a sort of toy castle, along with a moat, from used shell casings and presented it to the family's eight-year-old son. His squeal of glee at the improvised toy brought a smile to every person at the table.

Christmas had been enjoyable, despite the wreckage and death around us. I tried to get in the Christmas spirit, singing and dancing with the others, but it was hard to celebrate without my family. Henry had been a part of that family. I'd have to face the reality, whether here or at home, that he would never again celebrate in any festivities. A letter arrived from my cousin, Frank, late on Christmas Eve, the first from him since he'd left France. I quietly slipped outside to read it in private.

Dear Ron,
I wanted to let you know my recovery is going as expected. My knee is as good as it will ever be. My stomach

healed with not so ugly a scar, according to Joanie. She visits every day, and hasn't pestered me with unanswerable questions.

It's impossible for the city to be lively and in the Christmas mood. Uncle Tom cut down a tree for us yesterday and Mom decorated it right away. Remember how she always waited until Christmas Eve no matter how much anyone begged her?

Mr. Burke stopped by last week and offered to take me on in his office. I have to do something, and being a lawyer is as good a choice as any. He promised to keep your position open.

I'm sleeping a little better lately, the nightmares not so nightmarish. That's it for now.

Be safe.

Frank

I lowered the letter to my lap. The lack of enthusiasm in the words haunted me. In school, Frank's essays were pages long, elaborating on the most mundane issues, which was often the main criticism from the teachers. Children's laughter echoed in the icy air. A young boy and girl about six or seven were building a snowman. They placed a battered, discarded German helmet on its head. Did they realize it had belonged to their greatest enemy?

My gaze fell back to the letter flapping in the wind between my fingers. Frank's physical and emotional wounds were fresh, raw. Perhaps time would heal both enough for him to regain some of his old spark.

The front door of our billet creaked open and Harold came out with the sound of accordion music trailing behind him. He leaned against the side of the house and chewed on a piece of fruitcake. "Is Frank all right?"

"How'd you know the letter·is from him?"

"Your expression." Harold crossed his ankles. "You look concerned, upset even."

I passed the letter to him. "Read it for yourself."

When he finished he stared at the hills in the distance a minute or so, then handed it back to me. "The scars on the inside take much longer to heal. Joanie seems to understand that." Harold looked back toward the hills. "Good for her."

"Joanie is fifteen by now." I folded the letter and put it in my pocket. "She's not the little girl I left behind."

"Don't fret about it." Harold brightened up. "Be thankful she'll be there when the war's over." He peeked through the window of the house at Ches and Fred chomping down on pastries, the one delicacy remaining for the French in this town. "Let's get a croissant before those two devour every last one."

The back and forth between reserve and front-line trenches proceeded at regular intervals without a break. One night in April, sitting around a makeshift stove in the dugout Ches had christened "Home, Freezing Home," he brewed tea to warm us. "The big push on the Somme was a failure." He stirred the pot, the spoon hitting the sides with extra force. "What's the next big push?"

Harold blew on his hands to take away the chill. "There's talk about a major offensive around the town of Arras in northern France, near the Belgium border. The Canadians captured Vimy Ridge from the Germans, weakening their stronghold on that whole area."

Ches looked up from his task. "And where is Vimy Ridge?"

"A seven-kilometre ridge near Arras. Captain Burke said the French army will attack the German positions east of France."

Fred held out his tin cup for tea. "You don't fool with the Canadians. They haven't lost a battle yet."

Ches drank the hot tea in long slurps. "Good leadership is the answer."

I nearly choked on my tea at that statement. "Ches, your opinion about British generals has changed."

"Not at all. A Canadian general by the name of Arthur Currie leads the Canadian army." Ches poured himself more tea. "Obviously he has a better grip on how to plan and carry out an assault."

Fred downed the last of his tea. "Maybe we could all transfer to the Canadian army."

The following morning we headed for the firing trenches on the eastern outskirts of Monchy-le-Preux, a small fishing village eight kilometres southeast of Arras. At midnight we marched in single file through fields pockmarked from shelling. We were cold and tired, yet grateful for the knitted scarves and gloves from home. We had to tread around banks of dead horses scattered everywhere and covered in thin layers of snow. Ches blessed himself as we kept moving. The horses were like eerie white revenants in the black night.

John Shiwak stopped to look at a black stallion, its hind legs torn to shreds from shrapnel. "Innocent animals forced into battle." He gazed up at me, his eyes watery. "Such majestic creatures deserve to live in peace and not participate in man's war."

The futility of the terrible loss of such a noble creature washed over me. Our breath froze into clouds of mist as we turned away from the dead animal.

"Is the war ever going to end?" John mumbled to himself.

"I miss home, too."

"I miss my fiancée the most."

I was flattered by this rare disclosure of personal information.

We arrived at the front line by two in the morning and were immediately briefed on the mission. Lieutenant-Colonel Forbes-Robinson, the Newfoundland Regiment's commander, detailed the specifics. We were to advance behind a creeping barrage, accompanied by the Essex on the right flank, to take Shrapnel Trench a few metres away, then head for Infantry Hill Trench. The lesson learned from the last creeping barrage prepared the men to better adhere to the precise timing of each advance.

At five thirty, John Shiwak scouted ahead while we started the short walk for Shrapnel Trench, alert for any reflection of metal that would indicate snipers. We expected resistance from German artillery at any moment. John hurried back, surprise evident on his face. "Shrapnel Trench is empty."

Fred's gaze swept over the area. "Maybe Infantry Hill will be as well."

"Not likely," Captain Burke said. "It's only a thousand yards from Monchy-le-Preux. The town's in British hands and the Germans are determined to take it. John, go and see what the Germans are up to." John slithered away, quieter than a weasel.

We trudged on to Artillery Hill. John returned as the first shell exploded just short of us. "Fred, there's your proof Infantry Hill isn't empty," I said, skirting to the side with him. More artillery drove us into the ground, screeching toward us from every direction, like swarms of panicked hawks.

"All right, men," Captain Burke yelled. "We do whatever is necessary to keep the Germans from entering the town!" We launched hand bombs and returned gunfire, fighting like deranged men without let-up until we overtook the Germans and captured the trench.

John hurried off to scout out other German positions. He returned mere minutes later. "Bad news, sir. The Germans have us and the Essex cut off from Monchy. We're surrounded."

"Then we'd better be prepared to be overrun."

We waited, the one thing in war a soldier learns to do in silence. At eight o'clock, the counterattack commenced from all sides. Although we were trapped in the earth like wingless birds with little hope of holding them off, we resisted, firing back on machine gunners and artillery. Shrapnel whizzed through the air and men dropped around me, picked off in ones and twos until the majority of the regiment was either dead or wounded. There were too few men left alive to be effective, but we didn't— wouldn't—surrender. The Germans inched closer, capturing parts of the trench and taking prisoners. I didn't know if they included any of my friends. We suspected their next step would be an all-out advance on Monchy-le-Preux.

A shell landed nearby and I blacked out. When I awoke, my head throbbed and blood oozed from my ears and nose. A dead German soldier lay sprawled across me, a chunk of shrapnel ten inches long sticking out of his back. The absence of noise startled me. I wiped dirt from my face, pushed the soldier off me, and stood up. Dizzy, I dropped to my knees until the spell subsided. As far as I could tell, I was the only living person. A dread reached into my gut. Were all my friends dead?

I found my rifle, scrambled out of the trench, and headed for Monchy. Bodies from both sides were strewn along the ground, twisted and damaged corpses left to wither away to skeletons where they'd fallen. Crows cawed overhead. None of my friends were among the carnage. On the outskirts of the town, Colonel Forbes-Robertson and a group of about twenty Newfoundlanders ran down the hill toward me. Shells drilled into the town, and the men ran from side to side to avoid the blasts. One exploded on top of them, killing at least half. Captain Burke, Ches, Fred, and Harold were behind the colonel. "Two to three hundred Germans are advancing on Monchy," the colonel said. "We'll defend it to the last man."

We scrounged up weapons and ammunition from the dead

and wounded. "Hold up," the colonel said, and stopped at a house on the southeast corner of Monchy. "I need to get a better view of what we're up against." He scavenged a ladder from underneath a pile of tree branches, placed it against the house, and climbed to a hole in the wall. "The Germans have taken back the trenches you took this morning," he called down.

"How dumb does he think we are?" Ches grumbled to me. "A five-year-old would've reached that conclusion by now."

"Midway between this house and the trenches is a well-banked hedge," the colonel said, scurrying down the ladder. "It'll give us sufficient protection to hold back the Germans when they get this far."

"There's ten of us," Fred exclaimed. "What can we do against hundreds?"

"Our best." We followed the colonel, darting across a hundred yards of garden plots in full view of the Germans. Enemy fire dogged us. A shell burst a few feet away from Fred, who went down and didn't move. Every instinct in me ached to go to him.

By the time we reached the hedge, two more men had been cut down. Ches parted a portion of the hedge to see where the Germans were. "There's a soldier from the Essex heading this way," he said.

The man was fired upon and somehow dodged the bullets. Exhausted, he reached us, a small piece of shrapnel lodged in his shoulder. "None of the Essex blokes left standing," he said. "The bloody enemy kept coming, bulldozing through us. "

"Son," the colonel said. "Get that shoulder looked into."

"Beg your pardon, sir. I want to join you and the Newfoundlanders."

The colonel nodded. "Good man."

"They're here," Ches said in a calm voice.

The Germans rushed at us over the open field, determined to exterminate us and take the town.

"Don't waste bullets on men too far out," Harold said. "Fire at close range." Each burst of bullets found its mark. Harold and Ches trained their attention on the German scouts to prevent them from learning we were eleven men fighting off perhaps 200. As wave after wave of soldiers charged, we fired as rapidly as humanly possible. It astonished me how, during times of mortal danger, death is the furthest thing from your mind.

A hand touched my back and I spun around, ready to shoot. Fred crawled alongside me, his rifle slung across his back. His helmet was missing, and a huge welt ran from the left side of his forehead down his cheek to his chin, That would be a tender bruise tomorrow. His eyes were swollen and half-closed. "Need help?"

There weren't many occasions in this war to feel good, but this was one of them. "Any time you're ready," I said, firing off a shot.

Ches glanced over at Fred. "The townie finally made it."

At two o'clock, the German sniper activity and shelling slowed. "We can't hold them off much longer," the colonel said. "Ammunition's running low. Harold, go back for reinforcements and tell the gunners to fire on Machine Gun Wood. With all the movement from that direction, it has to be enemy headquarters."

"Yes, sir," Harold said, and turned to leave.

"And Harold," the colonel called. "You're to remain in Monchy. That's an order."

Harold hesitated, about to say something, but changed his mind. We continued to shoot, slowing the Germans' advance, each of us sneaking glances toward Monchy and willing help to arrive.

Ches fired five shots in a row. "Harold left forty-five minutes ago," he yelled. "What's keeping the reinforcements?"

Finally, we saw men running down the hill with Harold

in the lead. "Sorry, Colonel. I couldn't leave the boys stranded down here."

We held off the Germans for almost six more hours, working like efficient machinery programmed to run on maximum power. It was only when we were relieved that fatigue and weariness took hold.

"Before we leave," Captain Burke said, "I'd like two volunteers to accompany me to an unoccupied section of Assembly Trench to bring in five of our wounded." All stepped forward, but he chose Ches and Harold. They returned with all five injured men, who were physically drained yet still on their feet.

We were notified later that night that 166 of the regiment were killed, 141 wounded, and 150 taken prisoner. The Essex unit had fared no better. Heavy losses were never easy to bear for any unit, and as the months turned into years they became almost intolerable.

General de Lisle personally congratulated the Newfoundland Regiment on our bravery and determined effort. He declared in a proud voice that 40,000 soldiers would have been needed to retake Monchy-le-Preux if it had fallen into enemy hands.

As a soldier sworn to do my duty for king and country, at certain moments, such as in Beaumont Hamel and Arras, I questioned the purpose of war and the competence of leaders. We made some land advances during the Arras battles, which ended on May 16. Had the month-long campaign been worth the deaths of 160,000 men? Had the general's praise of our accomplishment been a tactic to assuage his guilt over so many casualties?

Men who'd held back the Germans with Colonel Forbes-Robinson received a Military Medal for bravery. When Ches heard the news, he grew quiet. "A medal for bravery. What man in this regiment hasn't been anything other than brave?"

In late June we were transferred to Belgium, where once again we dug and repaired trenches. Five hundred new recruits arrived in early July, eager and anxious to fight, like we had been in the beginning. August began with a series of battles raging around Passchendaele in which the Canadians, led by General Arthur Currie, scored a victory, yet suffered a staggering number of casualties. Some felt the victory softened the sting.

Vincent Monahue, "Skit" for short, the Essex soldier who assisted us at Monchy-le-Preux, planted himself beside me, Ches, and Harold, holding the London Gazette, dated July 9. "I thought you blokes might like to see this." It talked about the Military Medals we'd won and stated the citation for each man, quoting the reason for the medal and giving his name. Skit did us the honour of reading the article.

"For bravery in the field at Monchy-le-Preux, when an attack had failed and the enemy were advancing on the village, he displayed the greatest of gallantry as one of a small party hastily collected to oppose the hostile advance. This party maintained itself in the face of overwhelming odds, inflicted heavy losses on the enemy, and completely checked him on this part of the line."

Skit folded the paper twice and handed it to me. "It's been written up in other British papers." He gave a sly smile. "You blokes are all right for colonials."

CHAPTER 18

ST. JOHN'S, 1917

When the evening meal was over, Tom and Anne Marrie sat in the living room, both relaxing after a long day's work. Tom smoked a cigarette in the armchair across from his wife as he read a murder mystery. He challenged himself to see if he could figure out the murderer and the motive before the culprit was revealed. Anne lounged on the sofa, shoes off, feet on the flowered cushioned stool, knitting the heel of the second sock of a pair. Dust particles tumbled over each other in the rays of sun shining through the lace curtains. She felt its warmth on her hands as her needles clicked together in the silence. The smell of chimney smoke drifted in through the open window, mingling with the tobacco smoke's acrid odour.

"I used the last of the flour today," Anne said. "No more cakes or gravy for a while." She peeked over the knitting at her husband, expecting a reaction.

Tom's book dropped to his lap and he stared at her with wide eyes. "Anne, are you serious? How's a man supposed to survive without gravy on his potatoes? And poor Joanie. She'll fade away without your delicious cakes."

Anne's needles continued to click. "Sorry, but I refuse to pay triple for a bag of flour."

Tom squashed his cigarette in the glass ashtray on the mantel. "It's gotten that bad?"

"Indeed it has. If it keeps up, I don't how we'll afford food, let alone clothing and coal for the stove."

Tom placed his book on the side table and leaned back in his chair. He looked at his wife, both hands folded under his chin. "The merchants are responsible."

Anne's fingers stilled halfway in slipping a stitch from one needle to another. "What do you mean?"

"They sold their ships to the Russians. Why do that when they're essential for transporting needed supplies to fill your shelves?"

"You're suggesting they sold the ships to cause the shortage, which would inflate the prices to a scandalous amount?"

"We have to eat, therefore we are forced to pay the outrageous prices, as you said."

"What can be done about it?"

"Maybe stage a protest."

"All the good that will do. The Water Street merchants are powerful men." Anne's needles jumped into motion once again. "At least the codfish is somewhat affordable."

Tom eyed the *Evening Telegram* on the coffee table. "What's that doing here?"

"I forgot. Frank brought it over while I was getting supper ready. He said there's an article in it we both should read."

"What article?"

"Something about timber wanted in Britain. I don't see what that has to do with Newfoundland." The sun moved across the horizon, casting shadows into the room. "Doesn't Canada supply wood to Britain?"

"It's become too dangerous on the Atlantic with German

U-boats on the prowl. Some of the fishing schooners on the Grand Banks have been fired on. Fortunately, they escaped in their dories and were picked up by other schooners."

"The same problem would exist if the wood came from Newfoundland."

Tom glanced down at the paper. "It says April 7. That's from yesterday. Let's see what's so important."

TO THE MEN OF NEWFOUNDLAND

The King's Government calls for lumbermen and all skilled workmen not eligible for the Regiment or the Royal Naval Reserve for the service in the forests of the United Kingdom.

These men shall not be engaged in the fighting line. They are needed for the skilled work at home.

They will be under their own officers and need no military training duties beyond elementary drill. They will work with their friends and comrades as in Newfoundland.

The medical examination required for members of these Newfoundland Companies shall be modified so that all able-bodied men can be enrolled without limit of age or height. NO one shall be rejected for eyesight, flat feet, loss of fingers, deafness, etc.

No unmarried men of military age and fitness may be accepted; their place is in the fighting forces.

The pay, allowances, and pensions of the Newfoundland Companies shall be the same as the pay, allowances, and pensions of the Newfoundland Regiment.

Skilled workmen and mechanics such as mill-wrights, mill-sawyers, saw filers, cooks, etc., may be eligible for extra pay.

The period of enlistment shall be for the duration of the war; but arrangements may be made under which skilled workmen specially trained for Newfoundland industries may be released after six months.

W. E. Davidson
Governor
Government House
St. John's, April 4, 1917

Anne pushed the stool away and sat forward. "Why would Frank want you to see that?" A horrid thought made her blood go cold, and she threw her knitting aside. "He doesn't think you'll be interested in—"

"No," Tom said abruptly. "I don't believe it has anything to do with me."

"Then who in heaven's name?" The sun disappeared and the room darkened.

The front door opened, and Frank stood in the entrance to the living room. He looked at Tom. "You've read it."

"Have you broken the news to your mother?"

"I wanted to talk with you first."

Anne patted the cushion beside her. "Frank, come sit with me."

Frank slowly walked toward Anne, his right leg slightly bending at the knee. "Aunt Anne, I want to do this for the war effort."

"Frank, you've done your fair share. You fought and were wounded." Her eyes went to his damaged leg. "Scarred for life, even. No one expects more of you."

"Henry died. Ron's still over there. I have no purpose in life anymore."

Tom scratched the stubble on his chin. "And serving with the Forestry Corps will give you the purpose you crave?"

"The muddy trench floors are covered with wood." Frank looked out the window. He'd gone somewhere else. "The barbed wire requires stakes to keep them in place." He gave an intake of breath. "Railway ties are essential for transporting soldiers and ammunition to the front lines." He became quiet as he watched the curtains flutter in the breeze.

Tom turned on the light. "Why don't we go and have a chat with your mother? Now is as good a time as any."

Anne had finished knitting the second sock when Tom returned.

"How did it go?"

"Elsie listened to what Frank had to say, then hugged him and wished him well. I don't know if I would have been as supportive in her place."

"You love Frank like a son and you supported him. So there's your answer. Besides, he'll be far from the battlefields."

As expected, many men answered the call for help. Frank informed his aunt and uncle that 498 men were accepted, and 278 were rejected for medical reasons. "Uncle Tom, Aunt Anne, they were so disappointed. It was really sad to watch them leave knowing they'd failed once again to participate in the war effort." He paused, then smiled. "Plenty of mothers cried when their teenaged sons enrolled. Woodsmen too old for service in the regiment promised they'd look after the 'youngsters.'"

On May 19, the first set of recruits shipped out of St. John's harbour for Scotland aboard the *Florizel*. Frank hugged his mother tight. "Don't worry, Ma. I will come home safe and unhurt this time."

Elsie held back her tears. "Of course you will. Now go on and get on that boat before she sails without you."

As the *Florizel* chugged out through the Narrows, Tom put an arm around his sister. "He needed to know you were all right with his leaving."

She nodded, no longer able to hold back her tears.

The price of foods and other goods continued to rise. Poor Mr. Williams, the local grocer, felt the brunt of people's frustration. Unrest and grumbling continued throughout the city, like the eerie stillness before a blizzard. The lid blew off the boiling pot when William Coaker, the leader of the Fishermen's Protective Union, publicly accused the merchants of profiteering.

Tom and Anne discussed the matter one night during supper. "What does profiteering mean?" Joanie asked, spooning barley soup into her mouth.

Anne, fed up with spending three times the normal amount on groceries, answered the question. "The wholesaler and merchants are using the war as an excuse to charge whatever prices and rates they fancy, which is an unconscionable amount people can't afford."

"That's not fair," Joanie said.

"You're right," Tom said. "Sadly, there are people who care more about money and the power it wields."

The next week, Tom hurried home with the latest news spreading around the city. "The Prime Minister appointed a High Cost of Living Commission to investigate if the merchants really are profiting illegally from the war."

"Praise the Lord. Coaker's speaking out for the ordinary person trying to eke out a meagre existence finally paid off."

The commission's first report was published two weeks later. "Listen to this," Tom said, reading from the paper. "A flour combine is operating in St. John's, and importers have made more than six hundred thousand dollars in excess profit. A large shipping company increased its rates by over five hundred per cent."

Anne was shocked by the blatant misuse of the war efforts by men on whom the whole country depended. "What's the conclusion of the report?"

"They state there's no justification for the increases."

"Anything to be done about it?"

"Don't worry, Anne. Mr. Coaker isn't a man to let this matter drop. He'll see to it that prices reflect the true situation."

"Any recommendations made by the committee?"

"I've heard the government is going to impose a profits tax. That should give the merchants something to think about."

Elsie came running in waving an envelope. "I got a letter from Frank. He sounds excited, like his old self."

Tom scanned down the page. "The men are working on the pine plantation belonging to the Duke of Atholl. His estate is near Perth."

Elsie smiled. "He'll get strong again cutting down trees for the war."

Tom smiled as well. "He feels like he's helping Ron stay safer and more comfortable in the trenches and dugouts. And he's met up with some war buddies from around the bay who were injured and sent home just like him."

Tom passed the letter to Anne. "This is interesting," she said, zeroing in on the name Kathleen. "He's met a young Scottish lassie. By the way he talks about her, he's smitten. Isn't that lovely?"

Then, as abruptly as a sudden change in the wind bringing in a cloud of fog, Elsie burst into tears.

"Elsie, love," Tom said, "what's the matter?" He flashed Anne a helpless look.

Elsie wiped her face with the back of her hands. "I'm all right, Tom. It's just that I never thought my boy would be happy again."

CHAPTER 19

Tanks became the new weapon of war and a better safety net for the troops. In 1917, General Haig had been promoted to Field Marshal. He had wanted tanks for the Battle of the Somme. We never learned why they weren't made available. Another major offensive was in the plans, a sure bet, this time, to bring the war to an end. Neither side was making any satisfactory progress, and the Allies decided to take a ten-kilometre section of the German Hindenburg Line in northern France, which included the valley of the Escaut River, the St. Quentin Canal, and the unfinished Canal du Nord. The first line of defence consisted of trenches and barbed wire spread out over 3,000 yards. A second group of trenches lay 5,000 yards beyond. The goal was to reach the city of Cambrai, an important supply centre for the Germans. The Allies agreed a surprise attack was the way to go, using 278 tanks with six infantry divisions.

Captain Burke, a spring in his step, walked up and down the line of men. "The first thing is to train you how to move with tanks." He rubbed his hands together. "That will lessen the use of artillery, and hopefully there won't be as much loss of life."

The huge clunk of a machine was like something straight from a child's imagination. Close to two storeys high, they were powered by wide, flexible metal bands with notches that fit into toothed wheels. Small, square protrusions on either side held the guns which were operated by a man inside. When crossing a ditch, the front would lift up into the air and almost topple over backwards.

Several weeks of intensive instruction and training followed. "Obviously it's best suited for flat land," Harold said one day after walking in formation behind the machine. "Although it's strong enough to smash anything in its path."

Once Hadow was satisfied we'd become efficient at manoeuvring with the tank, we started the journey north for the Hindenburg Line. We marched to Boisleux-au-Mont for the train to Péronne. The following night, we marched for Moislains, near the Canal du Nord. At dusk we moved on to Sorelle Grand. To keep out of sight of enemy aircraft, we marched during the night and rested in huts during the day.

The weather had turned cold and we were grateful for the shelter from the bitter wind. Early one afternoon, Ches took a photograph from his breast pocket. "I can tell my little girl Lilly and the boys I played hide and seek over here." He kissed the photograph. "It's their favourite game."

I snatched the photograph from him and saw a beautiful woman with light hair and a dazzling smile. Next to her was a six-year-old version of the mother. The two younger boys had dark hair and Ches's dark eyes. "Why didn't you show us this before?"

"Never thought of it, I guess."

Harold glanced over my shoulder at the photo. "A very handsome family, Ches."

I held it out for Fred to take a look. "Your youngsters look real happy," he said.

"That was taken before I told them I was enlisting." Ches tucked the photograph into his pocket. "It's been three years. Too long to be away from your children."

November 20 rolled around, and at 6:30 a.m. the Newfoundland Regiment, along with the other units, followed tanks as they moved like overgrown beasts, groaning and moaning over the terrain. The barbed wire was easily trampled down, like it was made of paper instead of metal. Many of the German dugouts caved in under their hulking weight. Several German machine guns fired a few rounds before we took them out and crossed the first trenches of the Hindenburg Line. The Newfoundland Regiment's objective was to take St. Quentin Canal and the towns of Marcoing and Masnières.

The 29th Division began its advance with the aid of four tanks toward the Hindenburg Support Lines, which were another 5,000 yards farther on. Machine-gun fire broke out and several of our men were killed. We opened fire and stopped the guns, but not before more good men died. As we moved farther toward the second lines, a battery of artillery fire swept toward us, aimed at the tanks. The first took a direct hit, and the ground around the second tank erupted. The vehicle crawled ahead a few feet and sputtered to a standstill, damaged beyond repair. The two remaining tanks chugged forward at a walking man's pace, easy targets to set sights on. More fire slammed into the third tank. Only one tank remained to protect us.

"We have to keep moving," Captain Burke said, looking toward the remaining expanse to cover. "Be careful of small German garrisons hiding in the dugouts. We learned from Beaumont Hamel how very deep they can be."

"The Germans are like rats," Fred said. "They go deep and attack from nowhere when you least expect it." Many times we encountered the "rats" scurrying up from the bowels of the earth to fire on us.

The fourth tank made a grinding noise, slowed, then rattled to a stop. The side door opened and a soldier stepped out. "The damned thing just shut down." He kicked the monster. "Mechanical trouble is the last thing I expected."

All four tanks were disabled, mere husks of metal with no useful purpose. A warning sign, I thought to myself. An omen that this battle would finish in disaster like all the others.

Without support we lost precious time, and even more importantly, precious lives, in our efforts to shut down the machine guns. John Shiwak's aim was perfect as usual, and it was no surprise he'd earned a reputation as the premier sniper of the Newfoundland Regiment, a title which he humbly accepted.

We took prisoners trapped in dugouts and reached St. Quentin Canal, one thousand yards ahead over an open slope. The village of Masnières lay to the right, Marcoing to the left.

"Right," Captain Burke said. "Marcoing Copse is five hundred yards from the canal and the lock we need to cross." He stood tall, as tall as you can at five foot seven. Then again, even though I was over six feet tall, myself, the one lesson I learned from this war was that height had nothing to do with the measure of a man's honour or courage. "We're going to face heavy machine-gun fire and snipers."

The machine guns from the north bank of the canal fired on us with such rapidity it was like a hundred guns aimed on each man. A sniper's single bullet knocked my helmet off, which I quickly retrieved. I admit that close call started my heart racing.

"We're not getting out of this alive," Fred shouted, firing back at well-concealed men.

John directed his rifle toward a house. He fired, and a German crashed through the window from the top floor. Harold pointed across the canal. "There's a tank rolling toward the

Germans." It fired at the enemy and drew their attention away from us, giving us the opportunity to dash across the lock and secure the bridge ahead.

"I don't see any men from the Essex," Captain Burke said. "They were supposed to advance on Masnières from the right. Something must have slowed them down."

"What do we do?" Fred asked.

"We follow orders and attack Masnières from the left by proceeding along the banks of the canal."

As we started toward the town, a machine gun spat bullets at us, hindering our advance. We stole to the buildings along the canal and got a fix on the general area of the machine gun. Captain Burke sent John Shiwak out to mark the precise location. He blended in with the land in a way that only he could and soon returned with a report amid a blast of bullets. "The machine gun is by the railway, running parallel to the canal about sixty yards away. I couldn't get a clear shot at the gunner."

Captain Burke checked the bullets in his pistol. "We have no choice but to charge the station and take out that gun." We looked at one another, realizing he was serious. He ducked his head and moved out, the lawyer from St. John's, running at top speed with me, his former apprentice, a fisherman, a fireman, and a butcher, joined by a dozen other professions, but all wearing the same uniform, on one mission. A blur of bullets flew, downing men until the few left were out of range. John went ahead as we moved toward the town. A tank approached the bridge we had earlier secured from the other side.

"That weighs a ton," Harold said. "I hope the bridge is strong enough to . . ." His words were muffled by the creaking of wood as the bridge collapsed and the tank crashed into the canal.

"Good Jesus," Ches wailed. "That means armoured support is out of the question."

We pressed on and encountered another attack by a machine gun. In the open with no protection, two-thirds of our men were killed before the machine gun was stopped. I'd never gotten used to the quick, sudden loss of life, and I was grateful my humanity hadn't been chipped away. We reached the outskirts of the village by sunset.

All through the night, small groups of men from the regiment and other battalions sneaked into the town to rid it of any remaining Germans. By morning, very few sections of the village were in enemy hands. The British forces had advanced six kilometres, but this territory formed a salient, which meant we were surrounded on three sides by the enemy.

The Royal Newfoundland Regiment was ordered to go along the canal and head for a sugar factory on the other side of Masnières for the next phase of the assault. Free from artillery or machine-gun fire, we marched alongside the canal.

"A peaceful day so far," John said. "Maybe this time the fighting will end quickly."

The familiar shrill whistle sounded, and before anyone had time to react, a shell smashed into us. The blast lifted me off my feet and I ploughed into Captain Burke. I saw John Shiwak fall forward. When the smoke cleared, men were scrambling to help the wounded.

My ears rang. I thought the piercing noise would crush my skull. "John," I yelled, struggling to my feet, stumbling over to him. Even before I felt for a pulse I knew he was dead. He lay motionless on his stomach, one arm outstretched before him as if urging us to keep moving. The regiment would miss this quiet, unassuming man from Rigolet. He'd never again get to hold the fiancée he missed. I wished I had asked her name. Ches ran over and knelt at John's side. I couldn't hear what he said, but from reading his lips I ascertained it was something like, "I'm sorry, lad. It was a privilege to know you." Ten had died, fifteen were wounded.

While we assessed the situation, the captain received word to retreat back to Masnières. We gathered up the wounded and the dead and returned to the village.

Exhausted from lack of sleep for over twenty-four hours, we collapsed into heaps on the ground. Captain Burke left to get an update, and by the time he returned, looking dejected, I'd regained some of my hearing. "The attack has been stalled," he said.

"Stalled!" Fred shouted, in a high-pitched voice. "What's that supposed to mean?"

"Everyone, including us, are too tired to go on, and there aren't any reinforcements to replace casualties."

Ches slammed his fist against the hard ground. "John always wondered if the war would ever end. He believed the assault on Cambrai would bring that day closer." He snatched up a large rock and pounded it against a shrivelled tree stump. "Now the damn battle looks like another failure."

Captain Burke turned toward the bodies of the slain, which were laid out side by side. "For now we give our dead a decent burial."

I felt especially sad for John, hoping his spirit had travelled back to Labrador.

Shortly after the gruesome task was completed, heavy bombardment forced us into the caves and tunnels under the village, affording a short respite from the deafening noise.

"I hate to say it," Burke said. "This time we're the ones on the defensive to hold the territory we gained."

"Since the start of the Cambrai campaign," I said, "fifty-four of the regiment are dead and a hundred and eighty-four wounded. We can't keep losing men like that."

Fred lit up a cigarette. "Not to mention the casualties from the other units."

The morning came with news we were bound for reserve

in the town of Marcoing, which lasted three days. I'd taken the journal John Shiwak had written in on a daily basis, and I skimmed through it. The pages were filled with poetry he'd composed, his thoughts and feelings about the war and his unit, sketches of trees, flowing rivers, seals, icebergs, and watercolour paintings.

Ches thumbed through several of the paintings. "He was a gentle soul." He smiled to himself. "His family will treasure this."

On the morning of November 30, the Germans launched a counterattack, bombarding Marcoing while at the same time attacking southeast of Masnières.

Captain Burke kept us up to date on events. "I've received an urgent message that we're to help stop the German advance."

"Lose, win, lose, win, lose," Fred said. "Why can't we win and leave it at that?"

Under heavy shelling, we proceeded along the same route we'd taken toward Marcoing at the beginning of the battle. "I don't believe it," Harold said when the Germans came into view. "They've reached Marcoing Copse."

We engaged in hand-to-hand combat. Mortally wounding a man and watching him die in front of you leaves a mark that never goes away. The struggle continued, Allied and enemy soldiers fighting for country, fighting to stay alive. Other units arrived and held off the Germans for twenty-four hours. As usual, too many died in the process.

Skirmishes waged on for days. Then, on the third of December, the Germans began a formidable assault along the canal bank. Shells and machine guns tore the land to shreds. Unable to advance, we withdrew, with bombs chasing at our heels. Ches and I became separated from the regiment. "Don't worry, Ron, we'll get out of this mess in one—" His words were cut off by an explosion so close I felt the force it produced. He shoved me so hard I flew several feet, and as I fell to the ground a shell exploded behind me. My leg felt like someone had driven a hot poker through it. Ches lay on his back. I tried to stand, but my leg gave way. "Ches, are you all right?" He turned his head toward me. I crawled to him on one knee, dragging the other leg.

"Ron, lad." His voice was hoarse, his face whiter than cold marble.

"Ches!" My voice cracked.

He stared down at the place where his legs had been. Blood flowed from the stumps above the knees. He gripped my hand. "Ron, if Gord isn't alive, promise me you'll go see my wife. Tell her . . . I wasn't alone when . . ." He swallowed, his life force draining away. His grip tightened. "My boys . . . I don't want fishing for them." His breathing grew louder, heavier. "Too brutal a life."

I'd never noticed before how deeply brown his eyes were. The light was fading from them. "I'll see they have a better life." Something wet rolled down my cheeks.

"Medal . . . breast pocket," he gasped. "Give to Isabelle."

I opened the flap of his jacket pocket and took out a St. Christopher medal.

"Thank you." Ches's eyelids closed, then flickered open. "Tell Isabelle . . . love her. My little Lilly . . ." He shuddered out a long breath and his hand fell to the ground.

Tears dripping down my face, I closed his eyes.

There was movement behind me, and I shot a glance over my shoulder. A German soldier my father's age stood over me, the bayonet of his rifle ready to tear into me. He stared into my eyes, then slowly stepped back. Had he a son my age fighting in the war? Had my sorrow at the loss of a good friend touched him? Maybe it was a combination of those things.

He spoke words I didn't understand, yet I knew he was ordering me to stand up. I dragged my hand across my face to wipe my tears and looked one last time at the man who'd been like a father figure to me since the war began. I took a step and fell down. Blood seeped through my pants. I saw Harold in the distance take out a soldier about to pierce Fred in the heart. "Please, God," I mumbled under my breath. "Let them live to go home."

I looked away. I was now a prisoner of war.

Shelling intensified. One landed to the right of us. The German soldier slumped to the ground, the back of his head pierced with shrapnel. His rifle was trapped under his body with his hand still wrapped around it.

Harold ran toward me, Fred a few paces back. "We saw the German standing over you," Harold said.

"Oh, God no!" Fred stared down at Ches's broken body. "I really thought he'd make it to the end."

Harold didn't say a word as he knelt by Ches, shaking his head over and over.

Another shell struck. Fred pulled Harold to his feet. "We've got to get out of here."

CHAPTER 20

I spent Christmas and the next several months in a London hospital. The surgeons had taken two bullets out of my calf and one from my hip. When I recovered enough to walk with a cane, the nurses encouraged me to go sightseeing. Big Ben and the Tower of London had always fascinated me, and so I went, but it was a half-hearted attempt. I'd been notified that the king had agreed to grant the Newfoundland Regiment the title "Royal" in honour of our bravery and good work at Cambrai. Ches would have been pleased, though he would have made light of it despite the fact no other "colony" had been awarded the title.

Captain Burke paid me a visit several months into my convalescence. "Did you bury Ches?" I asked, once he reassured me Harold and Fred were well.

"I'm sorry. We weren't able to get to him."

"He hated the thought of being buried on foreign ground. He didn't even get that much."

We talked about Will's leave home a month earlier. "It's changed," he said. "There's unrest over soaring prices. The num-

227

bers killed at Beaumont Hamel have left the island devastated and angry. The desire to enlist has waned considerably. Father told me the government is thinking about bringing in conscription for men aged nineteen to thirty-nine."

"I don't blame anyone for not wanting to volunteer for a war that's gone on this long."

Will glanced at his watch. "One way or another, it has to end. Ron, my ride will be waiting. I'll visit again before going back to the front."

I didn't write to Isabelle. What I needed to say to the wife of the man who saved my life had to be done in person.

I received letters from my parents on a regular basis throughout the war in which they talked about everyday, ordinary things. It was plain they avoided any news that could upset or worry me. On the other hand, Joanie's letters laid out the facts, her beliefs, and feelings. Early March, a letter had came from her, the first since Christmas. Frank was never far from my thoughts, and I nervously opened the envelope, anxious to read the news.

> Dear Ronnie,
> Harold wrote Mom and Dad to let them know that Ches was killed. Harold said he was the kind of man who makes you a better person for knowing him. I wish I could have met him. He also said that Ches's brother Gord went missing on July 1, another man worth knowing, I'm sure. I can't imagine the heartache their family is going through.
>
> I taught Harold's mother to read and write. Don't tell him. She wants to surprise him with a letter she wrote herself.
>
> Harold also told us about your injuries because he didn't want us to worry in case we read about it in the

paper. He said you'll be pampered like a baby in England. Needless to say, Mom cried, but was happy to hear you're all right. So many of Dad's friends have lost their sons. Some as many as two and three. Ronnie, I hate this war and wish Newfoundland had stayed out of it. I told Dad how I felt. You won't believe his reaction. He never got mad at me, not one bit.

The Prime Minister was informed about the regiment's new title of "Royal." The whole island is so proud of all of you. That reminds me of something I forgot to mention in earlier letters. There's been a lot of men who volunteered to join and were rejected for medical reasons. I've heard people make fun of them by calling them slackers, accusing them of lying when they explained why they weren't accepted. The government solved the problem by issuing a badge which read "For King and Country I have Offered." It wasn't their fault they weren't fit to fight.

Ronnie, I have the best news for you. Mrs. Lawlor, Mr. Burke's secretary, just in case you forgot who she is, read in the paper one of her sons was missing in action. I know that usually means the person is dead. Mr. Tucker, Dad's friend at Government House, investigated and found out there'd been a mistake. Mrs. Lawlor hugged him so tightly she nearly crushed his ribs. Mr. Tucker needed something like that to break through the gloom he couldn't shake himself. Dad was so happy to see him smile.

Frank joined the Forestry Corps last year and is stationed in Scotland cutting down trees for the war. He writes every week and asks about you. We're looking forward to your coming home. I pray every night that it'll be soon.

Ronnie, there's something else I have to tell you. Mom and Dad were against it at first because they felt you have enough to worry about. I had a long talk with them and they finally agreed you should know.

I blinked. A long talk with a twelve-year-old! No. Joanie wasn't the child I left at home. She was almost sixteen, a young woman.

I'll finish grade eleven this June and have decided to become a nurse. There's been so many sick men returned from the war.
It's almost midnight and I have school tomorrow.

All my love,
Joanie

I returned to the regiment in early April, just in time to board a bus for Bailleul, a large French-Flemish town in northern France close to the Belgian border. The town was in British control, with an important railway head, air depot, and hospital. Our destination was La Crèche, a village a mile and a half north of Bailleul, and close to Steenwerck, which was occupied by the Germans. They were advancing toward Bailleul, and our objective was to stop them.

We moved into Steenwerck Station and spread out along a low embankment for one and a half miles of the track. Machine-gun fire blasted us, killing and wounding many. I dreaded that gun more than the shelling, as it had a capacity to kill and maim dozens in seconds. We fought with everything we had, as always, and succeeded in keeping the Germans back. As daylight faded we had no choice but to dig in with the 40th Division on the left and the 34th Division on the right. During the night the regiment was ordered into reserve. Sleep was a luxury, granted sparingly. We praised the stars when we awoke in one piece. Hunger and thirst, inseparable partners, tormented us on a daily basis.

The morning dawned with bad news. The Germans had pushed the British troops out of Estaires, a village just behind Bailleul.

Fred paled. "I never considered the possibility the Germans could actually win the war."

"It's only a setback," Harold said. "I have to believe that."

Captain Burke drank tea from a tin cup. "We've been ordered to the front line. The Hampshires will be on our right, Monmouth Regiment on the left."

All was quiet when we arrived at 4:00 p.m. and moved into position, anticipating an attack at any time. The roar of shelling sounded to the left. A runner arrived, panting, blood smeared across his cheeks. "The Monmouth Regiment is under fire." He paused to catch his breath. "Their orders are to hold tight despite being cut off from other British troops."

"If they're overtaken," Fred said, "the Germans will have an easy route to Bailleul."

The captain agreed. "We'll cover the open flank. Men, face west. The enemy will deal with us if they break through."

And break through they did, coming at us like machines fixated on one idea: to uproot us from our position. Side by side, strung out in a long line, we fired, killing many Germans. They charged, defiant in the wake of so many of their men falling, littering the land, around them.

"If this keeps up," Fred yelled, "there'll be no one left on either side to fight."

The strength of our line diminished as more and more men succumbed to bullets and shrapnel. Captain Burke climbed out of the trench firing his pistol. He raced at the Germans, striking one with every shot. Closing in on the enemy, he stopped and grabbed his leg. Blood flowed between his fingers. A momentary pause, and he fired again.

A bullet ripped into his shoulder. "Fall back to the railway station," he yelled.

Harold grabbed my arm. "We can't leave him."

"Fall back now!" Burke shouted as the butt of a German rifle hit him in the face. The captain wobbled like a broken toy as two Germans soldiers dragged him away.

We retreated to Steenwerck Station, where survivors from other units straggled in along with men from the reserve trenches. We had halted the advance at the cost of hundreds of lives from each regiment.

In reserve that night, I wrote a letter to Captain Burke's father to explain his son's bravery. Two of his four sons were dead in this war, and I wanted to confirm that Will was still alive. Sleep didn't come easy for any of us that night. Fred remained unusually quiet and didn't even light up a cigarette. He shoved his helmet back from his eyes. "I was thinking about the captain and Ches." He hugged his rifle to himself. "I'm tired of seeing good, decent men die."

In the front lines the battles raged on with a superhuman effort by the Germans, and by five o'clock the following evening they had overtaken the British lines, capturing Bailleul. Next they pushed on to De Broeken Road, which was close enough for us to see without a periscope. The Royal Newfoundland Regiment and the dwindled number of British soldiers fought back with equal ferocity to defeat the Germans, resulting in an enormous loss of life.

Without fail and as expected, the Germans commenced another advance. We fired on them, angered, bent on staying our ground with no time to think about home, lost friends, or survival. Sheer will gave us the upper hand. Fighting continued for days, but in the end, overcome by sheer German numbers, we were forced back. They claimed all the territory we had controlled.

Our unit at an all-time low, we marched to billets near Steenvoorde. We ate, hardly aware of what we were putting in our mouths. I blessed my fortune that two of my best friends, Harold Bartlett and Fred Thompson, were still alive. No one talked much that night. One thought stuck in my brain. Hundreds of Newfoundlanders and thousands of other Allied troops perished: lives wasted in the defeat. Weary, the next day we took a short bus drive to meet up with the remainder of the 29th Division.

"I'm sorry to say this," Steven Banters, our new captain, said. His deep voice contrasted with his small frame. "The regiment's numbers are far below normal and there's no immediate reinforcements. We've been taken out of line, which means we're no longer part of the 29th Division."

"Sir, what's next for us?" Fred asked.

"We're moving to Field Marshal Haig's headquarters at Montreuil to give Newfoundland time to send more recruits. We have to rebuild the unit before we can return to battle."

The Newfoundland Regiment had fought alongside the 29th Division since landing in England. We had deserted them.

At the end of April we travelled to Écuries, a village one mile from Montreuil. We remained there for four months. Our duties consisted of guarding the general while he was in the chateau and not allowing admittance to unauthorized personnel. Each morning he'd inspect the guards before taking a leisurely ride on his horse.

"It really annoys me," I said to Harold and Fred, "the way he rides around like a country squire who doesn't have any cares or concerns."

"Me too," Fred said. "The great lord of the manor, or in this case the chateau."

Harold chewed his bottom lip. "I used to wonder if he had sons killed on the front lines."

"What do you mean?" Fred asked.

"He's too content to have suffered the death of a child."

We spoke in whispers because many of the regiment held Field Marshal Haig in the highest esteem, those who hadn't lived through the hell of Beaumont Hamel.

Sport was the one activity every soldier shared, no matter his country of origin. One sunny afternoon, a British unit composed of professional footballers challenged us to a game. Soccer was Newfoundland's national sport, and we were more than happy to oblige. Even more so because Fred and several others were exceptional players.

I sat on the sidelines with Harold, rooting for our team. A player from our side butted the ball to Fred. He caught it with the toe of his right boot and dashed for the opposing net.

Harold jumped to his feet, yelling, "That's it, Fred! Show them what a Newfoundlander can do!"

Shouts and whistles erupted from both sides when Fred's fancy footwork left the professionals stunned. He stood to the side of the net and back-kicked the ball into the top right corner.

"A bloody good game," the goalie from the British team said, shaking Fred's hand at the end of the game. The opposing team won by a slight margin, which didn't bother us at all.

CHAPTER 21

By September the Allied forces were advancing into Belgium on their way to Germany. We were attached to the 28th Infantry Brigade and assigned to Ypres in Belgium. The town was close to the French border and the enemy's front line.

Much weighed on our minds during the four months in Montreuil, away from danger and the disasters of war. Had substantial progress been made? Would the war drag on for four more years?

On September 28, we moved toward Keiberg Ridge, situated halfway between the towns of Keiberg and Passchendaele. The objective was to cross the ridge and proceed over farmland, to capture the farms that had been strongly fortified by the Germans. Many of the farmers had fled, while those who resisted were killed or forced to leave. I was grateful my family would never face such cruelty and displacement.

Captain Banters separated us into small groups, to liberate one farm at a time. Germans fired on us from behind house and barn walls. Unprotected and in the open, we suffered many casualties. Young recruits fought with discipline and valour equal to the experienced. We covered nine miles of enemy territory in two days, with the loss of a hundred men.

As always, we went back to the reserve lines to recuperate. On October 2, we were directed to hold the railway line in the village of Ledeghem. The Germans attacked over the next four days. We held on, men dying, men wounded, hope eternal. By October 4, armistice talks had begun between the Germans and the Allies.

We returned to capturing one farmhouse at a time. "Why the hell are we still fighting?" Fred growled when another of our men was shot dead.

Harold threw a hand bomb into the back door of a house. "I'd guess it's because each side wants to strengthen its bargaining power. We're pushing closer toward Germany." Three Germans emerged through the smoke and debris, coughing and tripping over each other.

Fred fired two shots through a front window. "I prefer not be a bargaining tool." There was a cry of pain from inside the house, then silence.

"Don't worry," Harold said. "At this rate none of us will live long enough for that."

The Allied defensive continued, capturing and reclaiming more and more territory. For the first time since the war began, hope burned alive that we might win this conflict.

We advanced along the town of Courtrai, south of Ledeghem, and crossed over a stream. From out of nowhere a grey, dense mist surrounded the regiment. We stood still, unable to see our own boots. "Is this a new German weapon?" the men questioned among themselves.

Captain Banters sniffed the air. "It's not burning my eyes or affecting my breathing. If we can't see, neither can the Germans."

A new recruit by the first name Phillip cocked his head to one side. "Listen. I hear strange voices."

"It's German," Banters said. "Tread lightly. I don't want bullets flying in this."

We proceeded slowly, then literally bumped into a small group of enemy soldiers. Startled and confused by the mist, they dropped their weapons. In pairs we moved ahead, hands extended like blind men, shouting to each other to stay together.

The vague shape of a house appeared. "We don't know who controls the farm," Banters said. "I don't want to rush the house and get battered by Allied soldiers."

"I have an idea," Harold said, and yelled, "Newfoundland!"

"B'ys, it's us! This is some awful fog," a Newfoundland bay accent replied, certainly an accent no German could ever reproduce.

"Thank the Lord," Fred uttered. "I was afraid I might shoot myself in the foot."

Farther on, we came across another farmhouse. "My turn," Fred said, and called out the word "caribou." There was no reply.

A sound like a chair scraping across the floor came from inside. "Germans for sure," Harold said.

Captain Banters spoke distinctly, using proper English grammar, calling for the Germans to surrender. "If you don't," he added, "we have bombs to persuade you."

A door creaked open and ghostly spectres walked out, hands behind their heads. Two men were dispatched to escort the prisoners back to our line.

The morning wore on and we stuck to our task, calling to each other and groping around in the dense fog. A strong breeze stirred around mid-morning, and slowly the mist dissipated to reveal a wooded area directly before us. Immediately, machine gun bullets ripped into us, killing men caught off guard.

We hurried forward, the bullets felling more men as we sought shelter among bushes too little cover for anyone. "A lot of good a few twigs will do," Fred remarked.

On bended knee, Captain Banters searched the woods with his eyes. "I can't see any of the gunners."

Fred pointed his gun toward the trees. "John Shiwak would have spotted the devil before he got another belt of bullets away."

Stanley Newman, a store clerk from Gander, proposed a plan. "I'll take a small party of men and outflank the Germans, using a Lewis gun."

The captain gave him the go-ahead.

Newman glanced at me. "You up for this, Ron?"

"Yes sir."

"I'd like to go with you," Thomas Ricketts, a seventeen-year-old from White Bay, said. He had joined at fifteen and had proven to be as courageous as any man in the regiment.

Fred raised his eyebrows. "Captain, he's not much more than a youngster. I'll go in his place."

"I appreciate that," the captain said. "However, Ricketts is a soldier and has the right to perform his duty."

I scrambled away with the group and made our way into the woods, firing the Lewis gun as we went, in the hopes of getting behind the now invisible machine guns. We diverted some of the attack from our men and were getting closer to the guns when we ran out of ammunition.

Ricketts spoke up. "I'll go back for some." Without time for anyone to object and take his place, he rushed out of the trees and into full view of the machine guns. Every hidden gun trained on him. He sprinted like a gazelle, his feet lightly touching the ground.

We waited, unprotected like baby chicks with a predator prowling close by. The hail of bullets doubled, and through the trees we spotted Ricketts running toward us, loaded down with ammunition, the miracle we needed.

Fully armed again, we scoured the woods, shooting in every direction, driving the Germans away from their guns. Safe to advance without fear of casualties, the rest of the unit proceeded into the woods. As we moved we captured the fleeing Germans and their field guns.

With many more prisoners in tow, we trudged on for another mile and were ordered to stop for the night.

Fred took out a cigarette. "This is really something to write home about," he said. "We captured five hundred Germans in one day. Can you believe that?" He was about to strike a match but caught the captain's eye. "Wasn't thinking, sir," he said, and stuffed the matchbox and cigarette pack in his pocket. A flash of fire from a match could give away our location, especially on a clear night.

Harold lay back, pulled his helmet down over his forehead, and crossed his arms on his chest. "Five hundred Germans captured. Twenty-six of the regiment died in the process," he said quietly.

On October 20, the Royal Newfoundland Regiment arrived at the River Lys for another confrontation. Spirits had improved among the men, for we were almost at Germany's doorstep, and covering this great distance into enemy territory meant only one thing. The end of the war was in sight.

Many times we had to cross in deep water as bridges had been blown up by the retreating German army. We waded in calm water to the other side and pressed on, drawing closer to Germany. At the end of October we were relieved from the front line position and headed back to billets in Harlebeke, where rumours of peace pervaded the air like the smell of freshly baked bread.

On November 9, Harold and Fred burst into my room looking like they'd each been given a thousand dollars to spend. "The Kaiser abdicated," Fred shouted. He whooped and kicked up his heels.

"Are you sure?"

"Without a doubt," Harold said. Fred linked an arm with him and swung around.

"Does that mean the war's over?"

"Not yet," Harold said. "That'll be the next step."

Two days later, on the eleventh hour, on the eleventh day of the eleventh month, Germany officially surrendered. Bells rang out in every church in France. People danced and sang in the streets. Allied soldiers became revered heroes, thanked over and over for liberating their beloved country. French soldiers had suffered millions of casualties. Finally, the people were free from the constant threat of death that had become ingrained in the hearts and souls of every man, woman, and child.

The land itself had suffered extensive damage, which would take years to repair, to heal from the scars of bombs, shelling, and trenches that disfigured the countryside. Thousands of soldiers from both sides who hadn't been afforded an official burial lay somewhere beneath the bruised soil.

On the thirteenth of December, the Royal Newfoundland Regiment crossed the Rhine River into Germany. "It's an odd feeling," Harold said, "not to have to listen for every sound, to watch for every movement that might signal danger."

"Say that again," Fred piped in. "I can't wait to get back to Scotland and see my missus."

The people in Germany were subdued: a humbled, worn-out nation. Yet again, they'd been given no other recourse than to endure the whims of their leaders.

We were stationed in Hildon, near Cologne on the River Rhine. It was an old cathedral city and a military stronghold in northwestern Germany. The regiment was assigned to bridge-head duties, which consisted of guarding bridges leading into Germany.

"Police duty again," I complained to Harold and Fred. "I thoroughly dislike keeping troops in order."

Fred smiled to himself. "Remember the night both of you forced me and Ches to shake hands?"

"Yes. The townie and the bayman were at it again."

"What I don't relish," Fred said, "is enforcing the restrictions on German civilians."

Harold watched a woman holding the hand of a small child as they walked down the street. "I see the logic behind the no-fraternization rule with the Germans. Still, it's sad youngsters have to feel like they're a danger we have to avoid."

While off duty I took walks through the quaint alleys of the city, which were lined with centuries-old houses quite different from our wooden red or green painted houses back home. The old town hall was the oldest public building in Germany, dating back at least 200 years.

The Allied troops, taken prisoner over the course of the war, had been released. Uppermost on our minds were Gord Abbott and Captain William Burke. While coming off bridgehead duty one afternoon, a pale, thin man waved to me. "Ronnie, old friend. I heard you were here." He threw his arms around me. "It's great to see you alive and well." He drew back and shook my hand. The palms were hard, callused. "You look so much older than I recall."

I knew if I spoke at that moment I'd break into tears. A deep breath slowed my pounding heart. "Gord, we never gave up the hope you were alive."

He rubbed his thigh. "Let's go for a beer." I led him to a bar I frequented with Fred and Harold. We each drank a tankard of German brew. Gord broke the silence. "I thought you'd been killed at Beaumont Hamel."

"I was badly injured. A stay in a London hospital whipped me back into shape."

A barmaid asked if we needed refills. I declined, while Gord ordered another.

"Gord, Captain Will Burke was captured a few months back."

The tankard halfway to his mouth, Gord placed it back on the table. "Yes, I heard news of him. Gangrene set into his wounds. The German doctors did all they could. He died a month later."

"His poor parents. Two of his brothers were killed at Beaumont Hamel."

"When he knew the end was near, he asked me to give you a message for his parents. He didn't have the strength to write it down."

Gord related the last words of a dying man, pausing every now and again to take a drink. When he finished, he passed me an envelope. "This is for his wife. He penned it soon after his capture."

I sighed. "He'd gotten married a few months before enlisting."

"The German doctors took real good care of our wounds." Gord gulped down half the tankard. "Only because they wanted healthy strong men to work in the rock quarries. That's backbreaking work for sure."

Gord hadn't mentioned Ches. Perhaps he was scared to ask. I couldn't leave him in the dark any longer. "Ches didn't make it."

"What happened?"

"It was last year at Cambrai." I slowly pushed my beer from side to side on the table, vowing in my head never to reveal the extent of his injuries. "He died saving my life. I didn't hear the shell until Ches pushed me out of its path."

Gord looked even more haggard. "I'm glad his death saved another life."

I took out the medal and chain that Ches had entrusted to me. "He asked me to give this to his wife if you couldn't. Gord, even at the end he hadn't given up on you."

"Did he say anything else?"

"He wanted his children to go to school, to leave the fishing life behind. I promised to look after his family in your place if you didn't make it."

Gord took the medal. "Thank you, Ron. Isabelle will cherish this."

He rejoined the unit, a welcome Christmas treat for the few survivors of the First Five Hundred, the Blue Puttees. The name Joey Baker feared would be forgotten.

Two days later, following a performance of the Trooping of Colour, a ceremony which consisted of marching in public behind our military flag bearing the colours claret—a sort of reddish shade—and white, Major Bernard commanded us to form three sides of a square.

"Now what's the matter?" Fred asked, getting into formation. "It better not be bad news."

Bernard's face smacked of pride. "Hurry, men."

Fred grinned. "He looks like a youngster with his first lollipop."

The men quieted down and the major addressed us. "Field Marshal Haig has notified me that Private Thomas Ricketts has been awarded the Victoria Cross. The youngest man in the British army to ever receive it."

"That's the highest and most honoured medal ever given," Harold murmured from the side of his mouth.

Major Bernard turned toward Ricketts. "Private Ricketts, step forward. I would like to congratulate you."

Ricketts, the true, dignified soldier, marched to the major, saluted, and stood to attention. Bernard shook his hand and complimented his bravery.

Ricketts, displaying no visible reaction, marched back to his place in the ranks. We cheered as if we'd all won the medal, clapped him on the back, and shook his hand.

The official investiture took place on January 21, 1919 at York Cottage in Sandringham, England.

As we were unable to attend, we threw a thousand questions at Ricketts when he returned.

"Well," he began in his quiet, unobtrusive manner. "The king introduced me to his daughter, Princess Mary, as the youngest recipient of the Victoria Cross in his army. During a wonderful meal he asked about life in Newfoundland and commented on the excellent performance of our regiment."

CHAPTER 22

RETURN TO NEWFOUNDLAND
MAY 1919

High spirits abounded throughout the regiment when in early February our role as part of the occupation forces was terminated. On the eleventh we boarded the train for Rouen in France, a city situated on the River Seine, 130 kilometres northwest of Paris. I would soon see the very place Joan of Arc had been burned alive at the stake.

Fred sat down in a window seat. "Then on to England. I'll pick up my wife in Scotland, and we're off to good old Newfoundland." He stretched his feet out as best he could, considering the limited space. "My family will love her."

"Cherish her every day," Gord said.

"That I will. As I'm sure you will cherish your wife when you marry."

Gord simply smiled.

The men occupied themselves by playing cards and talking about their former jobs and loved ones waiting for them. I watched the River Rhine speed past, marvelling at the fact the war was over and I had survived. If only my cousin Henry and

Joey Baker were here. And Sid Tremblett. And Ches. Dark green forests replaced the river and I turned away to play cards with Harold and Fred.

When we arrived in Rouen, we discovered the regiment was to be stationed there for an indefinite period of time. Worse, our new role was to guard German prisoners around the clock.

"Goddamn it," Fred swore, his face redder than a boiled lobster. "The war's been over for months. Why the hell are there still prisoners of war, and why the hell are we burdened with guarding them?"

I shrugged. "Our injured have been sent home. That's a start."

Fred elbowed Gord. "I don't get why you refused to go home when you had the chance."

Gord gazed at the people milling around the station. "I wasn't ready."

He had talked very little about his time as a prisoner of war. I worried from the first time we reported together for guard duty. Close to three years as a captive had left him thin and weak. Time would take care of those things, but his humour and vitality had eroded, and learning about Ches's death hadn't improved his bleak mood.

The prisoners were in the courtyard, many of them as young as fourteen, scared, not knowing what fate lay in store for them. A German soldier crouched low in a corner, away from the other prisoners. He looked to be sixteen or seventeen and peered at us with pure terror in his eyes. His left cheek was badly bruised. Had he been mistreated by one of us?

"I'll be right back," Gord said, and walked toward him. The soldier stiffened. Gord took out a cigarette, lit it, and said a few words in German. The boy stood up and accepted the cigarette.

"You picked up a little German," I said when Gord sauntered back.

"Enough to get by."

I indicated the soldier with a nod. "Did a guard give him the bruise?"

"Not one of ours. I promised him he'll see home soon."

The boy put out the half-smoked cigarette with his fingers, stuffed it in his pocket, and joined a group of comrades playing cards.

Boredom breeds an exaggerated desire for home, which in turn breeds frustration. The men grew more restless with each day.

"We signed up for the duration," Fred said. "The war's been over for six months. I'll row across the ocean myself if we don't get out of here soon."

Even Harold didn't complain when we boarded a ship for Southampton, England. "What's a few hours?" he said, hanging over the side of the ship. Calm seas helped soothe the queasiness in my stomach, a minor complaint compared to Harold's gaunt, grey complexion. The ship docked, with Harold scurrying on to dry land before anyone else. We proceeded to Hazeley Down Camp, a few miles from Southampton. "I'd almost forgotten how awful seasickness is," he said on the short trek to the camp.

We settled into huts with the same question on every man's lips. "When are we going home?"

Captain Banters delivered the answer. "There are thousands of solders here, mostly Canadians, just as eager to return home. Sorry, boys. I'm afraid we'll have to wait a little longer."

"Jesus Christ!" Fred roared, and threw up his hands. "The transportation of the troops across the Atlantic is slower than the tanks were at Cambrai."

"How slow was that?" Gord asked with a serious face.

"Four miles an hour."

Banters smiled. "I have good news as well. You're all entitled to ten days leave anywhere in England or Scotland." He cocked an eyebrow at Fred. "I take it you'll skip this leave."

"The king himself wouldn't prevent me from going to Scotland." As soon as he procured the pass he rushed off to Scotland, clean shaven and wearing a fresh shirt. Most of the men chose Scotland to say goodbye to friendships forged there.

The day after leave began, I ran into Jean Lasalle, the French Canadian from New Brunswick I'd met while training in bayonet practice. A very pretty dark-haired girl held his arm.

"Ron, this is my wife, Lise. She's from Marcoing." He smiled at the girl. "Lise, je te presente Ron Marrie."

"Vous etes Francophone comme mon mari."

"She thinks you are a native French speaker like me because of your last name." Jean rambled off in French to Lise, then turned to me. "I explained the origin of your name."

Lise smiled. I couldn't help but notice a hint of sadness as well. "'Ello," she said with a thick accent. "'Appy to meet you."

"She speaks very little English." Jean patted her hand. "She has plenty of time to learn. A shell hit her house. Her parents and brother were killed, and I'm all she has now."

Innocents had suffered as much or more than the soldiers.

"We drink tea," Lise said, her voice softer than a cotton blanket. "You come us?"

"Avec plaisir," I said, remembering a few words from my limited knowledge of the language. We sat around a table in a small tea house and enjoyed tea and raisin scones. We talked about the friends lost and what we hoped to do in the future. The future was a concept I had never once dared indulge in during the war. We exchanged addresses and parted company. Many of the Canadian troops, including Jean and Lise's, left for Canada the next day.

The Victory Parade to celebrate the Allied win was scheduled for May 3 in London. The Royal Newfoundland Regiment was privileged to participate. I imagined what Ches's response would be to that. Privilege my arse. We more than earned the right to be in the parade. Sable Chief, a Newfoundland dog and the regiment's mascot, led us as we marched through the streets filled with throngs of spectators. The king saluted us as we passed, a positive memory to cling to when recalling the war years.

We went back to camp with no fixed date for our return home. The weeks dragged by, and the men were beginning to believe we'd disintegrate into this foreign land, forgotten by the people who'd brought us over.

One glorious sunny morning, Captain Banters clasped his hands in the air. "Pack your bags, boys! We're going home." On May 22, we boarded the SS *Corsican*, which would take us directly to Newfoundland, where the land and inhabitants were never far from our hearts and minds. The men who'd married foreigners had boarded earlier in the day with their new wives.

Harold breathed deeply as the ship pulled away from the dock. "Ten days on the water." He blew air through his lips. "Concentrating on the finish line will get me through it."

The first few days I attended concerts and played bridge while supplying Harold with dry bread and water. The simple effort of raising his head from the pillow caused him to vomit. Each day seemed longer than the one before, and my thoughts, as did those of my shipmates, centred on those left behind. I, one of the First Five Hundred, a Blue Puttee, was one of the very few survivors. Men who had loved Newfoundland would never again stand on its shores, laugh, love, cry, marry, have or see children grow, become prime minister, develop a cure for cancer. A generation of young men had been abandoned in a war-torn land. Would their bravery, their sacrifice, their names, fade from memory? Fade from history?

A woman's laugher, soft and sweet, penetrated the gloom that hung over me like a cold, wet overcoat.

Fred's firm hand gripped mine. "Come on, lad. A strong

drink will cheer you up." He winked at his wife. "What do you say, love?"

"Aye," Eileen said in her soft Scottish brogue. "And I'll pour it. We're on the way to a new, happier life."

On the last day of May, word went round the ship faster than a bird in flight that we were approaching St. John's. I stood at the rail with Fred, my hair damp from the fog blocking out the landscape. "This is absolute proof we're home," he said. "No place in the world produces fog thicker than thunderclouds."

The fog concealed the seagulls squawking above us. Uneven footsteps approached us, and Harold came out of the grey mist. He'd thinned out by a good ten pounds. "The ship's captain reduced speed to a crawl," he said, "to cut down the risk of colliding with other ships."

Fred hugged himself. "It's cold and damp. This time of year there's bound to be icebergs out there."

I caught a few hours of sleep during the night and was the first to stand on deck as the ship approached the Narrows. In no time, every soldier stood with me, their eyes on the thousands crowding the harbourfront. Rain pelted down. We saw dozens of small crafts surrounding the ship as if it were a king's carriage, their unfurled flags blowing in the wind. They blasted their whistles, the shrill noise sweet music.

We disembarked and marched through the downtown streets to the praise and applause of the people following us to Government House. The rain beat into the ground, the tap, tap keeping time with the marching tap, tap of our boots, but we stayed in formation as the rain stung our faces.

Gord stared into the crowd as if searching for someone. "It won't be long now," he said.

Sir Alexander Harris, the Governor, greeted us with all the rhetoric that politicians spew out and took custody of the Regiment's Colours, to be held in a place of honour in his official residence.

The cold air had restored a little colour to Harold's cheeks. "Thank God I lived to see this day. One more official duty and we're free," he said.

The rain bounced off roofs as we marched to the skating rink for another speech from the Prime Minister.

"He better keep his speech short," a man behind groaned.

"Yeah," another agreed.

The Prime Minister welcomed us home, and I knew we all held our collective breaths, hoping that would be the extent of his talk. Shoulders slumped ever so slightly when he spoke of our heroism and the Empire's pride.

Fred turned an angry shade of red. "For Jesus' sake, get it over with," he mumbled.

The Prime Minister concluded the speech and wished us well in civilian life. No longer soldiers of war, we turned in our rifles and bayonets to the quartermaster.

"Ronnie."

I turned. Joanie pushed aside strands of curly hair plastered to her forehead. A drop of rain hung from the tip of her nose like a teardrop. My little sister wasn't little anymore. She'd grown at least four inches taller and was more a woman than the child I'd longed to see.

She hugged me and I could feel her heart drum. "Ronnie, don't ever leave again."

"You have my word." An easy promise to keep.

My mother ran toward me, tears mingling with the rain running down her face. "My boy's home," she murmured softly into my ear.

My father held his salt and pepper cap in his hands despite the rain lashing at his head. "Son, it's grand to have you home." His voice trembled. "Jack told us about your injuries. You look well."

I looked around. "Jack is home?"

My mother took my arm. "He arrived a month ago. We're having Jiggs' dinner, your favourite. Aunt Elsie is keeping it hot."

I didn't see Frank. "The Forestry Corps aren't back?"

"Oh yes," my father said. "Both he and Jack wanted to give us time alone."

Gord stood a little behind me and to my right. He looked out of place, alone, hands in his pockets.

My mother followed my gaze. "A friend," she said.

"Gordon Abbott."

I opened my mouth to speak to him when a female voice called his name. I stared at the woman in Ches's photo. Tall, slim, a clear complexion, and blonde hair. "Gord," she said, a sad smile on her lips. "It's wonderful to see you." A young girl held the hands of young boys, who pulled free and jumped into Gord's arms. He lifted them high in the air as the girl leaned into her mother. Ches's Little Lilly would never see her daddy again.

My body shook. Waves of dizziness overwhelmed me. I was the reason the husband and father was dead.

Joanie watched me. Perceptive, even as a child, she somehow understood the emotions running through me. "Come on, Ronnie. Aunt Elsie is beside herself waiting to see you."

My father led the way. "We'll treat ourselves to a taxi."

"You all go ahead, Dad. I'd like to walk."

Mom kissed my cheek. "We'll see you at the house."

Joanie's hair hung in strings around her face and neck, and water pooled around her rubbed boots. "Can I walk with you?"

I nodded and turned up my collar against the wind and cold. Joanie strode alongside me, humming softly to herself. Her quiet company kept away unwanted thoughts that chewed at my insides. It was strange being home, like I was in the midst of a dream. Any second a shell or machine gun would yank me awake. Joanie spoke for the first time as we stopped outside our house. "Ronnie, Uncle Jack was badly hurt in the war. Mom and

Dad didn't want to tell you right away and spoil your homecoming. I wanted to warn you before we went in."

"How bad is it?"

The front door opened and my mother called us in. Joanie hurried inside.

Frank and Jack sat together on the sofa. Both looked up at me with a welcoming smile. My father lounged in the armchair by the fireplace. Flames crackled in the grate, producing a spitting noise not unlike the sound of a machine gun.

Frank stood up and came toward me, one leg straight, and shook my hand. He'd never done that before. Then again, we were no longer boys just out of high school. "It's been a long time, Ron." He looked much older, as I must have looked to him. There was also a maturity about him, imprinted by more than the passage of years.

I hadn't realized I was staring at his leg until he spoke. "A war souvenir."

My eyes went to Jack. A red and yellow checkered blanket covered his knees and reached down to the floor. Down to one shoe. My heart lurched. I couldn't believe it.

"My war souvenir," Jack said, his smile never wavering. "Thank God it wasn't my arm. Now that would've really hampered my role as a surgeon."

Aunt Elsie appeared from the kitchen and wrapped her arms around me. "Ron, you're a sight to behold." She'd lost considerable weight and I caught myself gaping at her hair, which had gone completely white. She was only forty-five.

She wound a few fine strands around her finger. "This is my war souvenir."

The front door opened and a pretty brunette with laughing eyes came directly to me. "You must be Ron." The quaint Scottish accent was barely detectable. "I'm Kathleen, Frank's wife. It's a pleasure to finally meet you."

Supper was filled with lively conversation about politics and the effect of the war on Newfoundland. I had nothing to say. Halfway through the meal I laid down my fork. "Please excuse me, everyone. I'm awfully tired."

"Of course," my mother said, as if it was the most normal thing for me to request.

My bedroom was the same as I'd left it. The binocular curtains in place, the hardcover book sitting on the bedside table, opened to the page I'd last read. All the gifts Joanie had saved for me rested on the bed. I put them on the floor and lay on top of the bed, fully clothed in my uniform. The hours ticked by with me staring at the ceiling, my mind blank. The house was so quiet it kept me awake. During the war I slept whenever the opportunity presented itself. I turned to look through the hole in the curtain. The sky was overcast with not a single star visible. There weren't any Germans to fear, no gas, shells, or machine guns would strike when least suspected. My brain had registered that new reality, but my body hadn't had time to catch up. The floor outside my room creaked and I pretended to be asleep. My door slowly opened, and I knew it was Mom. I opened my eyes when the door closed, feeling guilty for not wanting to talk to anyone.

Someone coughed. I bolted upright, alert, eyes darting around the room. My room, not a dugout. I lay back down and rolled onto my side. The first rays of early morning sun cast shadows along the wall. Morning sounds penetrated through the window: birds chirped, a car engine stalled and caught again.

I closed my eyes.

The roar of guns boomed overhead, the whistling noise signalling the shells were close. The sky was black with smoke. I huddled into the side of the trench. The ground shook, and clay spilled over me. Another explosion sent dirt flying into the air. Then silence, unbearable silence. I heard the gagging noise of someone struggling to breathe. A hand clawed at my arm. It was

Charlie Paterson's; his mouth and nose were plugged with mud. He can't be here, he died in Gallipoli. I reached for him, but he vanished.

There was movement outside the trench. I peered over the top. A face stared down at me. I aimed my rifle.

"Ron, it's me. Jack."

"Oh, God," I whispered. I was crouching on the floor next to my bed.

"It's all right, Ron. The nightmares will fade with time."

CHAPTER 23

PROMISES TO KEEP

I accompanied Frank to work the following day. The sights and sounds were familiar and unfamiliar all at once. We walked at a brisk pace despite Frank's lame leg. "You like working for Mr. Burke?" I asked.

"It surprised me, but I do. He says I have a natural ability and thinks I'm best suited for criminal law." Frank glanced sideways at me. "Mr. Burke would welcome you back to the office." We crossed the street, weaving between cars. "If your heart is in it," Frank added when we stepped onto the sidewalk.

"My heart's not into much these days." The words spilled out, a sentiment I hadn't been able to define until now.

Frank didn't miss a stride in his steady gait. "Ron, I promise, purpose will come back to you. Give it time."

Mrs. Lawlor pulled me into an embrace as soon as I came through the door. "Ron, my boy, you look grand. I'm delighted you made it home. Let me make you a nice cup of tea."

I disengaged myself from her stranglehold. "Thank you, but no, Mrs. Lawlor. Is Mr. Burke in?"

"He'll be delighted to see you." She wiped at her softly falling tears. "He took Will's death awfully hard, especially after losing two of his other . . ." She rushed out of the office, openly sobbing.

"Poor Mrs. Lawlor," Frank said. "She's been like that since her own son was mistakenly reported killed at Beaumont Hamel." He indicated Mr. Burke's office. "Go ahead. He'll welcome the interruption."

I tapped on the door and opened it. "Mr. Burke, I hope I'm not bothering you."

He looked at me a long moment without speaking. "Come in, Ron and have a seat." He took off his glasses and laid them on his desk.

He'd aged. There were new wrinkles around his eyes and his cheeks were sunken. The loss of loved ones, especially in the prime of life, added an extra weight to grief.

"Will wrote me often about you. He was proud of your performance."

"I wanted to tell you how Will was captured." I paused, surprised by the tears welling in my eyes, which I managed to hold back.

Mr. Burke took a handkerchief from his pocket and blew his nose. It's funny how men pretend their noses are running when in reality it's how they fight through emotion.

"He fought off the enemy despite being wounded, giving his men the chance to escape with their lives."

Mr. Burke blew his nose again.

"Gordon Abbott, one of the Blue Puttees captured at Beaumont Hamel, was with Will when he died. Gangrene set into his wounds. Before he . . . passed, he asked Gord to tell me that he wanted you to know he didn't regret signing up to fight. He did what he thought was right and would do it all over again. He loved you and knew you'd take care of his wife."

Mr. Burke stood and went to the window. "Then he never knew Charlotte became with child on his one leave home."

"Yes, he did know. He received the letter the day he was captured. I'd never seen a happier man."

Mr. Burke turned to me. The harsh lines around his mouth had suddenly smoothed. "Ron, the thought my son died without knowing he was a father has tortured me." He turned back to the window. "Thank you for letting me know."

"I'm sorry about and Ted and Wayne. Beaumont Hamel was a difficult battle."

"Thank you. At least Gus made it home uninjured. His safe return and our new grandchild has given me and Mrs. Burke the strength to go on."

I took Will's letter from my coat. "Will wrote this to his wife shortly after his capture."

"Poor Charlotte. She hasn't quite forgiven him for leaving her here. Please God this letter will help." Mr. Burke returned to his desk and put the letter in the top drawer. "You can start back to work whenever you're ready."

"That's kind of you, sir, but I'm going to pursue journalism."

"I'd sensed that working here wasn't really in your future." Mr. Burke reached across the desk and shook my hand. "Good luck in your new endeavour, Ron."

I bade him farewell and headed for home to fill my father in on my new career choice. Along the way I stopped off to see Harold Bartlett. He was in the backyard repairing the picket fence. Five years of neglect had loosened half of the pickets.

"How'd you sleep last night?" I asked, holding out a handful of nails.

He yawned. "By the dark circles under your eyes I'd guess about the same as you."

I strode to the back steps and sat down. Harold laid down

his hammer and sat with me. "Everything's the same, yet different in a way I can't explain," he said, stretching out his legs.

"For me, too. Maybe everything will return to normal once we get used to being home."

Harold looked at a maple tree in the far corner, where a roped swing hung from a branch. "I put that there for Lucy. Mom had the hardest time getting her off it." His gaze wandered back to me. "My baby sister's gone. It won't ever be normal without her."

I stood and leaned against the house. Staying still was difficult for me these days. "Have you made any decisions about your future?"

"I thought a lot about that on the ship home." Harold pulled a blade of grass from the ground. "It may sound stupid, but I want to work at something that makes people's lives better."

"Anything particular in mind?"

"A teacher. Being able to read and write can lead to many opportunities." Harold smiled, one of his rare ones. "You couldn't be a journalist without those skills."

I unbuttoned my coat and threw it on the steps. "Got another hammer?"

My father was still at work when I arrived home and broached the subject of a career in journalism with my mother while she set the table. "I'm happy you haven't let that dream go by the wayside."

"Dad will be disappointed."

"Not at all."

"Mom, he's always wanted me to be a lawyer."

The pea soup bubbled on the stove. She lifted the lid and tasted it. "Almost done." She stepped around me. "He got over that years ago. I told him the day you shipped out about your dream to pursue journalism."

"What did he say?"

"Ron, your father isn't as stubborn as you think. Besides, I warned him to get over it and move on."

The next day, Gord showed up around mid-morning with Isabelle, Ches's wife. A cup of tea in hand, we sat at the kitchen table. "The children and I are staying with my parents for a few weeks," she said. "Gord thinks me and the children should move to St. John's permanently." She raised the cup to her lips, then lowered it before drinking any tea. "Bonavista is . . . was Ches's home. That's where he'd want his children raised." She swallowed to keep the tears from welling up.

"Ron," Gord said, "I told Isabelle you were with Ches when he died. She needs to hear what he said to you about, wished for, the children."

Isabelle's fingers tightened around the cup. "Did Ches suffer?"

"No." I believed that to be true.

"Ches told me he didn't want the boys to be fishermen, said it was too hard a life."

"And that's all they'll be if they stay where they are," Gord said.

"Your mother and younger brother are there."

"Ron, I'm moving them to St. John's with me."

Gord reached into his pants pockets and took out the St. Christopher medal, and turned to Isabelle. "Ches passed this on to Ron to be given to you." He placed it in the palm of Isabelle's hand. "It was important to him that you have it."

Isabelle smiled, and she became even more beautiful. "We met in Mass on Easter Sunday. He gave me this medal on our first date." She folded her hand around it and held it to her heart. "As a keepsake of where he'd first seen me."

I looked at Gord. "I didn't know you were Catholic."

"I'm not. Ches saw Isabelle going into the church and followed her in. He told me he knew right then he wanted to marry her."

She laughed, a sound as smooth as honey. "I couldn't be mad at him when he told me that."

"Ches married in the Catholic Church," Gord said, "and agreed to raise his children in the Catholic faith. Our mother took a bit of time getting used to that."

"He kept his promise," Isabelle said. "Ches was a man of his word." She smiled again. "My parents didn't approve of him at first. A fisherman from around the bay who couldn't read or write, and a Protestant! They changed their minds when they saw what a good husband and wonderful father he was."

We drank our tea in silence, a sort of reverence to Ches.

I approached the *Daily News* with my desire to work for the paper. My standing as a Blue Puttee and survivor of Beaumont Hamel gained me immediate access to the owner. He was doubly impressed with my high school diploma and offered me a job on the spot. I'd been afforded the means and opportunity to work my way up the ranks to journalist. I conveyed the news to my family at supper that night. Although in my twenties, I was nervous about my father's reaction.

He buttered a slice of bread. "I guess that means we'll hear the latest goings-on before anyone else in town." He glanced at Joanie, then back to me. "There'll be a journalist and a nurse in the family. No man could be prouder of his children."

When everyone had gone to bed, I sat in the living room, gazing into the fireplace. The flames licked high into the chimney, taking away the chill. A knock came on the door around ten and I hurried to open it. Four of my fighting comrades stood before me: Fred, Frank, Harold, and Gord. I moved aside for them to come in, neither of us uttering a word.

Gord was the first to speak once we were seated in the living room. "I missed you fellows. We were a family over there. I wanted to get together with all of you before heading back to Bonavista to see my mother and younger brother."

"Are Isabelle and the children going with you?" I asked.

Gord held his hands out to the fire to warm them. "She decided to stay in St. John's, to give the children a better life, like Ches wanted. I have no idea how I'll make a living once I'm back here."

My father's employment popped into my head. "You can check out working on the docks as a stevedore."

"Unloading ships can't be any harder than setting and hauling fishing nets and trawls."

Fred leaned back in the armchair and folded his hands behind his head. "My family adores Eileen. She was worried what they'd think of her." He smiled. "She's already calling my mother 'Mom.'"

"Harold," Frank said, "how has it been coming home with your sister Lucy gone?"

"I'm still getting used to it."

Frank sighed. "It's like a part of you is missing."

"It's funny," I said. "I can't bring myself to talk to anyone who wasn't in the war about my experiences there."

"I know what you mean," Gord said. "Isabelle has asked me to talk about the war with regards to Ches, but I don't where to start."

Frank leaned forward, hands clutching the ends of the armrests, his face hidden in the shadows. "When Henry was shot, I knew even before he went down that he was dead. It sounds strange, but I felt his life force ebb away."

Fred chuckled. "Ron, remember the night in France when Sid Tremblett was getting ready to go to a certain residence? Sid begged you to go with him, but Ches made up an excuse for you."

"Later, he encouraged me to go, and I did. Ches was like a father to many of us. I know when Charlie Paterson died, he was really upset."

"Being older and a father," Gord said, "he had a protective side. Although the man could be a grumpy sod, and short-tempered, except with Isabelle and his children."

"True," I muttered.

Fred stared down at the floor. "I really thought Ches and Sid would make it."

Gord went to the fireplace. "I ran into Captain Wakefield's mother this morning. I don't know who told her, but she thanked me for trying to save him."

"In all likelihood it was Chaplain Murray," I said. "He's been going around visiting the families of soldiers killed over there."

Harold dropped his chin into his hands, an expression of contempt on his face. "I wonder if Field Marshal Haig still takes his morning jaunts?"

"Hmph," Fred said. "The war didn't interfere with his leisure time. Why the hell would peacetime stop him?"

Frank reached for his cane. "I'll be right back," he said, and went into the kitchen. He returned with five glasses and passed one to each of us.

"What's this about?" I asked.

He pulled out a bottle of overproof rum. "Let's drink to our absent comrades, the men we left behind." He poured three fingers into each glass. "We were all well aware we didn't stand much of a chance at Beaumont Hamel."

"You can say that again," Fred said.

Frank held out his glass. "We went over regardless, frightened, none of us never having fought before."

"To brave men lost," Harold said.

Fred went next. "To the ultimate sacrifice."

We looked at Gord. "Never forget those who died."

All eyes turned to me. "To everlasting peace."

We each threw back our heads and downed the liquor in one swallow.

CHAPTER 24

THE EVENING TELEGRAM
St. John's, Newfoundland
July 7, 1970

Another veteran has answered the last roll call. Comrade Gordon Abbott, 81 years young, passed away at his residence, 15 Flower Hill, St. John's, last week.

Comrade Abbott and his older brother, Ches, served with the Royal Newfoundland Regiment, each having been a Blue Puttee with a distinguished record. Gordon and Ches served in Gallipoli, Gordon evacuated to England with life-threatening dysentery.

During the first day of the Battle of the Somme, July 1, at Beaumont Hamel, Gordon reached the enemy front line trench, was captured and taken prisoner for the rest of the war. It is worthy to note his brother gave his life to save that of another Blue Puttee during the Cambrai campaign of 1917.

To the exact day that Comrade Abbott was laid to rest, we are honouring his former comrades in the Royal Newfoundland Regiment who were killed July 1, 1916, when approximately 800 men went over the top and only 68 answered roll call the next day.

Comrade Abbott was laid to rest at Holy Sepulchre Cemetery after Requiem Mass at St. Patrick's R.C. Church, Patrick Street. Former comrades who served in the Regiment and Blue Puttees were in attendance. Comrade Abbott was a well-known member of the Knights of Columbus, who offered themselves as pall-bearers. The family thanked the Knights for their kindness, but Gordon Abbott's two nephews, Philip Abbott and Wesley Abbott, and four godsons—Henry Marrie, James Thompson, Norman Bartlett, and Herbert Corcoran—undertook the privilege.

Fred Thompson, a Blue Puttee, a close friend and member of the Royal Canadian Legion, recited the Legion ritual at the gravesite.

Days of danger, nights of waking
Dream of battlefields no more
Sleep the sleep that knows no waking
Veterans rest their warfare o'er

I closed the newspaper and laid it on the coffee table. The house was quiet and I was alone with my thoughts. My dear wife, Sheila, passed away five years before, soon after my retirement from the *Daily News*, where I served as editor-in-chief. I was thankful all but one of my children lived in the city and stopped by on a regular basis.

Jean Lasalle and his family often visited and vacationed in Newfoundland. My youngest girl, Emma, married one of his boys and moved to New Brunswick. Their three children speak French like a native. Ches, my middle child, was killed in World War II, underaged and not much older than I when I enlisted. Sheila was furious, and although I wanted to lock him away for the duration, I persuaded her to allow him to choose his own course. The war I had participated in was supposed to end all wars, yet in reality it triggered more conflicts around the world.

We sent our son off to war with feigned smiles. I now understood with a gut-wrenching ache my parents' fear at my departure. Each morning waking up sick with anxiety that this might be the day you learn the tragic news: your child was dead or reported missing in action. I got down on my knees and prayed that Britain's military leaders had learned from their mistakes in the Great War.

On a bleak, cloudy day, the dreaded news arrived. Ches had been killed evacuating a wounded man to safety. The soldier he saved came to see Sheila and me after the war, to tell us about the day our son died. Life is ironic with its unexpected twists and turns. Ches, my good friend, and Ches, my son, both lost in a World War saving the life of another. I'd once questioned if events occurred for a reason or if they were simply fate. The answer still eludes me.

Times were hard for the country in the years following the war to end all wars. Twenty per cent of the young men who signed up had died. Thousands more returned, requiring medical treatment, rehabilitation or long-term care. Medical care and pensions for veterans drained the government. None of this compared to the grief over a loved one never recovered or buried thousands of miles away. There's a measure of comfort in visiting a gravesite. I was robbed of that comfort with my own son.

Years later, excerpts from Haig's diary and letters to his wife during the war were published. I shed tears over one comment he'd written about the first day of the Battle of the Somme, when

20,000 men died and 40,000 were wounded. The words caused me to tremble for years after. Such a figure cannot be considered severe in view of the numbers engaged, and the length of the front attacked, wrote General Rawlinson, also high up in the chain of command. Although the casualties had been "heavy," there were plenty of fresh divisions behind.

Fred Thompson had five children, four daughters and one son. He danced with joy at the birth of each girl. "I don't want boys," he told me after the birth of his fourth daughter. "Girls aren't obliged to fight in wars." His luck seemed to have run out on the fifth when his son, James, arrived, a healthy ten-pounder. We didn't know then, but his luck held because James was born in 1936; he was much too young to even realize that a war raged in Europe.

Once a month I got together with my Blue Puttee buddies for a few drinks and conversation. Today would be the first time without Gord.

The doorbell sang its musical tune, and before I had time to rise from the armchair, Frank, Harold, and Fred shuffled in, old men like me.

Frank's cane rhythmically tapped the hardwood floor as he led the way into the living room. He carried something in a paper bag. "Fred, go get four glasses from the kitchen."

Fred placed two fingers against the side of his forehead and saluted. "Righty-o, Commander," he said, and went down the hall.

Harold stepped around Frank. "You've taught Freddy well, old man."

Frank's knee was stiffer with the passage of time. He eased himself down into the sofa, and hung his cane off the arm.

Fred hurried back with the glasses rattling in his hands. "Come on, Frank. Break out the Screech. I've got an awful thirst."

Frank opened the paper bag and took out a forty-ounce

bottle. "Overproof rum, they called it in our day." I detected a sadness in his voice.

Fred reached for the bottle and studied the dark liquid. "Screech better describes its effect on you, in my opinion."

Harold chuckled. "And who better to comment than the former rum-runner?"

"Now, hold on. I was part of a legitimate trade in my youth, not like the crowd who smuggled liquor out of Saint Pierre."

We each retained a full head of hair, though white as primer paint it may be. Harold was as straight-shouldered and slim as in his youth. Joanie had set her cap for him shortly after our return, and they married two weeks after she graduated from nursing. His mother had started a seamstress business, thanks to a contribution from the Women's Patriotic Association, and had cut and sewn the wedding dress herself. Harold retired from teaching at sixty-five, having refused many times the position as principal. He preferred to teach, not supervise those who did.

The gluck, gluck of alcohol into a glass drew my attention to Frank. His hand was steady as he poured. Due to his lame leg in later years, walking became a challenge, and as a result he'd developed a beer belly. He'd stayed on with Mr. Burke's law office and eventually opened his own firm specializing in criminal law, which his two daughters now ran. Herbert, his son, went the financial route and opened an accounting firm.

"We've all come a long way since the war," I said.

Harold clinked his glass with mine. "To Gord Abbott. It won't be the same without him."

"To Gord," the rest of us said in unison, and drank.

"He was a determined man," Fred said. "He wanted to break the fishing tradition in his family, and by God he succeeded in spades. He couldn't read or write, yet within ten years of coming home he was elected to parliament."

Harold topped up the glasses. "He was quite the flirt, but no woman was able to put a ring on his finger. Never understood that."

I swirled the dark liquid in my glass. "During the war, he told me about his wife and child."

All three stared at me like I'd stripped down to my shorts. "His wife and child!" Fred said.

"Rosie was her name. Gord said he'd never love another like her and would never remarry." I sipped at my drink. "I used to think he'd change his mind with time."

Fred laid his empty glass on the coffee table and rubbed his knuckles, thickened and gnarled with arthritis. "It's got to be mighty tough getting over the death of your young wife and infant child."

Frank massaged his bad knee. "In every way that matters, Gord had a family. He as good as raised Ches's children. He even became a Catholic in order to take them to church. They were fortunate to have him when Isabelle passed away with breast cancer four years after the war."

"You can say that again," Fred said. "Her parents were too old to take on three active youngsters."

Frank raised his glass. "I want to toast another fine fellow who is no longer with us. To Uncle Jack, the best psychiatrist in the country." We drank to his memory. Frank continued. "Dedication to his patients was second nature to him, proven by his dying of a massive stroke during a consultation, at seventy-five years of age."

Strokes were prevalent in my mother's family. My mother and my grandmother had suffered one in their early seventies.

I rested my head against the back of the armchair and closed my eyes.

"You all right?" Frank asked.

I rolled my head to the side to look at him. "I drank the Screech a little too fast. It's made me a little dizzy."

Fred chuckled. "You were never much of a drinker."

The clock on the mantel chimed eleven times. I hadn't bothered to turn on a lamp. Light from the full moon streamed in through the window and fell across my three friends. Silver sparkles danced around their hair like twinkling stars. I'd always loved the night sky, and I had stationed a telescope in my bedroom and spent hours exploring the black expanse lined with the beautiful objects.

"Don't you agree, Ron?"

"What?"

Fred grinned. "I asked if you agreed with . . ."

I really had indulged too much this evening. His voice faded as another, gentler, sweeter voice filled the room.

Dream my sweet boy of chocolate bunnies in a land of candy.

I felt drowsy and fought the urge to close my eyes. A gentle breeze blew over me, cool, refreshing, and I turned my eyes to the window. Henry sat on the ledge dressed in his uniform, young, his horrific wounds gone. He smiled. "Hello, Ron. I've missed you." I tried to call out to Frank to let him know Henry was here. The effort was too great.

We have all missed you. Ches had spoken, young, in uniform, his legs intact. He indicated the fireplace with a nod of his head.

Look who else is here. Sid stood with his hands in his pockets next to young Charlie Paterson, who'd suffocated under clay and rocks in Gallipoli.

Sid winked. Don't be afraid, Ron. We've come to take you with us.

Young Charlie took a step forward. Is that all right with you, Ron?

Yes.

Charlie sighed softly. It won't be long now.

The glass in my hand weighed a ton. Where's Jack and Gord?

Ches smiled. They're waiting for you.

My glass shattered in the distance.

"Ron, what's wrong?" Through the darkening haze I saw Frank hobble over to me. He knocked his bad knee on the corner of the coffee table. He kept moving toward me.

Frank, don't worry. If only I could summon the strength to speak. This is what I want to do.

Harold hopped to his feet, his chest heaving. "I'll call an ambulance."

No. It's all right. The boys are here for me.

The haze before my eyes darkened. I perceived moving shadows.

"Ron." Frank's voice, frantic. "Don't leave us."

"Dear Jesus," Fred cried out. "He's had a stroke."

I can't see her, but I know it's Mom caressing my cheek.

There's not a sound. Everything is black.

Dream my sweet boy of chocolate bunnies in a land of candy
Where twinkling stars sprinkle strawberry gumdrops
All through the night.

Acknowledgements

To Ann and Clifford, my two favourite writing buddies, thanks so much for your great suggestions.

Linda Abbott was born in St. John's, the eighth in a family of ten children. She is a graduate of Memorial University, with a Bachelor of Arts and Education. She holds a Certificate in French from Laval University, Quebec City, and attended the Frecker Institute in Saint Pierre. She is a retired French Immersion teacher, having spent most of her career at Holy Trinity Elementary School in Torbay. *The Tin Triangle* is her third novel. *The Hull Home Fire* is her second, and her first novel is the critically acclaimed bestseller *The Loss of the Marion*. She resides in St. John's.